THE HOODED FALCON

The Hooded Falcon is a medieval story, set on the wild border of England and Wales just after Owen Glendower's rebellion. Prudence Andrew shows a most unusual capacity for vivid and imaginative writing. Her plot is worked out with great skill and ranges widely, but never irrelevantly, over many aspects of life in the fifteenth century – Lollards, plague, bear-baiting, superstitions. The 'hooded falcon' of the title refers to the Welsh people, temporarily subdued but always ready to rise and strike again. In the March of Abercibbi they are ruled by the Beaumont family, one of whose younger members, Simon, is torn by the dilemma of his English blood and the lure of the Welsh magic. There is tenderness, passion, treachery and horror as the story moves to its exciting climax.

THE HOODED FALCON

Prudence Andrew

CEDRIC CHIVERS
PORTWAY
BATH

First published 1960
by
New Authors Limited
An Imprint of the Hutchinson Publishing Group
This edition published
by
Cedric Chivers Ltd
by arrangement with the copyright holder
at the request of
The London & Home Counties Branch
of
The Library Association
1975

ISBN 0 85997 096 5

Printed in Great Britain by
Redwood Press Ltd, Trowbridge, Wiltshire
Bound by Cedric Chivers Ltd, Bath

I

SIMON BEAUMONT sat perched unsteadily on his father's stallion and watched the Welshmen struggling in the stream. He lifted first one shoulder and then the other, inclining his head from side to side until the lobes of his ears touched his coat. It was just the same. Nothing had altered. He had lit candles to St Giles every feast day since Michaelmas. He had told Huw to collect a score of snails from the castle walls, as the wise woman had said, and had eaten, retching, their raw and mucous flesh. He had slept with a dried baby's thumb round his neck to please his mother, and still one shoulder was higher than the other, one arm a dry stick, one leg a flimsy reed. He had scarcely to incline his head to feel the fur of his collar on his right ear. The leathers of his right stirrup were shorter than the left. He held the reins gathered into his strong left hand and hid his right hand in the folds of his coat lest the lone Welshman should see it.

'*Y nefoedd, mae'n oer*,' shouted the Welshmen, with the water swirling about their thighs.

Every day he heard of miracles, an egg with the imprint of Our Lady's face; a bladder stone melted; a novice cured of his pox even before his knees touched the chancel steps; but there was no miracle for him. For seventeen years he had sought a miracle. As a baby he had been carried from one holy well to another; as a child he had been jolted from one shrine to the next, even as far as Our Lady of Walsingham and the bones of the holy martyr at Canterbury. During twelve hot midsummer nights he had knelt at the foot of the wooden statue in the parish church, praying with the sick children of the town, for legend said that once long ago a baby had been cured of the whoop before this very statue. But he remained unchanged. For the seventeen years of his life twelve Herefordshire monks had been saying Masses for his healing, paid by his father, the great baron of Abercibbi, to do nothing else from Matins to Vespers. But nothing happened. Nothing had done him any good.

They had the cross in the water now, dragging it back to its ancient socket on the other side of the stream.

He watched the Welshmen slipping on the smooth stones, cursing the weight of the cross, and he thought of his little sister Blanche, buried a year this Ascension Day in the Benedictine nunnery at Usk. He had gone with Richard to take her, the dowry chinking in his saddlebag, and had seen the great door close upon her. It was the only thing to be done. There was no husband who could face her. He tried to picture her in her habit, her deformity mercilessly framed in white linen, the lovely sad eyes, the tiny hands, the lip cleft not once but twice, so that a red channel of gum disappeared into each nostril. God had marked her just as He had marked himself. But not for their own sin.

He stirred in the saddle. The men had the cross on the further bank, out of the rushing water. They must think me a fool, he thought, glancing at the lone Welshman with his dog beside him. But my eyes are sharp, even if my body was marred in the making. Did they really think I would not notice? I saw what they had done even before Huw spoke. They had moved the boundary cross to the other bank in order to have my father's trout. They must think their English masters very stupid if they expect us not to notice the fresh earth and the trampled grass. There is even a pickaxe leaning against a thorn bush. Odd to have caught them in the act, he mused, and he wondered whether this strange Welshman had lent a shoulder or had stood aloof on the bank, watching.

He thought of him as the Welshman because he had noticed him at once, a small dark man with hot black eyes like coals, standing with a dog at his heels watching their approach with his hand against the sun. He did not move as they jingled to a standstill, simply nodded at their greeting. Strange, thought Simon, to think of him as *the* Welshman when there are so many Welshmen here.

They were in the Welshry now, the Welsh half of his father's great border lordship. Here were vast upland sweeps of pasture and forest and huge hills crowned with bracken. Here they were ten miles and a whole world away from the Englishry, from the English castle and the English town, the English manor houses and the neat English walls. Here they were ten miles from his father's seat of barony and the nerve centre of the March of Abercibbi.

'Go and check the boundaries,' his father had told him, looking at him sharply over his winecup and his chalky knuckles. 'Those Welsh of mine want watching and it is time you stopped mooning about with cures and got your legs over a horse. Take Merlin, take Huw and Thomas'—Thomas was the chaplain—'take a dozen stout fellows and do the thing properly. Take John Upton, he knows those boundaries like the lines on his hand. It is time you learned the duties of your station, Simon. It is time to forget your affliction and thank God that you have a fair face and a pair of legs fit to go round a horse's belly.'

He had glanced wryly at his own legs as he spoke, at the swollen joints and spindly shins. Simon had stopped trickling the salt through his fingers and looked fondly past his mother's frozen face to his brother Richard, who was tearing the meat from a mutton bone with grease glistening on his chin. He was glad that his father had trusted him with such a commission. He loved the Welshry. He had always felt its magic. He had been here many times, in the Welsh part of the March, to watch the cattle herding or to stand in Thomas' skirts at the renewal of oaths, and he had always loved it. As a child he had felt its magic as one of all the other magics that filled his childish days. As he had grown to manhood magic had departed from the Englishry, from the soft lowlands, the snug town and the familiar rhythm of ploughing and sowing and reaping; but up here in the Welshry the magic had persisted. It had never died away. Now, as he watched the Welshmen struggling up the steep bank, exchanging God knew what blasphemies in their strange musical language, the magic was as strong as ever.

These Welsh people were dreamers. Their allegiance was to the past, to the glorious days of Arthur and to the memory of Llewellyn ap Gruffyd, who was the only Welshman to rule the

Welsh people as their chosen king and who died at the command of an English sovereign. Llewellyn it was who had commanded Wales from Anglesey to the Bristol Channel and won the heart of Abercibbi, only to fall to the swords of the English soldiers in the bloody meadows of Builth. Well might Simon's father fear the memory of Llewellyn ap Gruffyd! He had been dead now for a hundred and twenty years but his memory was green and it was only seven short years since a flame had run the length of Wales scarcely less terrible than Llewellyn's; a flame that had burned up the country like barley stubble and stretched its evil fingers into the March of Abercibbi, even to the walls of the town.

Hither had marched the fabulous Glendower, heralded by the bards as Llewellyn born again, rushing like a meteor across the March with his golden dragon fluttering before him and half the men of Wales streaming in his wake. Among them had been men from the Welshry, men who had sworn with a sacred oath to be his father's men, bewitched by the same magic that drew Welshmen from every town of England, from Oxford, Norwich, Chester, Canterbury and York, even from London itself. They had thrown down their sickles, their hoes, their manuscripts and their quills, their tallies and their weights, and hastened by foot or horse to their golden leader, ready to die for a dream of Welsh independence.

No wonder his father did not trust them! Were they not the finest bowmen in the world? Had he not to send regularly to view the boundary crosses? The rebellion was over long ago, Glendower a ghost wandering in the Welsh hills, the Welshry quiet once more, the rebels taken or fled to the caves of the Black Mountains. There was nothing in these beautiful hills to mark Glendower's passage, for he had not touched the Welshry. There were no scars on the face of these slopes as there were in the Englishry and on Richard's face. But there were scars in the people's minds. There were dreams there that could mean danger, dreams of a golden past that might become a golden future.

What did they really think, these Welshmen? Did they remember Glendower's torches? Had they cousins perhaps who had joined the rebels?

Simon remembered Glendower's torches well. He had been

ten when the news had come of the rebels' approach. Huw had been his servant even then, the only pure Welshman his father dared employ within the castle walls, loyal as only a loyal Welshman can be. Huw had taken him on his back up the damp winding stairway to the roof of the keep. It was dusk, he remembered, a soft spring dusk, and he had been afraid, confused by the activity in the courtyard, by the roar of the smiths' furnaces, the heavy hammer of iron, the sanding of arrows, the scream of the grindstone. They climbed slowly and he was glad to feel Huw's stubble pricking his wrists. At the top of the stairway he slid to the ground, landing heavily on his sound leg, and Huw unbolted the heavy trap. The door creaked back, letting gloom into the blackness, and they crawled out on to the leads.

It was a sight Simon would never forget, a picture that he was to carry in his mind to the day of his death. It was like a scene in a window, a scene of hell, each detail outlined in black, one colour separated sharply from the next. It was still light enough to see the south gate, clogged with wagons and packhorses, the people like frantic ants running for the shelter of the stone. A litter had slipped from one of the horses and a bundle—man? woman?—spilt over into the road and disappeared beneath a heavy cart. As far as Simon could see to the south, as far as the bend in the river and the black curtain of forest, torches flickered like fireflies as the people of the Englishry rushed for the haven of the town walls.

Below him men ran to and fro in the dying light, buckling their leather jackets and thrusting their daggers into their belts. Others seized quivers and bows from the armoury and flexed their bow muscles. In the corner by the well he could just make out the chaplain confessing those in mortal sin, and he guessed his friend the priest would be equally busy in his church, no less than the prior in his. The evening was filled with the cries of the lambs and calves being herded into the pound, with the shrieks of hysterical maids and with his father's huge voice, so surprising in that crippled body. There was a stench of simmering tar, a clash of iron buckets, a rocky noise of boulders being assembled inside the gates. He caught glimpses of Richard being inserted into his new breast-plate and helmet, swearing when Old Peter nipped his neck in the joints.

As long as Simon could remember the two bells had been ringing the alarm, the bell of the parish church and the bell of the priory church, both within walls. He pictured the two, both God's houses, but the one so poor and plain, the other stuffed with riches. He pictured the two men, each doubtless listening now to the confessions of terrified souls and sending up prayers for deliverance; Martin the priest so thin and holy, William the prior so fat and worldly. He loved the priest, to whom he went to learn his letters, and he hated the prior, who had fat white hands like slugs. He loved Martin with all the love of a lonely sensitive boy set apart by the injuries inflicted by his perilous birth, and he had always regarded the prior as his enemy. He looked at the priory, built into the south-east angle of the town, and wondered inconsequently whether the two lepers hidden there were as afraid as he.

Then he had looked due east to the east gate, seeing past the dim gallows the stream of torches, and he had heard a sudden scream as a woman's hair caught fire. It was a scene from hell, an illumination in gold and black with the added horror of noise—shrieks, shouts, the clank of armour, the twanging of gut, the rumble of the scaffolds being wheeled against the north wall, then, suddenly, the shutting of the gates.

Thud, thud, went the south gate. There was a grind as the great bolts shot home, four thumps as the huge bars dropped into their sockets, a fiendish wail from those shut out in the road. Thud, thud, went the east gate, as those from the south came frantic with fear to join the dangerous throng in the eastern roadway. Thud, thud, went the north gate, but here there was no forsaken wail. There was no stream of villagers from the north. These would be cowering in the depths of the woods, holding their hands over their children's mouths, cursing the lost goat and the fretful grandmother, their nostrils filled with the smell of their burning homes. For from the north marched the enemy Glendower with his stream of Welshmen, not a few from the Welshry of Abercibbi. They were exhilarated by the sacking of Brecon and the spoiling of the monastery, gorged but not sated by the pleasures of plunder, eager for another nut to crack, another jewel to set in their leader's crown. It was known that a hundred from the Welshry had come down the mountain of Blorys to join them, rushing like bewitched swine down the slopes and swimming the river with their bows over their shoulders.

Now Simon could see the torches of the enemy, a double line of golden specks a mile upriver on the east bank, a sight for a feast day did he not know that the hands that grasped the smoking torches were red with English blood.

'Will they get in, Huw?' he asked fearfully.

'There's chicken-hearted you are, boy,' said Huw. 'I shouldn't like your da to hear you speak so. Get in, is it? No, they'll not get in.'

He laid both hands on the battlement with one of his graceful gestures and said, 'It's lusty fighters they are, those boys, but they'll not be getting in.'

'Have you not to go down, Huw?' asked Simon, pointing with his sound hand to the hell below.

Huw slowly shook his head.

'I'd be fighting my own kindred, see, your da could not ask it. Cousin against cousin, that's not a good fight. A Frenchie or an infidel, there's heart in a fight like that, made to be beaten they were, but there's evil in me to send an arrow into a Welshman's heart. There's a sin now no penance could wipe away.'

'The prior would absolve you. He is an easy confessor, Martin says.' Simon still kept his eyes apprehensively on the golden specks, but not even fear could dull the edge of his acute mind.

'Give me easy penance, is it?'

'Nothing worse than a journey on your knees and a gift to the brothers. The bigger the gift, the shorter the journey, that's what Martin says. He is angry with the prior's absolution. He says there is no true repentance.'

Huw turned his head to look at this extraordinary child, this lop-sided angel earnestly criticizing a holy father with the enemy not a mile from his father's gates. Not a day went by but he was astonished by the things that Simon said. In all his forty years he had known no boy like him. Timid in movement, audacious in utterance, sometimes he wondered if he were quite right in the head. Look at his mother now, there was a queer one, and they did say that a twisted body meant a twisted mind.

'It is not within me to kill a Welshman,' he said again, and at that moment through the hubbub came the sergeant's horn for the mounting of the scaffold. Before his eyes the scornful youth became a frightened child and Simon tried to clasp Huw's arm with his withered claw. It was a measure of his fright that he had unconsciously taken it from the folds of his tunic.

'Come you, Master Simon, time for the cellars, boy, and the moaning of women.'

No, no wonder his father did not trust his Welsh. For four hours the Welshmen battered at the north gate, while Simon trembled among the wine casks in the dripping cellar and watched his mother's face assume the rigidity of a stone image in the rushlight. Blanche knelt at her feet, her poor split mouth hidden in her mother's gown. Ceaselessly one thin hand smoothed the little girl's hair, while the other soothed the squirrel in her pocket. Simon noticed the bulge where the tail was and wondered if the squirrel were as frightened as he. He remembered Thomas in the corner, rattling his rosary and gabbling unintelligble supplications; and he remembered the way the ground trembled minutely, the shock of the battering-ram communicating itself through four hundred paces of rock.

By midnight they had gone, leaving the town untaken. They streamed away to the south to set light to the bishop's palace at Landaff. They set their torches to the hayricks, the mills, the abandoned cottages and the woods. They snatched treasures from the parish churches, slashed the hamstrings of the cattle and draped their necks with dead hens, each man a knot in a many-tailed scourge ripping the fair back of the countryside.

The town was safe but the enemy left in its wake a devastation unknown in the history of the March, a blackened trail of smoke and ruin such as the Englishry had never dreamed of. Even the millstones were smashed. In that one night his father's hair turned from gold to white, Richard received an arrow that carved a groove from eye to mouth wide enough to fit his little finger, and his mother spoke her last word. When Richard appeared at the top of the steps with blood gushing like a spring through his fingers his mother had started to her feet and shrieked: 'He has marked them all! God has marked them all!' She had never spoken another word from that day to this.

No, his father could not trust these his Welsh people. Where the Welshry began, danger began. For seven years there had been peace, but it was an uneasy peace. It lay over the land like leather over a falcon's head. The bird was quiet but beneath the plumed hood were watchful eyes and a cruel beak. The English heron could not afford to forget them.

Simon watched Huw on the far bank, calling directions in his high-pitched, musical Welsh, and he could feel the eyes of the lone Welshman upon him. His scrutiny made him nervous, almost guilty. There was no doubt about it. There was not even any need to swear witnesses. There had been the empty socket for anyone to see. They had not even had time to fill it in. Why should this Welshman watch him? Did he hate him, scorn him, wonder that such a weakling should be sent to view the boundaries? Had he perhaps a brother, a cousin, who had swum the Usk to join Glendower seven years ago? Had he a kinsman among the three score whose brains had mingled with the dust of the northern roadway or whose blood had stained his father's arrows? Or did he harbour friendship for the son of a just ruler who from the year he had entered into his wife's inheritance had chosen to leave the bland meadows of Herefordshire and make his home in this remote lordship; who honoured their ancient customs; and who never squeezed a cow too many? He could not tell. Those hot eyes told him nothing.

He shifted his eyes to the cross and saw it drop heavily into its ancient hole.

'See that it does not happen again,' he said, with sufficient sternness, to the bailiff and kicked Merlin with his sound leg.

They moved on slowly, a cluster of Welshmen at their horses' rumps and the lone Welshman watched them out of sight, his dog like a statue at his feet. He had not uttered a word. When Simon turned at the bend in the track he was still there and another man was urinating against the cross. He asked the bailiff the man's name and was told Llewellyn ap Thomas, from the neighbouring commote of Pwll-du. When he asked what in that case the man was doing out of his district he was told that Llewellyn was an unlikely man, a soothsayer some said, born with a caul in a storm of wind that had taken the roof from the church and whirled it away never to be seen again; a clever man, look you, who wrote both Welsh and English and was clerk to the lord of Pwll-du.

Simon rode thoughtfully on with Huw at his knee and wondered why, knowing all that he knew, he was not afraid of these Welshmen. Thomas feared them, not their bows nor their daggers but their spells. He kept crossing himself and glancing fearfully round as if he expected the devil to step from a thicket with a leek in his bonnet. Richard too preferred the Englishry and came here only on essential business. He never chose to hunt in his father's forests here, not even when one of the charcoal-burners saw a stag with three antlers, one behind each ear and one in the middle of his forehead. 'I am afraid of the witch-women,' he said. 'They dance naked in the forest and suck a man's soul.'

Simon was different, in this as in everything. He could never think as others thought. He should have remembered Richard's cheek and his mother's frozen face and the murderous progress of Glendower's army, but whenever he passed the boundary cross the bitter memories faded and he saw only a fair country and a bewitching people. He could take nothing at its face value. Always he had to probe until the canker was found or the jewel uncovered. It was the same at home. He should have reverenced the holy prior and he could only hate him. He should have laughed when they pulled Old Peter's stool from under him and all he could feel was his pain in his body. He glanced back at John Upton, square, strong, unimaginative, and longed to be inside him, content in that sturdy body and incurious mind. He wanted to look at the world through those unglazed eyes, so like Richard's. He did not want to be different.

Sometimes when he heard the bears being baited in the market or was forced to watch the hangman leap for the felon's shoulders or saw the prior return from the hunt with blood on his cheek, he felt a terrible sickness that only the sacramental bread could take away. How many times had he limped from a hanging, his ears full of the victim's shrieks, and sat on a tombstone waiting in a daze of nausea for Martin to ring the bell for Mass. He never went to Mass at the priory, not even to please his father. He could not bear those fat white hands near his face.

Yet no one else seemed to mind. Cruelty was a part of life, like gout and scurvy and scab. It had to be accepted. But he could not accept it any more than he could accept his hideous body. He must forever be seeking a remedy.

Thus he wrapped his melancholy about him, while they left the boundary cross behind and rode on. When the sun was high they halted in the shade of some mountain thorns and ate their bread and meat, relishing its sweetness after the salty winter months. The sound of cow-bells mingled with the tinkle of the streams where the fat trout lay. The Welshmen sat apart, talking quietly among themselves, watching them out of the corners of their eyes. Simon shifted so that the sun struck his neck and savoured the peace and the quietness. A skylark sang above him. Over the brown water bumbled a bee. Down in the English valley he never found this peace. Even outside the walls of the town there was seldom any peace in the bustling arable life of the English farms. There was always the creaking of wagons, the chip-chip of the mason's hammer, the roaring of forges, the shouts of bird-scarers, the clip-clip of wooden clogs, the sharpening of sickles. Never, never this blessed peace.

Presently they remounted. They moved methodically from one boundary cross to another, along a narrow track levelled by the Welsh picks for the baron's convenience. They exchanged one bailiff for the next, one group of Welshmen for another, as they rode from commote to commote. The sun was directly in their eyes when they reached the southernmost cross in Lasgarn and John Upton swung his horse's head eastwards in preparation for the descent, for there was level riding along the valley that was kinder to the horse's legs. But Simon did not follow. He did not want to leave the Welshry so soon. His haunches ached from the saddle and the reins had worn a groove between the fingers of his left hand but he looked back over his hunched shoulder and said they would return the way they had come. 'You cannot know,' he said, 'they may have moved the cross back again.'

'Aye, maybe,' said John. 'There is no knowing the tricks of the Welsh.' And Huw roared with laughter.

Simon did not really expect the Welshman to be still standing like a statue with his dog beside him, but he was disappointed none the less when he approached the place and found it empty. No one had touched the cross so they went on, with the pastures on their left and the forest on their right, hearing the dying tinkle of the cattle bells as the cows were driven home for milking and feeling the stares of stray Welsh children. When they reached the track they swung their horses into the gloom of the trees, but Simon paused a moment and gazed over Merlin's ears at the scene spread before him. At his feet lay his father's treasure, the Englishry, the lovely plain of the Usk. Far to his left glimmered the dark mountains of Wales, home of the ghost Glendower. Before him, across the rich valley, rose the peak of Pen-y-val, the northern boundary of his father's March, its bald brown head glowing above the trees like a tonsure. Below him lay the valley, drowned in the unearthly evening light and watered by the beautiful river Usk. This was his father's dove, dearer than the meadows of Herefordshire because it crouched at the feet of an alien people who eyed it scornfully and despised its arable pleasures. He twitched the reins and Merlin moved forward, stiff-legged on the slope.

Now they were in the Englishry. The forest was full of shadows and the domes of charcoal-burners. Silence was gone. The echoes of their harness were flung from tree to tree. Twigs snapped under the hooves. They passed barefoot children, with fair English heads, gleaning the winter's droppings of dead wood. A herd of swine crashed out of the undergrowth, their young trotting at their heels. On the fringe of the trees they saw the mouths of the iron workings and even as they watched a truck came up with a rumble, pulled by six filthy men on their knees. The smeltings on the roadside roared and rang and before they crossed the bridge they had passed two ox-carts laden with bars of iron for the castle smithy. Simon sighed and thought, as he often did when he set foot on this road, of the wild night of the Welsh attack. I feared them then, he thought, but I do not fear them now. Now I am a man I do not fear them.

The north gate of the town stood open and the gate-keeper lounged in the last of the daylight, sucking a piece of straw.

'Good evening, my lord,' he said, touching his temple. 'Rare do at the church.'

Then Simon noticed people hurrying towards the tiny parish church, Martin's church, a woman pinning up her hair as she ran, a man with only one arm in his jacket, a child with a crust. He could see heads round the porch, figures climbing on the tombstones to peer through the windows. He urged Merlin up the path to the porch, the people falling away on either side. Word must have passed of his coming because as he drew rein Martin rushed out with his cassock flapping about his ankles and grasped his bridle.

'A miracle!' he gasped. 'By God's holy grace, a miracle!'

2

SIMON's heart jumped. A miracle? A miracle here? A miracle in the church? If one miracle why not another? A miracle for his stricken body, a miracle for his restless mind? Miracle, miracle, the blessed word rang in his mind.

'A miracle!' Martin cried, plucking at his withered knee. 'A miraculous light at the altar. I have sent for your father. I have sent for the prior. . . .' Ah yes, the prior. He would never believe it unless he saw it for himself. 'Come quickly, Simon, and see the miracle.'

Simon dragged his weak leg over Merlin's rump and slipped to the ground, but he would have fallen had not Huw been there to catch him, he was so tired from the day in the saddle. The people pressed so close on either side that he had to edge his way through them shoulder first, like a crab with a damaged claw. A miracle? If this were a miracle, it would be a blow to the prior. It was good to have relics but it was better to have a miracle. There had never been a miracle in the priory church, not even at the altar where the relics were buried. He looked at Martin's dark-cropped head, at his tonsure shining like a full moon in the gloom of the porch, and absentmindedly passed his hand over his own hair. It was fair, like his father's used to be, and curled thickly about his ears. They shaved a priest's head to set him apart, so they said. He needed no such insignia. He was set apart from birth by his mother's sin.

He limped up the nave at Martin's heels, feeling the smoothness of the brasses under his feet, peering. There were shadowy shapes against the walls, kneeling he thought. He caught glimpses of pale faces turned towards the plain east window and he heard the click-click of the rosaries and a dying whisper of prayers mouthed below the breath. They passed through the screen. At the chancel steps Martin stopped and sank on to his knees, pointing.

'Look,' he whispered. 'There.'

Simon went down heavily on to his sound knee and stared. At first he could see nothing, but presently, gazing into the shadows of the altar, he became aware of a tiny golden light, so faint that when he looked directly at it it disappeared altogether, like a distant star on a dark night. Only when he shifted his eyes to one side did it reappear on the edge of his sight.

'You see it?' breathed Martin in his ear. 'On the altar step, directly under the chalice.'

Simon stared. There was a small commotion behind them, a shuffle of footsteps, a grunt as a huge figure dropped on its knees beside them. The prior had arrived.

Simon edged away, the stones boring into his withered knee. As a child he had hated this man, with a child's unreasonable hatred, for no better reason than that he had heard Martin speak of him as an easy confessor and that his hands smelt of soap. As a youth, and now as a man, he disliked him for the riches of his priory, for his roasted swans, his servants, his hunting horses, his dogs and his cellar; for his corpulent flesh and his little piggy's eyes; for the tombs of the past lords of Abercibbi that lined the walls of his priory church and for the richly coloured windows and the splinters of the true cross that Martin would love to have had.

This habit of dislike was so ingrained that when he eventually turned his head to look at the prior Simon could scarcely believe what he saw. The prior was crying. He had clasped his hands under his chin and the tears ran down his fat cheeks and dripped on to his fat fingers.

Suddenly the light disappeared. One instant it was there, the next it was gone. Now his father would never see it. They had not been able to get him to the church in time. At his side the prior stirred and sniffed and blew through his nose. Subdued gabblings broke out behind them. Simon could feel the tremors of excitement through the stuff of Martin's cassock. 'They have never had a miracle at the priory,' he heard him whisper. The prior gathered his skirts into one hand and rose stiffly, pressing heavily on his knee. He spoke a low word to the brother at his side, who moved towards the altar.

'They are going to verify the miracle,' thought Simon. They all rose and moved forward. Someone came running with a taper and lit the altar candles. Simon looked back and saw the faces behind the screen, peering through the spaces at the mysteries of the chancel, already adoring. Out of the corner of his eye he saw Brother Gregory squat down with the palms of his hands flat on the stone, and he did likewise, determined that if there was anything to find Brother Gregory should not find it. They knelt one on each side of the altar, their fingers inching forward like caterpillars. Martin was nervously plaiting his cord, the prior stood like a statue, the faces whispered and waited beyond the screen. For hours, as it seemed, their fingers crawled over the stones. The only sounds were the whispers of the people and the occasional scraping of a nail. At last they rose to their feet and the brother approached his master.

'There is nothing, my lord prior,' said Brother Gregory.

The prior turned his little eyes on Simon.

'There is nothing, my lord prior,' said Simon.

The prior crossed himself, his rings flashing in the light of the candles. 'A miracle!' he announced. 'By God's Holy Grace, a miracle!' and kissed Martin on both cheeks.

A miracle! The word ran through the church and out into the churchyard, where it became like a flame to the stubble. A miracle, a miracle! they cried, falling on each others' necks and dancing on the tombstones. Oh blessed day! A shining light in their grey days! God had once more chosen their church for a miracle. He had sent this sign of His favour into their humdrum lives and there was not a living soul but rejoiced.

Save one.

'The bells,' cried Martin, and Sexton's sandals flapped up the staircase. Praise Him, praise Him, sang the bell, and even the felon in the castle cellar heard it and wondered. The churchyard was filled with people, old and young, men and women, lay and religious. There was the baby tethered to his mother's breast with a ragged shawl; there was the blind man groping along the wall; there were the toothless, the earless, the man in mortal sin, the constable, the Seneschal, the woman with the pot in her hand still smoking from the fire, the child with his teeth in a bacon bone. Sinner and saved, there was not a soul but rejoiced.

Save one.

'Come,' said the prior, 'we must record this blessed event.' And Martin led the way to his own room, that stood out on the shady side of the church like a wart on a man's nose. But Simon stood still on the chancel steps, picturing them fussing over the ink and the quill and the parchment, calling in one or two lay witnesses to make their shaky crosses. He followed in his mind the angular script, the long tails of the aitches, the elaborate capitals. He pictured the date at the bottom, May 3rd, the third day after the Invention of the Holy Cross, 1411, and the polite tussle as to who should write to the bishop. He saw the shining excitement of his friend's face and the envious glances of Brother Gregory. He could not picture the prior. The prior had surprised him. And all the while his left hand was in his pocket and he turned over in his fingers something dry and small.

One by one the shadowy shapes left the church to join their friends outside, until he was left quite alone. The church door slammed. Suddenly the bell stopped. He could hear the hubbub faintly as a man in a dungeon hears the life of the town. He limped over to the altar. Slowly he drew his closed hand from his pocket. Slowly he uncurled his fingers and gazed in the light of a candle at what lay in the palm of his hand.

It was a glow-worm.

He poked it with his powerless forefinger and wondered which end made the light and what chance had led its crawling legs over the pitted stones and smooth brasses of the nave and up the steps to the altar. He knew it was a glow-worm because Huw had showed him one when he was a child, unhappy because he could never bend a bow. He had never cried, even as a child, but Huw had known he was unhappy and had shown him the glow-worm, taking it from the bank on just such a May evening as tonight. He had smiled, then, to give Huw pleasure, but he had wanted to lay down his head and weep away his sorrow. But he had never been able to cry. He could not remember ever crying in all his seventeen years of life. Sometimes he longed for the relief of tears. Everyone cried, even the prior, even his father had cried on the night that his mother lost her reason and her tongue to the devil. Even Huw, even John Upton, but never Simon.

The church door creaked open and his father came in, carried in a chair by two stout men with his spindle legs swinging. Simon put the beetle back in his pocket and came down to meet him. At that moment the bell started ringing again but he went through the pantomime of showing his father what had happened and the chair was carried up to the altar.

'Here? Why here?' wondered his father, mouthing without sound. He was puzzled, Simon could see, that God should have chosen the humble parish church for such a sign of grace rather than the holy priory of distinguished history, with its twenty meek monks and its capable prior and its splinters of the true cross buried under the altar stone, not to mention the coloured windows presented by the former lords of the March and their watchful figures on the lids of their tombs. What was there here in this plain building to attract such a gracious sign? Why Martin's church? Simon could see the questions in his father's mind as plainly as if his forehead had been a window. To his father, Martin was of scarcely more account than the ploughman whose brother he was. He was a man of God, it is true. He could put God into a man's mouth. He could read and write in Latin and the vulgar tongue; he could intone the services at a true pitch, for his mother had been a Welshwoman and had bequeathed to her son her musical ear. But did he not dig his own cabbage patch like any peasant, with earth between his toes? Did he not blow his nose on his fingers, like any cottager? Was he not as poor as the black rat that lived behind the altar and had once eaten the sacramental bread? Why Martin? Why, indeed?

When they came out into the churchyard, the deformed father and the deformed son, it was quite dark. The prior and his monks had gone, the people had gone, the town gates were shut and Martin pored happily over his handwriting. Only Huw was waiting to attend them, with his father's servants. 'Home,' said his father, and Simon limped wearily beside the bobbing chair while Huw followed with the horses. But he kept his left hand in his pocket still and stroked the dry beetle with the tip of his finger.

. . . . .

At dinner that night they could talk of nothing but the miracle. The hall, the buttery, the pantry, even the seething kitchen was full of the miraculous light. They breathed it with the smoke from the fire, they gnawed it with their marrow bones, they cut it up with their knives. It hopped with the fleas in the rushes, crawled with the lice in Old Peter's hair, scratched where they scratched, spat where they spat. Only his mother was unmoved, dipping her bread into the sauce and licking her fingers without interest. Everyone was chattering, everyone hopeful. Richard's wife Alice, barren these three years, was going first thing in the morning to pray for a child on the spot where the light was seen. Richard as usual had no thoughts but he was pleased none the less when he saw all so pleased about him and said he would give Martin a present, see if he would not. The Seneschal had visions of pilgrims coming to visit the scene of another authenticated miracle and licked his lips over their tolls. The Pardoner, a mean hateful man with greasy hair hanging on his shoulders, determined to attend early Mass and scrape up some of the dirt with his knife for selling. Thomas the chaplain bit his nails between courses and considered that it would almost be worth slaving in a parish church if one could be sure of a miracle. Huw hoped with the fervency of a loyal and devout heart that some of God's grace would spill over his young master and was puzzled that the lord Simon should look so miserable, today of all days. Even the great baron himself, William Beaumont, master of these twenty-five thousand fair acres, cracked a joke about his old bones and swore that he would talk no business for an hour. But his son sat as silent as his mother, taking morsels of meat from the tip of his knife and feeling with every bite as if he were crunching the beetle between his teeth.

'A day to remember, my lord,' cried the Seneschal, a plain man fervent for business, and lifted his goblet.

'You are right, Seneschal,' said the baron, 'a blessed day indeed. Although I cannot but wonder,' he added, being a man used to speaking his mind, 'that the priory should be so honoured.'

'Indeed, my lord,' broke in Thomas the chaplain, who disliked Martin for his strictness and wished to keep on the right side of the prior. 'Indeed, my lord, I do not doubt that it is a foretaste of greater things to come. It was but a little miracle,' he added hopefully, 'after all.'

'Little?' thought Simon, with his finger on the ridges of the beetle's back. 'You will never know how little.'

'A miracle is a miracle,' said Seneschal in his soft Herefordshire voice, 'little or no, Master Thomas.' He glanced down the tables to where the Pardoner sat picking his teeth with his knife. 'I do not doubt the news will travel fast and we will have a fine spate of pilgrims knocking at our gates.' He rubbed his thumbs as if he felt the coins between them already.

'Will you let in the Welshmen, Father?' asked Simon, thinking of the strange Welshman he had seen that day, Llewellyn ap Thomas, and wondering if he would want to visit the scene of the miracle.

'Of course, boy, when have I ever kept them out? If they pay their toll like Christian men, and if they leave their arms at the gates, are they not free to come as they please? Do they not come to the market?'

'But they never come to the church, Father, so Martin says.'

'Heathens, no doubt,' said Thomas maliciously, and quailed before the baron's look.

'Heathens you say, Thomas? And was your father a heathen?'

'Nay, a true Christian,' stammered the unfortunate Thomas, who was always hoping people would forget he had had a Welshman for a father.

'And do not the Welshmen have Christian churches with Christian priests?'

'Aye, my lord, I spoke only in jest.'

'Do they not go to Mass every Sunday, as a Christian should, and confess to their priest lest they die in mortal sin and go to everlasting hell?'

'They do, my lord, they do truly.'

'Then let us hear no more of heathens. If the Welshmen wish to visit the place of the miracle, and if they leave their arms at the gates, they shall come without hindrance. May it never be said that the lord of this March barred the gate to those that came in peace.'

There were Welshmen in the hall now, small dark men grouped round a rushlight at the second table, too far away, Simon hoped, to hear Thomas's remarks. He would like to have spoken to them but knew his father would not wish it. He gave them justice but not love, hospitality but not friendship, and would be glad when they were gone. Simon watched them from under his lashes, wondering if they knew Llewellyn ap Thomas, and all the while he turned the beetle over between his fingers. It was dead now. There was no movement in it. He wondered what he was going to do with it. It did not seem right to toss it among the dogs. It was a kind of miracle, he supposed, that it should have left the green grass and crawled through the gates and found its perilous way to the church and the altar.

There was movement at the high table. His mother and Alice rose and withdrew to the solar and Richard called for a tray of sand. He would now spend the rest of the evening rolling his new chain mitts in the sand to clean them. He could never sit inactive for long. Servants came and cleared the table of its linen, leaving only the rushlights, the great mazing cup and its ladle, the pewter mugs and the three salt-cellars, each standing on one foot. The baron leant his gouty elbows on the smooth wood and Seneschal laid before him the parchments that filled his life, the receipts of the Englishry. Each parchment made its own tight roll and when they wished to read they had to pin down the four corners with mugs. Every night it was the same, his mother and Alice in the solar, Alice sewing and his mother playing with her squirrel; Richard sanding his armour or whittling wood, waiting only for instructions; his father and Seneschal poring in the rushlight over the crisp parchments. And he?

He wandered down among the chattering groups, dragging the rushes with his lame foot, rubbing the ears of the dogs. Even in May a fire smouldered on the round hearth, making his eyes smart with its smoke. He took a stick and stirred the ashes until he had uncovered a patch of red embers. Then he took the dead glow-worm from his pocket and dropped it into the heat. It flared an instant and was gone.

'Simon!' It was his father's voice and he went back to the dais.

Noise never worried his father. He did business in the bustle of the hall at the cleared table, with the servants clattering the platters and half a dozen soldiers throwing dice among the rushes and the cook screaming from the kitchen and humble guests like these Welshmen watching from the door. Through this dim chattering world Simon limped night after night, restless and unhappy. He was uneasy among the men, feeling that they watched him and wondered why God had struck him so. He could not bear to sit and watch his mother with her squirrel, ceaselessly smoothing the coat from ears to tail, again and again and again, heedless of its droppings on her dress. Alice was stupid, a giggling girl, Richard had no conversation. He had no place, he felt, with his father and Seneschal. He could not give to the administration of the lordship the passionate devotion of the baron. Often he and Huw used to slip away and visit Martin or climb the stairway to the ramparts or the roof of the keep or on fine summer nights to wander in his mother's little garden and smell the herbs. But not tonight.

'Simon,' called his father from the high table. 'Come here. Sit down. Tell me about the boundaries.'

So Simon told his father about the moving of the boundary cross.

'Which commote?' asked Seneschal, his quill poised over his map.

'Blaen-avon.'

'Which kindred?'

'The kindred of Iago.'

The quill darted like a swallow on to the map but Seneschal was puzzled. 'Moving the boundary cross, you say? We have never had any trouble with Blaen-avon, not since the rebellion that is, and then they were all troublesome.' He glanced ruefully at his left hand, from which three fingers were missing. 'Now if it had been Pwll-du . . .' He moved the dry quill to the next commote, the northernmost commote of the Welshry, the commote of Llewellyn ap Thomas. 'Pwll-du I could understand. There are some hotheads there, in Garndyrrys for sure, but Blaen-avon . . .' He gazed at the map, sucking the quill.

'Well, it is back in its socket and that is all to be said,' said the baron, impatient for the rolls of parchment. 'Threaten them with a communal fine if they touch it again. Now, Seneschal, the rolls. Which first? Ah, Llanwenarth.'

An unrolling of parchment, a pinning of corners, and his father was lost in the purpose of his life.

Huw slid along the bench towards him and Simon called for the chessmen.

'A game now, is it?' asked Huw and began to put out the pieces.

They played, but only a fraction of Simon's attention was on the game. He heard the regular scraping of Richard's mittens in the sand-tray; he heard the occasional click of a chessman on the board; he heard the rough-and-tumble of the hall where a game of blind man's buff was in progress; he heard the quick shuffle of feet in the rushes and the yelp of a trodden dog, the shouts of laughter, but these were but a background of sound, as familiar as the tapestry in his mother's chamber. All these sounds he heard, but through them all he heard his father's voice, sharp and clear, and the soft rumble of Seneschal's replies. His hand was with the chequered board, but his mind was with the two men behind him, stimulated into unwonted attention by the extraordinary happenings of the day.

They were speaking of the Englishry, where the baron's heart lay. 'Now Tregoythel, my lord . . . trouble getting in the rents . . . only twenty shillings this quarter instead of thirty . . . the lord of the manor there asks to be allowed to pay two quarters together on the Nativity of the Blessed Mary . . . a bad harvest, my lord . . . a bad district for cattle disease . . . the flooding of three fields of winter wheat . . . ten acres still not reclaimed since the rebellion. John Strangway pleads his father and two brothers killed by Glendower's men . . . only his sister to help him . . . pleads for time. Receipts down on your mill there, my lord. Little corn was harvested, most of it to be kept for seed . . . a bad winter for Tregoythel . . . pleads for time to pay the rents. Llanddakoc, my lord . . . four acres reclaimed from the waste made by Glendower's men . . . receipts from the fisheries improved . . . the bailiff found a stranger from Gloucester to rent them . . . Good receipts for running swine in the forest there. The forester reports two hawks' nests and five wild bees' nests, the honey of which he will send to the kitchens in due season . . . weeders did demand a penny a day which the bailiff was not willing to pay, but the weeds growing so high and there being no man willing he was perforce to pay what they asked . . . he makes due note. . . . Penros, better news.

A fine growth of wheat, like to render eight or nine loads, God sparing us storm and drought . . . six more acres brought under plough, the first time since the Glendower rebellion, and sown with peas for the enriching of the ground. . . .'

So the tale went on, a tale of struggles to reclaim land wasted by Glendower's men, to resow woods fired by Glendower's men, to replace millstones broken by Glendower's men; a tale of families fatherless from Glendower's swords, and houseless still from his torches; a tale of hard times and empty stomachs and debts. Everyone was feeling the pinch still, seven years after the murderous passage of Glendower's army, all but the people of the Welshry whose lands and stock he had not touched. None felt it more than the baron himself, who had been living since the rebellion on the rents from his Herefordshire estates and who felt every injury to his Englishry as if it were another stab in his painful joints. The night that Glendower's men had streamed away to the south in a whirlwind of destruction, he had sworn that he would never leave the lordship until the English farms were restocked, the people rehoused, the woods resown and the waste reclaimed. He had never broken his vow. Even before his disease had crippled his legs he had never left the March nor his ceaseless preoccupation with its refurbishing. His people had cause to bless him indeed who never cursed for his rents any more than Martin cursed for his tithes and who sent his own carpenters and masons to help them repair their churches, his own oxen to lug the new millstones from the quarries. He had sent Richard to fight for the king while he struggled painfully on Merlin down the rutted tracks to view one blasted manor after another or along the upland slopes of the Welshry, hounding lurking rebels over the mountains into Brecknock or hanging them from convenient trees. He was harsh with his Welshmen then, increasing the tribute of cows that year and the next and imposing communal fines, commote by commote, paid in coin on the boundary of Pwll-du on the feast of St James the Apostle. He was a hard master to his Welsh then, but he did not fire the standing crops like the lord of Wentloog nor take Welsh hostages as the king himself had done, a thousand terrified children from the rebellious lands.

Now, for seven years there had been peace in the lordship

while the land slowly healed its wounds and trees grew to hide the scars. Each year, as Simon trotted along the valley paths with Huw at his knee, he saw new acres taken from the waste, clean earth lie where there were nothing but weeds before. Children grew and families multiplied. Here a church sprouted a new tower, here a roofless house was made whole, in the black expanses there suddenly glimmered the green of seedling trees. But Simon could not feel for these stricken English people the love his father felt. Even with the ashes of Glendower's fires scarcely cool under his feet he felt his eyes pulled always towards the hills, where lived the Welsh, and he was never nearer happiness than when he was allowed to ride with Seneschal to a commote court or with John Upton to a cattle-herding. Once over the boundary he seemed to breathe more freely. Sometimes he could swear he felt his right leg stronger, his mind less troubled, as he entered the Welshry. He used to watch the Welsh ways—the ploughs pulled by teams of four with the ploughman walking backwards, the cows with bells on their necks, the towerless churches—and think that he was in another world, a faery world of singing and fresh breezes and dark faery people. To come down into the trees and pass the hole of the ironworkings was like coming down into a prison. That was why he found it so surprising that tonight he should feel such an interest in what his father was saying to the Seneschal. He had heard it so many times before, the arrears of rents, the pleas for time, the flooding due to inadequate drains, the drains neglected through a shortage of labour, so many cattle attacked by the dreaded murrain, so many swine with fever, so many oxen with galls—it was like a calamitous nursery tale that had lost by its familiarity all its horror. Why should it interest him tonight? Why tonight?

The voices went on, his father's, Seneschal's, Huw's, his own, blended like one of those strange songs he had heard the Welsh sing, with parts for different voices; and in listening to them he forgot the glow-worm and the miracle that he could not bring himself to expose and his own longing for a miracle of healing for himself.

'Pleads for time, my lord, until the feast of the Blessed Mary. . . .'

'There is slow you are. Move you now.'

'We must have more waste under plough, it is the only way . . .'

'Did you see the prior crying?'

'Got my old castle, is it?'

'You must get what you can for the fisheries.'

'Adam Ewan's gift cow had swollen udders.'

'Which end of a glow-worm has the light?'

'You must tell them I will not accept diseased cattle.'

'Hisht now, it's quiet I must have.'

'I must have him at the next court, my lord. . . .'

'Did you see how pleased Martin was?'

Then suddenly without warning came the name he wanted to hear, the reason for his stretched ears.

'Llewellyn ap Thomas.' Like a false note, it struck across the harmony. And again, 'Llewellyn ap Thomas.'

'Ah, the clerk at the Pwll-du court. But he speaks both Welsh and English, you tell me. And surely many of the Pwll-du commote speak the English tongue.'

'I do not trust them, my lord. I think many plead in Welsh that have the English. And how am I to tell if Llewellyn ap Thomas translates correctly?'

'The bailiff understands Welsh, surely?'

'Aye, he does, my lord, but he is a timid man, like a rabbit. I would have him from there if I could find a man to replace him.'

'Take Huw. Then you will be sure.'

'I will be glad, my lord. He is the only Welshman I can find it in my heart to trust.'

Simon felt his father turning painfully in his chair and remained as if turned to ice, his hand stone still an inch from his queen. Then he felt his father's hand on his shoulder and his muscles melted.

'Father, please let me go to the commote court with the Seneschal. Please.'

His father looked at him in pleased surprise. He loved this son and wanted to make him happy, but he was so difficult to please. He was the dearest of his children, brought up at home in the March and not sent, as Richard had been sent and as all normal boys were sent, to a great English castle to get an education. His cousin the great Earl of Warwick would have had him, if with reluctance, but William Beaumont would not expose his stricken son to the jeers and glances of his contemporaries. He loved this boy, but he did not understand him nor have the power to move his melancholy. He remained unmoved by the ordinary pleasures of his years. He could neither bend a bow nor hold a lance; he showed no interest in women; he was quick to anger and seldom smiled; he felt none of his father's pride in the administration of the March; he hated to hunt, farming bored him, he could not fight, he disliked and criticized the monks and spent too much time seeking cures and miracles. What was to be done with him? A good marriage might be the making of him, but could the boy . . . He had yet to prove . . .

'So be it,' he said at last, and was rewarded by his son's rare smile.

So intent had they been on their business that they only now became aware that the accustomed hubbub of the hall had risen to an uproar. Simon looked down and was surprised to find the game of blind man's buff still in progress. Old Peter, his head bound up in a rag, was spinning blindly from one hand to another, stumbling from one tormentor to the next amidst shouts of laughter.

'Here, here, send him by here!'

'Twirlum, twistum, like a bloody top.'

'Up a dando now!'

'Right you, I got him.'

'Over!'

'Mish mash, mish mash!'

'Here, here, by here!'

Every face was split in a grin. Mouths gaped. The dogs cowered under the trestles. Suddenly Old Peter ran blindly into the centre of the hall, caught his foot on the stone hearth and fell with a shriek into the fire. He was up in an instant, running up and down like a chicken with his coat smouldering, tearing at the knots of the rag. The shouts of laughter became a roar. Men doubled over the benches with their hands on their bellies; others leant helpless with mirth against the walls. The shoulders of boys heaved over their mugs; fists beat weakly in the air. Seneschal shook with laughter over his map. The baron made no move. Even Huw was smiling. Up and down Old Peter rushed, frantic with fear and pain, smoke rising from his behind, and no man stretched out a hand to help him.

Suddenly Simon lurched to his feet and sent the chessboard clattering to the floor in a shower of ivory men.

'Stop him!' he cried. 'For the love of God, stop him!'

3

So Huw stopped him. He tore off his smouldering coat and undid the knots of the rags, while Simon called for goose-grease and the grins wavered along the wall. The baron and Seneschal went back to their business and Richard returned to his sanding, straightening his face when he met his brother's furious eyes. The skin beneath Old Peter's grimy drawers was red and shining but unbroken and he was soon happily snoring face downwards in a swaddle of grease among the rushes, fuddled with more spiced ale than he had drunk in a quarter.

He never thought, not Old Peter. He never wondered why he was the butt of the castle, a living target for the men's shafts of humour. He accepted the kicks and the mockery as a part of life, like the rotting teeth that he could waggle with his tongue and the vermin that crawled in the folds of his clothes. He was a natural, was Old Peter, born to carry water from the well-house to the kitchen until his arms stretched in their sockets and his hands came down to his knees. A simple soul who toiled to Mass on his ingrowing nails because the cook told him he must and who confessed once a year sins of which he was ignorant because the cook told him he ought. He took the bread because he saw others take it and wondered why the priest should feed him when he was soon going to have his breakfast. He wondered too where God was and had decided after many years that He was in the wooden statue just inside the door of the parish church. It was a nice statue, Peter thought, a man as thin as himself with just such long toes stretched out on a cross and with great nails in his hands. A bad man, Peter supposed, to be punished so. He would rather have his ears lopped than be nailed to a cross like that. But he could see no other stranger in the church and he had seen women kneeling at the foot of the statue with babies in bundles, so he supposed that if God was anywhere He was there.

Now Old Peter loved God because the only certainty in his poor muddled mind was the certainty that his Saviour loved him. He knew nothing about Him, nothing about his Church, but he loved Him. He loved Him because nobody else in all his fifty years of painful existence had ever loved him or even seen him for an instant of time as anything better than a mule or a packhorse. The household ignored him, the men tormented him, the cook beat him. His days were a slow bewilderment of pain and stupidity, his suffering worse than the suffering of a dog. Until tonight, the night of the miracle. Tonight another certainty had clicked like a lock in Old Peter's brain, the certainty that he loved the lord Simon. Through all the terror and the smart and the shouting, choked by a stinking rag until he could scarcely breath, dizzy from those spinning hands, he heard the cry of the queer young master and it was like the cry of an angel. That night Simon fastened to himself a human soul, loyal not as Huw was loyal, with intelligence and strength, but loyal as a limpet is loyal to the rock. It was the end for Old Peter of the path from the well-house to the kitchen. He simply attached himself to Simon like a shadow, and when twice he had been found beaten senseless by the cook with the scummer Simon spoke to his father. Henceforth he was allowed to hobble after his young master as best he could, lug water for his washing and sleep across the sill of his door and if Simon had asked him to murder the baron in his bed Old Peter would unhesitatingly have done so.

So he slept happily on his stomach among the rushes on the night of the miracle, an old man with a purpose. But not so Simon. He tossed on his mattress and was haunted by dreams. Once again he rode past the boundary cross as he had done that day, with the sinking sun behind him, and his heart leapt with joy to see the Welshman still standing like a statue, with his dog at his feet. He stood on a mound to the left of the track and Simon twitched Merlin's head only to find with horror that both his hands were claws, both his legs reeds. He sat powerless on the great horse, forced to watch the Welshman slowly turn away and vanish over the hill. Wait! Wait! he screamed, but he could not move one withered muscle and he knew he had lost him whom he wanted for his friend. He opened his mouth to scream again and found words issuing from his mouth like a stream.

'Quia tu es, Deus, fortitudo mea; quare me repulisti et quare tristis incedo, dum affligit me inimicus. . . .'

He was in the tiny parish church standing as Martin's server in the celebration of the Mass.

'*Emitte lucam tuam et veritatem tuam*,' said Martin.

'*Spera in Deo, quoniam ad huc confitebor illi*,' replied Simon.

He had the responses pat in his brain and they glided off his tongue without hesitation, but as the age-old conversation proceeded he became aware of something wrong.

'*Confitebor tibi in cathara, Deus, Deus meus; quare tristis es, anima mea, et quare conturbas me?*' said Martin.

'*Sicut erat in principio et nunc et semper, et in saecula saeculorum*. Amen.' answered Simon.

As he puzzled what was amiss he saw a black snout peep out from behind the crucifix and a black rat sprang out on to the altar.

'*Domine, exaudi oratorionem meam er salutare tuum da nobis*.'

The rat hesitated, twitched his whiskers over the sacramental bread, then leapt down on to the altar steps, where the glow-worm crawled. With a snap he swallowed it and at that moment Simon knew what was wrong. He was giving the wrong responses. Always he gave the wrong responses. Horrified lest his failure invalidate the Mass, he shouted, 'Stop him, stop him!' and all the people began to chase the rat round the chancel, until he woke to find himself muttering, 'Stop him, stop him!' with sweat running down his thighs. The wrong responses! Always the wrong responses. As in dreams, so in life. Always he could be relied upon for the wrong responses.

When he heard the priory bell ringing for Prime he got up and went out alone by the back stairway, leaving Huw snoring on the floor by his bed. Instinctively he turned his face towards the church. He waited while the porter, still rubbing sleep from his red eyes, opened the castle gate, then limped slowly up to the church, the toe of his right foot bumping softly over the cobbles. He would go to Martin. Martin would reassure him, tell him that his dream meant nothing. But in the churchyard he found the Pardoner, sitting in the cool sunlight on a flat tomb picking his nose. He looked at him intently. He had the face of a fox, a stinking fox fit only to be shot like vermin. He had the face of a fox even to the red hair and the yellow fangs.

'Good morning, my lord,' said the fox, pulling his greasy fringe but not rising from the tombstone. 'Can I interest you in anything today? An indulgence hot from the Pope's own hand? A snippet of Our Lady's veil? A bone from the toe of the blessed martyr St Peter? Or . . .' Here he eyed the withered leg, the hunch-shoulder, the dragging foot . . . 'a cure? I got here a magic mitten, to cure a man of what brings sorrow and disappointment to his wife. No? A balm then? A balm for sore bodies, a balm for sore minds, only one penny. . . .'

'I want nothing,' said Simon, but he did not move away.

The Pardoner quickly unslung a wallet from his shoulder and laid it beside him on the tomb. 'A pardon then? Pardons here for all sins, blessed by the bishop and signed by the Pope. You eaten meat on a Friday? Here . . .' He scrabbled among the dirty bits of parchment and held one up in the sunlight between his filthy finger and thumb. 'You lain with your maid? Here . . .' And another mockery was hauled into the pure light. 'Here and here.' He dealt them out in rows like cards, each one marked with a cross. 'Buy a pardon, my lord, a pardon for sin!'

Simon looked down at the dirty pieces of parchment and retched to think of God's pardon travestied and made into a traffic. A pardon? He did not need a pardon. His affliction was not the result of his own sin but of his mother's and she was beyond God's pardon. She must have sinned after Richard's birth, but she had never confessed her sin and so in Simon she had given birth to a deformed child. Even then she could have saved herself by confession but still she had not confessed her sin and she had born another deformed child. Even then God's pardon was open to her had she but confessed her sin, but she had not done so and on the night of the Welsh attack the devil had entered her and chained her tongue. It was his mother needed God's pardon, not he, and she could never have it while the devil inhabited her. The stain of his mother's sin lay over him as over Blanche and he felt that only a miracle could take it away.

But others needed pardons and many would buy them rather than face the priest and do proper penance.

'You expect to sell these?' he asked, pointing to the shabby pardons. 'Do people buy them?'

'Buy them? 'Course they buy them. A penny for venial sin, tuppence for mortal sin. Why shouldn't they buy them?'

'And they give absolution without penance?'

'Penance?' he cackled. 'Penance, you say? Money's penance, ain't it? Copper and silver, there's all the penance I need,' and he tickled his scabby palm.

Simon turned away, sick at heart, but the Pardoner clawed at his coat and showed him a little bag tied up with hairy string.

'Know what that is, my lord? Dust from the altar, where the light was. Penny a pinch that'll fetch, see if it don't.'

'And Our Lady's veil?' mocked Simon, 'and the toe of the blessed martyr? Who can afford such luxuries when dirt is a penny a pinch?'

'Oh, my lord!' The fox was hurt. 'I give good value, you can't deny. Only fourpence for a bit of veil. It's sixpence for a bit of St Stephen's loincloth, I'll allow, but then it's got blood on it.' He leered through his hanging hair and slowly, deliberately, winked his right eye. 'Worth sixpence, ain't they? Bloodstains is rare.' He wiped his nose with his hand and went on: 'Cures, now, they don't seldom come so dear, not being religious, see, but here . . .' He drew from his pocket a curious little pot stoppered with wax. 'Now this here is something very special, my lord. An elixir, that's what. I got it from a shipman in the port of Bristol. And what can it cure? Why, anything, my lord, be it hot humour or cold, wet or dry, scab, plague, the falling evil, pox, fever, gout, melancholy. But it's dear. Elixirs don't come cheap. A shilling, my lord. What you say to a shilling? A shilling for a cure?'

Simon looked at the pot. It was a pretty colour, blue like a periwinkle, with the wax neatly levelled in the mouth. He looked at the scabby hand that held it, he smelt the stinking breath. A shilling? Well, it could do him no harm. It could not make him worse. And who knows, it might, it just might . . .

He did not really believe that this ointment would cure either his lopsided body or his lopsided mind. He no more believed in it than he believed that the bloody rag in the Pardoner's wallet was the loincloth of St Stephen, or that the shreds of blue linen came from the Blessed Virgin's veil, or that those dirty bits of parchment could give pardon for sin. But the frauds of a hundred pardoners could not alter the truth. True relics did exist, although they were not hawked about the countryside like trinkets. True absolution could be obtained, although not by the scribble of a quill on grubby parchment. Somewhere lay hidden the miraculous power that could cure him, strengthen his limbs, straighten his mind, and if it did not lie in this little pot at least it was better than raw snails.

'Here,' he said, and tossed the shilling on to the tombstone, where it spun among the pardons and came to rest in the exact centre of a purple cross.

He had hardly time to hide the pot in his purse when Martin appeared, hot and angry with a besom raised in both hands. One sweep and the parchments fluttered like dirty snowflakes in the grass and the Pardoner was down on his sharp knees frantically salvaging his stock-in-trade.

'There! There! There!' cried Martin, bringing the besom down on to the mean upturned behind. 'Out of here, you filthy toad. Defile my churchyard, will you?' Again and again the besom descended, while the Pardoner shrieked and scrabbled in the grass. One last snatch, a final desperate lunge for the shilling, and he was off, streaking over the cobbles like a felon fox with his wallet bumping on his back.

'There,' said Martin, and threw down his broom. He breathed heavily and dusted one hand against the other and wiped them carefully on his skirts lest they should have been polluted. 'There's the last of him, I trust. Just let him show his face in my churchyard again and God save me but I will bloody his nose.'

A scrap of parchment came floating down from the yew tree like a bedraggled feather. It came to rest at Martin's feet and he picked it up with the tip of his finger and thumb, wrinkling his face in disgust. 'A pardon? Eh dear, he will be putting me out of business just now with his tuppenny absolutions. Blessed by the Pope too. Now which Pope will that be, I wonder,' and he cracked the parchment across and across, as a man breaks a twig.

'Hot from the Pope's own hand, that's what he said.'

'Ah, but there are two Popes at this time, as you very well know, Simon. A French Pope at Avignon and an Italian Pope at Rome. Which will you have now, eh?' He looked at his friend shrewdly, noting the furrow between his eyebrows so deep it was like a scar, and his haunted eyes. 'Do not mind him, Simon. He is not worth your disgust. He is a louse, that one. He breeds only where there is dirt. He cannot harm the truth of Holy Church.' He laid his hand on Simon's shoulder, his sound shoulder, and drew him towards the church. 'Come, you shall share my breakfast. I have pulled a cabbage with the dew still on it. You shall watch me cook it and then we shall talk.' They passed through the porch and made a circuit of the font on their way to the priest's room. The chill of the nave struck cold on Simon's forehead where the holy water glistened. Martin chattered on. 'Now there is a fine cabbage for you. I will add chives and bacon and make a noble dish. A dish of hot food is better than all your cures. If I had the money I should be fat enough to stop a barrel.'

'Like the prior,' said Simon.

'Aye, he likes his food, does the prior. Three cooks and a man for the sauces, but I will wager none made a better sauce than my mother. A good cook was my mother and a lovely voice, although she never could get her tongue round the sharp English words. Beat her my father did for speaking Welsh.' He sighed, and began shredding the cabbage with his fingers. 'It is sad to have had a Welsh mother and not speak the Welsh. To speak English with the Welsh music, it is not the same.' He went down on his knees and began blowing on the embers so that the white ash flew about his cropped head. A flame leapt and he fed it with the Pope's pardon. 'Food,' he said, and threw sticks on the fire. 'Better than simples, eh, Simon? Better than cures?'

'Aye,' said Simon, guiltily feeling the little pot through the leather of his purse.

He returned to the castle in time to take his mother for her morning walk on the battlements. She would never leave the castle grounds, had never done so for seven years, but he thought she liked to look over the great fields and the dark woods and peep into the priory grounds. She used to hold up her squirrel to see the view, careful first to loop his golden chain round her wrist. She clucked in her throat now and then, the nearest the devil would allow her to speech. He watched her, as he watched her every day, and wondered for the thousandth time what her sin had been. A terrible sin, he had no doubt, a mortal sin, one of the deadly seven. Well, she had been punished for it, he thought, hearing the clucks and feeling his toe dragging on the lead and noting the sores on her chin where the drooling was. But he could not hate his mother, not even when he looked at Blanche. It must be terrible to live with a devil inside you, denied the consolation of the Mass, cut off from God, and to see in every fire the leaping flames of hell.

Presently they went down the winding stairway, having narrow glimpses of summer at every turn. The sunlight cut through the darkness as if a golden knife were thrust through every window. At the bottom they found Margaret waiting for her mistress, and Huw.

'Come you, my lord,' said Huw. 'There's wanting you your da is.'

They found the baron in the solar, hunched over his sops. His old enemy was active today, ready with his thrusts, and when Simon limped over to him it was some time before he spoke. 'Go,' he said to Huw and Huw went, leaving them alone. Simon watched his father, feeling something of his suffering and wishing that he were not such a disappointment to him. If only there were something . . .

'Simon,' his father's words cut through his pity, 'have you ever lain with a woman?'

Simon winced as if a finger had touched a secret wound.

'A woman, Father? No. No, I have never lain with a woman.'

'Come now, boy. I am no priest. I shall give you no penance. Tell me the truth now. Have you ever lain with a woman so that you were like to get her with child?'

'No, Father, truly.'

'Nor wished to, eh? Or have you wished and never done?'

Had he wished? Had he? He stood with his forehead against the warm stone of the mantle and nudged the embers with his foot. What had he wished? He thought of how Richard looked at Alice. He thought of the ungainly humps among the rushes at night, the whimpers of pleasure. He thought of Margaret's high round breasts and the white thighs of the reed-cutters and he knew that he did indeed wish. But he was afraid; afraid that in love, as in everything, he would fail in the doing. Halt in limb, lacking the right responses, who was he to lie with a woman and be told to go and buy a magic mitten?

'Yes. Father. I have wished, but not done.'

The baron swallowed the last of his sops and laid the bowl across his shapeless knees. 'A man in your station,' he said thoughtfully, 'must either marry or become a monk.'

The words hung in the air between them, heavy with portent. 'It is your duty to marry and have children, Simon, if it is within your power. Richard's wife is barren and like to remain so'—Simon thought of poor Alice hopefully on her knees where the beetle had crawled—'and I shall never rest quiet in my tomb if the March passes to Warwick. Have I given the best part of twenty years to the nursing of this lordship only to see it snatched away like a sucking child from the breast? Nay, I will get Richard an annulment first.' He looked at his son, purposefully keeping his eyes on his face. 'God has marked you for your mother's sin, but there is nothing in your face for women to shrink from, and as to the body'—he viewed his own with a glint of humour—'I have never found an ugly body a hurdle in the way of a woman's heart. There is only one thing, one lack, that can separate her from you.' He shifted in his chair and the bowl clattered on to the stone in a dribble of milk. Simon limped across the hearth to pick it up and felt his father's hand on his head, among the tight curls. 'My son, I wish you to go down to the priory and see Brother Gregory. I have spoken to the prior. Brother Gregory is a learned man in anatomy and the workings of the body.' Simon jerked his head away, appalled. Brother Gregory? That worm, that snake? Were those beastly fingers to crawl over him as they had crawled over the altar step, inching into his secret places? And for what? To pronounce him a gelding? To shut him up in a monastery like his sister Blanche?

'Do it for me, Simon,' urged his father, watching him. 'You are the best-loved of my children. Do it for me.' And Simon never thought that it might be for his own sake too. He paused on his way to the door and looked at his father and thought what his life must have been these twenty years and more with a wife in mortal sin and a body held in a vice. He pictured him gazing at the deformed boy, the deformed girl, setting all his hopes on his first-born and his first-born's children. He imagined the waiting, the covert looks at Alice's belly, Richard's bewilderment, the charms, the candles, the prayers, the cures. He remembered the terrible day that his father entered his chamber when Huw was rubbing the balm into his side, the secret glances while he blushed with shame. And now Brother Gregory. Well, he would go. He would endure that groping for his father's sake, whatever the verdict, so that his father might know. He hoped for Alice's sake as well as his own that Brother Gregory would not pronounce him impotent. For him it would mean the cloister, for Alice a papal dispensation for Richard's remarriage. Well, he would go. Brother Gregory would not dare to tell his father a lie, and supposing . . .

'So be it,' he said to his father with his hand on the door, 'I will go.'

He went. Alone, for he did not count Old Peter who hobbled on his heels in his swaddling and waited for him in the courtyard, kneeling for the hurt in his behind. To the day of his death he remembered the look of the priory that morning, the shining horses in the stables, the seething fish-pond, the smell of baking and roasting, a brother on his knees clipping the grass, a wagon coming in from the estates loaded with wood, a greyhound with a silver collar, three novices pacing the cloisters with their missals in their hands and rosaries swinging against their knees; the door to the church, the library, the infirmary, the prior's lodging with its door mercifully shut, and finally the gloomy parlour where he was to be examined. He went through the doorway as a felon goes to the gallows and the door closed heavily behind him.

When he came out an hour later the priory bell was ringing for High Mass but he could not make his feet carry him up that nave to that altar to have God put into his mouth by those scented hands. Instead he drew down a shutter in his mind over his humiliation and went in to his father with the blessed news. It was the only time in his life that he saw his father move quickly. He started out of his chair at his son's words and grasped him by the arms with a surprising strength. He was bent like a bow but he peered up into Simon's face and laughed. 'Heathy, eh, boy? Sound and strong? We shall make a father of you yet.' He chuckled and exalted and Simon distinctly heard one of his own burdens drop to the floor. He had many burdens tied to his crooked shoulders and now he heard one of them go. Not the heaviest, but he felt the easier for its going. His father levered himself back into his chair, but he had the breath for another word of advice.

'Take a woman, Simon,' he said at last. 'Do not be afraid. And tell me when you have done so.'

As if his day had not taken shocks enough, at dinner Simon was forced to eat next to the Summoner, come on one of his periodic visits with summonses to the bishop's court. If the Pardoner was a fox, the Summoner was a wolf, a dangerous animal with a long nose for sin. Sin was his business, to smell out spiritual crimes and lug them before the bishop. Never mind if a man had confessed to his priest and done penance; if the Summoner came to hear of it he would ferret the man out and serve him with a summons. Not that he was a merciless man, oh no. He could be persuaded to forget the sin and the summons for a money payment, if it was not of too serious a nature. Heresy, now, did not admit of payment, nor the lapsing of a priest, but many an adulterous ploughman purchased his escape with a week's wages placed in the wolf's paw.

The man even ate like a wolf, guzzling his meat and licking the blood from his mouth with a sickly tongue. Simon wondered whom he was trailing today. He was not long left in doubt.

'Do you know a man named Stephen Oxted, my lord?' asked the Summoner, chewing.

'I may do,' said Simon cautiously. 'Why do you want him?'

'A sad case, my lord, a very sad case. Given to unnatural and evil practices. His name has come to the bishop's ears,' and he looked at Simon out of the corners of his eyes, that were like little black knobs in his smooth white face. 'Aye,' he said slowly, sucking his teeth, 'his name has come to the bishop.'

'What has he done?'

The Summoner glanced along the chattering line and drawing nearer breathed something into Simon's ear.

'How do you know?'

'I have evidence, my lord. I have reason to believe the other man will talk.'

Simon crumbled his bread and began rolling it into little balls on the tablecloth. Stephen Oxted? That jolly man who slept with Merlin and could lift a man in each hand?

'And what will the bishop do to him, if he finds him guilty?'

'It's not what the bishop will do, my lord, not in a case like this, but what the bishop's officer will do.'

'What? Will the bishop not take his money, then? Since when had the bishop had scruples about taking the money of sinners?'

'You mistake me, my lord. This is not a case of money payment, not once it has reached the bishop.' He paused with a chicken leg in his hand and inspected it as if he suspected it too of unnatural behaviour. 'Not once it has reached the bishop,' he repeated with another sidelong glance, and Simon understood him. Evidently even sodomy had its price.

'It is bound to reach the bishop, surely. If he has the man's name——'

'Ah, I see you are a clever one, my lord, the Lord has blessed you with brains, sure enough. But the bishop is old, quite seventy summers if a day, and what if I cannot find this Stephen Oxted? Fled to the woods maybe or over into the next diocese? Is the bishop to take horse and look for him?'

Simon turned and looked the man full in the face, the sloping forehead and knobby eyes, the dead whiteness of skin like something under a stone, the greedy mouth with shreds of chicken hanging from it. Here was a man worse than the souls he hounded, more sinning than the sinners, a deceiver and a blackmailer. Here was one more evidence of the cruelty and horror that filled the world, lurking even in the skirts of Holy Church. A louse, like the Pardoner, but what had Martin said? 'He breeds only in the dirt.' Was there dirt then between the toes of the church that such a man should have a place in it? A bishop's officer, a man in minor orders, a blackmailer and extortioner, growing fat on the farthings of frail widows and tempted hostlers?

'And what,' he asked again, with coldness in his voice, 'will be done to him, if the bishop finds him guilty?'

The Summoner did not reply but picked up his knife and slashed the air in a circular movement of sickening significance. 'Remove the cause of offence, my lord; what else?'

Simon shuddered, shutting his eyes on the damage no magic mitten could repair. Manhood given, manhood taken away. It was too much for one day.

'How much?' he asked, and put his hand to his purse.

The Summoner pretended not to hear.

'How much?' he asked again.

The knobs swivelled in their sockets as if appraising their man. 'You must understand,' he said softly, in a dreadful confidence, 'the bishop having the man's name it comes more expensive.'

'How much?' asked Simon, bending his back to be out of the other man's breath.

'And the offence, the horrible nature of the offence, flying in the face of nature, as you might say——'

'How much?' asked Simon patiently, knowing that they would come to a figure in the end.

'Ten shillings, my lord, and cheap at the price.'

So Simon bought the safety of Stephen Oxted for ten shillings to save him from the gelder's knife.

His hand still burned from the Summoner's touch when he dragged himself up to the altar at the evening Mass, as a man drags himself through the desert to a sweet pool of water. This was his moment of peace, when he felt God on his tongue and all the doubts and uncertainties of his life fell away. This was the only moment when he forgot his affliction and lost sight of his unhappiness.

The world was looking very lovely when he came out of the church into the soft evening light and collected his shadow from the tombstone. The north gate was not yet shut and he strolled out on to the highway for a last glimpse of the lovely curve of the river and the steep sides of Blorys down which he had ridden only yesterday. As he stood there, relishing the beauty before him, two figures approached out of the gloom, a man and a woman. As they drew nearer he could hear the soft shuffle of their feet in the dust. They came level with him and passed and he recognized the man, who gave him a civil greeting. It was the tailor Philip Win, a dimpled apple-cheeked man who lived in his wish-bone house against the east wall and made the livery for his father's men. The woman he did not know. She was tall, taller than he, with long black hair unbound on her shoulders and a face such as he had seen only in dreams, long and white with eyes like dark diamonds. They passed in at the gate and vanished and he was alone with his faithful shadow.

Presently he turned to go in and found the gate-keeper waiting to shut the gates.

'Who was that, Rufus?' he asked.

'Who was who, my lord?'

'That woman. The one with Philip Win.'

'Her? Why, it's his daughter, my lord. Been to fetch her home, he has. She been in service up in the Welshry these three years. She got the Welsh, you see, seeing as her dad married a Welshwoman. From Pwll-du, so they say, but she's been dead these many years. The daughter she finished her term so he bring her home.'

'And her name?'

'Eva, my lord.'

'Ah. Good night, Rufus.'

'Good night, my lord.'

They passed in at the gate, Simon and his shadow, and the great doors shut them in.

4

NEXT morning the sun shone brilliantly, making a shining star of the mirror, and Simon nudged Huw with his foot. He had not felt so light-hearted for many months. It must be Brother Gregory's news, he thought, the assurance of his manhood. Perhaps he was not so different from other men as he thought. They ate their breakfast in the great hall, with light streaming through the open doors and the long windows. An early swallow swooped among the beams of the roof. The cook scolded in the kitchen, too sleepy to be shrill. The fire had been cleared of its ashes and a clean cold flame burnt on the hearth. A freshness lay over the familiar scene, even over Old Peter, who had ducked his head in his master's water and who brought them their sops with the wet making runnels in his neck. The Summoner had gone, sniffing his way downriver to Usk. The Pardoner had departed to chew offal elsewhere, and the air was the sweeter for their going. The day was so lovely that Simon did not feel the accustomed stab of envy when his father came creeping from the solar on the arms of two men and said that Richard should go to see to the sheep-dipping.

He never questioned his father's right to order his life, and the lives of all of them, wife, sons, daughter, servants, Welsh and English. Was he not the lord of the March, a Marcher baron holding his lordship by right of the conquest of his predecessors? Had he not greater powers within his boundaries than the king himself in the English shires? The king's writ did not run in the March. The king's justices had to turn back at the boundary. The powers of life and death lay in the baron's gouty hand. The baron's word was the law; and it was well for King Henry IV that his shaky throne had such a secure buttress in the loyalty of the Baron Abercibbi. He sat now, bent-backed at the high table, obsessed with his rents and his tenants and his farms, while his sons stood before him for the ordering of their day.

He was puzzled what to do with Simon. He looked at his son, the dearest of his children, his fair head shining in the sunlight from the window. He had so many gifts, a compassionate heart, a gentle nature. He was clever, too. He saw things Richard never saw. But he was a dreamer, a thinker in a world where thought was dangerous. Sometimes the baron woke in the night and shuddered to think where his son's thoughts might lead him.

He gave his orders. Richard was to go to the dipping and the baron himself was going to the weir in a litter to supervise the setting of the fish-traps. Seneschal must go to Llanvetherine, to see after a tardy death duty due last Holy Week, and never brought to the castle as custom demanded. 'I will have his best beast if I have to take his affer out of the wagon,' he grumbled. 'I'll not have him thwarting my lord of his just rights. Slippery, that David Morgan. He had a Welsh grandfather, so can you wonder?'

They were all busy, full of plans. And Simon? Simon was to go to Ty-Mawr to the parish church to find how much lead was needed for the roof tower. And on his way back round the skirts of Blorys he was to stop at the ironworkings and order another load of iron bars. A courier, a messenger, fit only to carry orders. But the sun was still on the day and he and Huw set off with the priory bell in their ears and Old Peter at their horses' heels. Nothing would persuade him to stay behind. It pained Simon to see his hobbled haste to keep up with horses and when Old Peter's feet began to bleed he put his spurs to Merlin's flanks and with a word to Huw broke into a canter to spare the old man the agony of pursuit. Soon he was lost to them in a cloud of white dust and presently they came within sound of the ironworkings. Here the winches rattled, the great bellows blew, the puddling poles hissed in the fire. A huge mound of iron ore, red rocks the size of a man's fist, rose like a giant mole-hill at the side of the road. Further along, past the smelting barn, were the iron bars, stacked like a dark honeycomb as high as a man's head. There was a sturdy Welsh wagon ready loading with iron for the Welshry, the eight oxen standing patiently in the shafts blinking at the flies. For the Wesh were bound to fetch their iron in the bar and were forbidden by the law of the March to dig for their own. Every quarter the wagons came down from the commotes and their quota of iron was checked on a tally; so much for ploughshares, so much for hoes, so much for horseshoes, so much for nails, for arrow-tips and for knives. For the baron lived yet with the sound of iron at the north gate and the only iron he allowed the Welshry was iron for its necessities. Arrow-tips, now, he could not deny them those. It was well known that when the old king died the young Prince Harry would spring straight from his coronation stone to a war-horse and would be skewering the French dogs within the year; and were not the Welsh the finest archers in the world, many of them ready to earn their tuppence a day in the service of the hot Lord Harry in the hope of glory and plunder? For a hundred years it had been the law of the land that men should practise at the butts. No, the baron could not deny them their arrow-tips, nor knives for their daily usage, but he could deny them iron for swords and armour, and the bars from the workings were carefully checked.

Simon watched the bars being taken from the honeycomb to build a smaller honeycomb on the wagon. Welshmen darted here and there on their stocky Welsh ponies, many of whom still carried the tatters of their winter coats. They were small and dark like gnomes, with secret faces, and to Simon they spelled magic. Their hair hung to their shoulders and their faces were scraped clean and their eyes looked through a man to his backbone. They rode without spurs, twisting in the saddles like mountebanks, urging the oxen with strange Welsh cries: '*Tynnwch! Nol!*'

Now the last bar was lugged and chains rattled across the load to prevent it slipping. It was a scene of confusion; only the patient oxen stood still. There was another wagon waiting for the ascent, a team of eight with a load of herrings. Simon caught the whiff of fish as he approached it. Eight oxen for a load of herrings? Eight oxen for a load of iron? He looked from one wagon to the other, faint stirrings of doubt in his mind. He was confused by the clatter of hammers, the heavy breathing of the bellows, the darting ponies. He looked for Huw but suddenly the word was given, the whips cracked over the oxen's heads and the beasts set their weight against their loads. Shoulders bunched, haunches braced, they lowered their broad heads and threw their weight forward.

'*Dere mla'n!*'

The shafts creaked, the timbers groaned, but the Welsh elm was sturdy and suddenly the wheels moved.

'*Tynnwch! Tynnwch!*' shouted the Welshmen, urging their ponies forward while the grimy English ironworkers paused to watch them go.

'*Dere mla'n.*'

Slowly the wheels turned and the oxen set their small feet on the hem of Blorys' skirts and began the long haul up through the forest to the Welshry. To Simon's surprise the herring wagon toiled as slowly as the other, although it was drawn by eight oxen and was in the lead. The wheels crawled like snails in their baked ruts. One of the oxen suddenly made water and the urine ran down the rut like a little river pushing dust before it. The leading wagon was nearly in the trees now. Time only for a Paternoster before the leading pair was in the shadow. Horsemen made a procession either side with chocks ready across their saddles but the wagons crept steadily up without pause. Curious and uneasy Simon looked again for Huw and saw him at some distance, dismounted and bending over a bundle in the roadway. Heat rose in waves from Merlin's neck, making the fields waver. A fly settled on Simon's mouth and an insupportable depression suddenly overcame him. A fly, a prick of doubt, sweat in his armpits, the glare of the fires, these were the sparks that fired him to shake the reins irritably about Merlin's head and follow the wagons into the coolness of the forest.

Here the light was sieved through the branches and Simon had to thread his way carefully among the trees with his head bent, for he knew that if a branch swept him from the saddle he could not mount again without Huw's help. He could see the procession of wagons and horsemen through the trees to his right and he spurred Merlin on so as to come out on the track above them. He came out at the head of the leading pair and waited for the waggon to draw level, curious to peer over its high sides at the herring baskets. A whip snapped over his head but he swung Merlin's rump so that his withered knee touched the side of the wagon. A Welshman urged his pony past him but did not turn his head and Simon peered over his hunched shoulder at the baskets. They were filled with herrings, right enough, netted off the Irish coast three days before and still smelling of the sea. The fish gleamed dully with dead eyes. But the baskets were packed close on a bed of brushwood that he thought strangely thick and the tops of the baskets were high up the sides for such a deep wagon. He leant away to measure the sides with his eye and suddenly found himself slipping between the horse and the wheel. A hub had rasped Merlin's shank and his buck had thrown his master off his precarious balance. Simon's limp right foot slid from the stirrup and he fell in a heap a hand's breadth from the back wheel, his left arm thrown up to save his face.

There were shouts and the slipping of hooves and the wheel mercifully jolted to a stop. Welsh voices surrounded him. '*Beth ar y ddaear y mae e'n gwneud yma?*' they said. The sound of the chocks travelled along the ground to Simon's ear but he lay half-stunned on his back seeing but not noticing the red dust that trickled through the bottom of the wagon. Then he felt a hand on his arm and he struggled into a sitting position more worried about the humiliation of mounting his horse than any hurt. He grasped the wheel and pulled himself upright on to his sound leg. His only thought now was to be gone. The Welshmen watched him from their ponies and it was suddenly very quiet, the only sounds the blowing of the oxen and the click of a hoof. Someone fetched Merlin and Simon looked wildly round, caught in a nightmare of mortification. He tried to hide his hand in the folds of his tunic but a little wind blew and exposed it. He looked at Merlin, suddenly thirty hands high. Then there was a movement and he found a dark Welsh head bent at his side and a pair of hard Welsh hands linked for his mounting. Thankfully he placed his knee in that proffered crook and was lifted into the saddle. The man's touch was strange, as if there were no stuff between the flesh of the fingers and the flesh of the leg. 'My thanks,' said Simon, and the man straightened his back.

It was Llewellyn ap Thomas.

His eyes glowed like coals and there was no doubt now of their meaning. These were the eyes of a friend. Gazing, Simon forgot all about the herring baskets, as Llewellyn intended him to do. Moons waxed and waned as he gazed into those hot eyes; quarters passed, the seasons fell away. Llewellyn stood with his hand on Merlin's neck. It was like a tableau in a church, the wooden oxen and the carved figures, the iron honeycomb and the silver-painted fish. Then Merlin twitched his ears and Llewellyn withdrew his hand.

'My thanks,' said Simon again and turned his horse. He left them levering the chocks away from the wheels and jolted back between the ruts. He had forgotten the herrings and the suspicious heaviness of the wagon. He did not remember the red trickles of dust. He was only conscious of something about his right knee, Llewellyn's hands lifting him up. Even when Merlin kicked a ball of red earth with his hoof and it rolled with a metallic click into last year's leaves he did not suspect. His doubts had been wiped away by the fire of Llewellyn's eyes just as an imprint is melted from the wax.

When he reached the highway and found Huw waiting for him with a bundle he simply said he had ridden into the shadows to cool himself.

The bundle was Old Peter. He was thick with dust. Little stones had worked their way into his feet, which were a mess of blood and dirt. Flies fed at the corners of his eyes. He was too weak to stand but he would have crawled after his master until he died had not Simon set a man to watch him. They propped him in the shadow of the iron heap, drenched him with water from the stream and rode on into Ty-Mawr to view the roof-tower. They saw the parson, viewed the tower and rode back in the noontide sun. They found old Peter dozing with his back against the iron and hoisted him onto Huw's horse where he sagged like a sack. Simon was quiet and Huw, as always, suited his mood to his master, riding in his master's shadow as he had done since his master was nine years old. As they walked their horses home Old Peter thought of nothing, Huw thought of Simon and Simon thought of Llewellyn ap Thomas. He was slipping furlong by furlong back into his customary sense of unsuitability but if the gay mood of the morning was gone so was the terrible oppression that had come over him at the iron-workings. He had seen Llewellyn and knew him for a friend. He felt that he was on the threshold of new things. He heard the creaking of hinges in his mind. He felt excited, hopeful. Watching him, Huw felt that their morning had been a success.

There wanted still an hour before meat and they sat awhile in the herb garden, having left Old Peter with Stephen Oxted in the stable with instructions to tend his feet. To please the man who had saved him from the gelder's knife Stephen Oxted would have washed the feet of a leper.

'Huw,' said Simon, 'have you ever had a woman?'

'There is funny you are, boy. There's not many indeed have reached my age and not had a woman.'

'Many women, Huw?'

'Aye, a tidy few. But fleeting, mind. No wives for old Huw.

'Did you not like one enough then?'

Huw considered, with a sprig of thyme between his teeth. 'Well now,' he said at length, 'where would she be sleeping if I had a wife? Am I to lie with her in the rushes for all to see? Or in the bracken like a green boy? Or in the stable like a whore? There's a house she'd be wanting and a babe in a cot of rushes and old Huw at the end of a spit and my lord sleeping alone with only Old Peter's snores in his ears. Nay, there is men for marriage and men for service, look you, and I am not one to be wanting a wife.'

'And what is it like, Huw, to lie with a woman?'

Huw looked startled, as well he might. Here was a queer one indeed, expecting a dark tower to be flooded with light. 'Like, my lord?' He scratched his head and glanced at the shrunken haunch beside him. 'There's no man can say what it's like. You will be after finding soon enough.'

Simon was silent, unrolling the petals of an apple bud, and Huw thought of Alice and Jenny, of Bronwen and Ceinwen, of all the lasses English and Welsh that he had known in his forty-seven years of life. 'There is softness in a woman,' he said with his eyes on the torn petals, 'and fire and whiteness and lips to stop a man's breathing. There is an arrow and a sword to pierce a man through.'

They sat quietly in the warm sun until they heard the cluck-cluck of his mother's throat and saw her dead face through the pink and white of the apple blossom. But as they rose Simon put his hand on Huw's arm, feeling the stuff, and said: 'Huw, you shall have a new livery. We will go down to see the tailor.'

Towards Vespers they came out of the castle and paused, drinking in the sweet evening. It had been fair weather since Palm Sunday and the rooks had built high. Three times during Lent Simon had seen a falling star, portent of a favourable summer. Please God there would be a good harvest. It bewildered Simon sometimes to think how they were all at God's mercy, little insects fearful of the falling stone or the descending foot. Pray as they might, they could not hold back the hailstones that stripped the trees of their blossom or the cloudburst that carried the young wheat in a flood of destruction into the ditches or the dreaded murrain that struck the standing cattle as surely as the knacker's hammer. It was a merciful God, so Martin said, but Simon could see little mercy in the world either for himself or for others. Disease, disfigurement, cruelty, melancholy and poverty were everywhere around him pulling at his heart-strings until he was like to be torn in pieces by his pity. Every drop of blood shouted for mercy, for an easing of the weight that crushed man's shoulders. Yet they all thought it odd that he should resent the brutishness of life. Life was short, life was painful. It had always been so, it would never be any different. It was not for man to question God's will or the workings of God's mind. Simon laid his sound hand on Huw's shoulder to assure himself of one man's affection and looked about him. With the human touch his mood changed. The world seemed fair enough tonight. It glowed in the evening sun, all save Blorys which lay with its back to the light, black as the whale that swallowed Jonah. A golden cloud rose slowly from its ridged back and drifted into the shape of a crucifix. Simon hastily crossed himself. The cross dissolved into a cloud of golden feathers and suddenly the sun slipped behind Blorys, going to its sleep behind the Welshry.

'Come you now,' said Huw, and they went down the cobbled slope into the town. They passed a row of cruck houses with mud walls and tattered thatch, each with its tethered hen and a dozen cabbage plants before its door. Once clear of the castle wall they had the pound on their right, empty now save for three unmarked lambs and the death duty of David Morgan. It was a fine cow calf. Seneschal had had a successful day at Llanvetherine. At the last house they paused to exchange a greeting with the wise woman. She was a huge woman with a lucky mole on her chin as big as a shilling and she bent over her herbs as a mother bends over a cradle.

'The portents is right for rue,' she wheezed as they drew near. 'Six sparrows on the roof-tree last Sabbath and a toad across the sill in the night. You shall have it Saturday, my lord, if the devil does not put out the fire.'

Simon's tongue curled as if he felt the bitter herb already and he spat among the entrails on the path. 'May I sweeten it with honey, Mother?' he asked. 'Will honey spoil the simple?'

'What a child it is! Have I not told you that the virtue dwells in the gall? If you want a cure, my lord, you must swallow bitterness.'

Swallow bitterness? Well, he would do it. He would suffer smally that he might benefit greatly. 'Bring it then,' he cried over his hunched shoulder. 'I shall drink it and Huw shall hold my nose!'

A few steps brought them to the road only an arrow's flight from the south gate. Before them lay the market square, slippery with dung and black with flies, and beyond its streaming filth were the gallows, the stocks and the baiting-post, with a wisp of bear's hair still hanging on a splinter. Beyond the gallows, out of sight and snug against the east wall, was the tailor's house with an upstairs room as befitted his prosperity and oiled linen in the window. They stepped aside as a pair of driven geese hissed at their heels and Simon watched in amusement the waggling tails and the waggling buttocks. His moods passed like the moods of the river in the breeze and since Brother Gregory had whispered in his ear one sore place was healed for ever. The goose-girl had tucked up her skirts to be free of the muck and her calves swelled like moons. Only one hand for love, thought Simon wryly, but the old fear was gone.

Intent on the lusty figure before them they had reached the crossroads before the noise struck them. At the crossing stood a stack of last year's hay, the height of a man's head. It hid them from the source of the noise, which came from the direction of the east gate. There was a snarling and a snapping of empty teeth, animal screams and the shouts of men torn between fear and amusement. They hurried round the hay and looked down the road towards the east gate. There was cruelty somewhere, Simon knew. He smelt it before he saw it. At first they saw nothing but a rabble of men, some leaping to see over the others' heads, some peering through a forest of legs. The din was fantastic. 'Have his guts, boy, tear his bloody guts out,' they shouted. A big man with no hair screamed, 'Go on, you dogs,' and clutched his head. Suddenly they saw a dog hurled up above the heads of the crowd with its back broken. It fell kicking like a rabbit on to the bald man's shoulders and knocked him full length in the dust. Then Simon saw that every man in the inner ring held a hoe or rake, pointed like a Welsh pike into the centre of the circle. Another dog shot screaming into the air amidst a roar of rough voices and fell back out of sight.

'What is it?' he cried frantically. 'Are they piking the dogs?' Huw rushed forward and tore a gap in the wall of men. It closed in an instant as a huge brown shape lunged forward, but Simon had seen the whole picture with his extraordinary sight. One piercing glance, sharpened by horror, had told him everything. It was a bear come for the baiting, a shabby bear sent mad by the town dogs.

Dogs one by one he was used to. For years he had cuffed a cur here or there and amused the crowd with a docile contempt, a few scars the price of his keep. This evening he had ambled through the gate behind his master dragging his chain in the dust and thinking of his supper when suddenly they had been upon him, a score of mangy devils snuffling the streets for offal. His master had been powerless to protect him. He was tired and shabby but he fought for his life. He reared on his hind legs with four dogs fastened on his back and shook them off with his fur in their bloody mouths. Two more leapt for his throat and he ripped their bellies with his claws.

'Call them off!' screamed Simon, trying to make himself heard in the tumult, but these dogs knew no masters and they fought the bear as they fought a rat, to kill, and no man dared risk their jaws. The bear's master, a little white-faced man with red hair, ran in a frantic circle pulling coats and kicking heels but he might as well have kicked a wall. As the bear's roars dwindled to a mutter and he sank beneath a mound of gobbling dogs the little man sank too, dying the same death until his mouth was in the dust. Simon crouched against the baiting-post and vomited. He tried to shut out the terrible sounds with his hands but his withered hand would not cover his ear. Nothing could muffle the bear's agony and he crouched, powerless to do ought but listen, until he had heard the last dog driven away and the scraping of shovels on the baked ground. When he felt Huw's hand, he rose and wiped his mouth, feeling the curious stares between his shoulder-blades. He had determined not to turn his head but he heard an odd sound and he felt his neck twist as if it had been worked by a string. The little man, the bear's master, was crying. He lay with his face in the dust making a damp patch with his tears. Watching him Simon felt a curious comfort that there was one other man who felt as he did and shared his own distress.

'Lost his trade, see,' said Huw, and felt in his belt for a farthing. A little heap of copper dropped beside the sobbing man and one by one the men drifted away, all save those who waited to bury the bear. But Simon did not take money from his purse. He knew as surely as if his soul inhabited the red-haired man's body that he wept not for a lost livelihood but for a murdered friend and all the cruelties of life. For the first time in his seventeen years he felt that he was looking at a man who felt cruelty as he felt it and who could no more accept the pains of existence than he could himself. Perhaps I am not so different after all, he thought with a faint stirring of hope. That man is as stricken as I. Lucky fellow that he can weep it away in tears.

He watched Huw drop his farthing and determined to give his prayers instead. It was prayers the man needed now.

Wise from a long experience of such occasions Huw expected his master to make all haste for the church, but to his surprise Simon turned his face in the direction of the tailor's house and began to plough ankle-deep through the muck of the market square, making a furrow with his lame foot. With a shrug Huw followed his master, treading in the furrow his master had ploughed.

The tailor's door stood open and on the threshold sat Master Win himself, sewing in the last of the light. He must have heard the tumult but he had not gone to see it and he did not speak of it now. He leapt to his feet at the young lord's approach, not without a surprised glance at the beslubbered legs whose progress through the market had been hidden by the houses opposite.

'A livery, my lord? I got the very thing, a sweet bolt of worsted from Norwich. Norfolk green, a brave colour.' He hesitated, not daring to invite the baron's son within doors, but Simon was determined to see his daughter, the Welshwoman's daughter, Eva, and he stepped over the threshold.

She stood in the shadows at the back of the room with her hand to her throat. What she saw framed in the light of the doorway no man ever knew. What Simon saw was his heart's desire, the balm for his lonely heart.

5

YET he did nothing, simply stared at her while she fetched the cloth from the chest and carried it out into the light. She was tall for a woman, taller than he. When she straightened her back her deep dark eyes looked into his own. She did not speak, but as she moved he felt his heart tied to her by a string. There was talk about the livery, how long the tunic, how wide the sleeves, but he spoke mechanically and his eyes never left her, her long white face and the long white lobes of her ears and her long black hair. He had only to look at her to forget the gobbling dogs and the bear. Even the taste of vomit left his mouth. There were measurings and jottings and Simon leant against the door-post watching her with the tape in her hand and wishing it was he she was touching. For an instant, as her eyes met his, he forgot his deformity. It was the first time outside a church that he had ever done so. She was like no woman he had ever seen. Even the dark Welshwomen of the Welshry had not this magic. Soon, too soon, the measuring was done and Eva carried the cloth back into the house, her skirt brushing his thigh. It was the nearest he came to touching her.

'Four days, my lord,' said Philip Win, 'and my daughter shall bring it to the castle.'

Simon counted the days. Saturday, Sunday, Monday, Tuesday.

'Nay, we shall be from home, at the commote court. Let her bring it the fifth day from this.'

'So be it, my lord.'

The days passed slowly, crawling towards Tuesday.

Tuesday was overcast. Heavy clouds rolled up the Usk valley from the sea, full of rain. They set off with the first light, Simon, Huw, Seneschal, Thomas the chaplain with his heavy Bible in one pannier and ink and quills in the other, John Upton with his back bristling with parchment rolls and a stout coil of rope over his pommel. Next came the two clerks with tallies, bumping clumsily on heavy nags, and after them the escort, a score of strong fair men with bows over their shoulders and daggers in their belts, men from Herefordshire and Warwickshire from the baron's English estates, some of them twenty years in his service. There was no Old Peter today hobbling in their wake on ingrowing nails, for Simon had sent him into the stables with instructions to Stephen Oxted to keep him until they were safely away.

They turned into the trees at the ironworkings and the gloom of early morning became darkness. They bent forward over the horses' ears and plodded slowly up between the ruts. It was quiet at this hour, the swine still within hurdles and the charcoal-burners still munching, sleepy-eyed, their bacon and beans. Simon was silent, waiting for his spirits to lift at the boundary and thinking of Eva. Huw matched his mood to his master. Seneschal was silent, occupied with the business of the day. Thomas was silent because he was repeating Ave Marias under his breath and praying at the same time that there would be no unpleasantness. John Upton was silent because it was his habit and the men were silent because they were sleepy and the day was dark and they had not yet digested their breakfasts. A wood pigeon flapping over their heads made them all start but it was gone before a bow could be drawn.

It was a day like other days. There was a duty to perform, a court to be held, disputes to be settled and felons to be punished. Justice must be administered, in the Welshry as in the Englishry, by the baron's officer if not by the baron himself. Seneschal carried his master's justice quarter by quarter up the steep tracks to the Welshmen's courts, bearing in his strong hands his master's powers of life and death. His master's word was law in the March both to English and Welsh. But his law was good. His decisions were final but he listened—or Seneschal listened and that was the same thing—to sworn witnesses and was not deaf to Welsh custom and his punishments were those common throughout the whole of England. He favoured swift death and had never had a traitor torn apart by horses, like the lord of Striguil.

Yet Seneschal was not at ease. He smelt trouble as a greyhound smells the hare, as Simon smelt cruelty. This moving of the boundary cross, now, he did not like the sound of that. Blaen-avon was a law-abiding commote, like Lasgarn where Huw came from, like Tillery and Carn-y-cefn and Llanhilleth. To move a boundary cross! They would never, he knew, do such a thing without incitement and he could guess where the incitement came from. It came from Pwll-du. He had never been sure of Pwll-du. There were many hotheads there, looking on the English with hostility behind their eyes. Sixty of the men who had charged like bewitched swine down Blorys and swum the Usk to join Glendower had come from Pwll-du, a full score from the kindred of Garndyrrys, whose lands lay at the mouth of the Welshry, where the track they now trod came out above the trees. This was the kindred of Llewellyn ap Thomas, the strange man who was clerk and steward to the lord of the commote and who was, some said, a soothsayer. It was no chance, thought Seneschal, that young Simon should have seen him at the boundary cross, out of his own commote. He needed watching, did Master Llewellyn ap Thomas.

At last they came out above the trees and crossed the boundary into the Welshry. The mountains to north and east were lost in mist, the valley was seen through a veil, and from the south rolled the great clouds like dirty fleeces. The rain had reached Llanellen already and would soon be watering the young wheat of Llanfoist and leaking with a hiss into the puddling fires at the ironworks. Soon it would sweep over the forest of Blorys and wet their parchments and Thomas's Bible, so they set spurs to the horses and turned their heads due west into the rolling slopes of the Welshry.

Simon stirred and looked about him, seeing this land through the eyes of Llewellyn ap Thomas, as Llewellyn intended him to do. He had always loved this upland. He had loved it six days before when he had ridden with Huw and John Upton to view the boundaries, but he had not loved it as he suddenly came to love it now. He fell in love with it as he had fallen in love with Eva Win, with its magic and its beauty and its quietness. Miraculously, as he turned to look at the rain-clouds, he felt his self-consciousness slough like an old skin. He did not entirely forget his deformity but for this magic day it ceased to obsess him and when they passed the spring which was said to run red on Good Friday he crossed himself mechanically and actually forgot to pray for a miracle. The truth was that once he had crossed the boundary he seemed to draw in assurance from the pure Welsh air and today with the storm-clouds chasing them from the south he felt for at least a few hours his fatal otherness drop away.

After all, did not the word Welsh mean 'other'? What wonder that he should feel at home here, he who spent his days in the English valley wondering if men watched him and pitied him for being different. Surely on this springy Welsh turf he would never dream of giving the wrong responses! He saw the cattle not with his own English eyes but with Llewellyn's, so he did not think them thin. He saw the scraggy mountain sheep but did not think them ragged, although their wool hung in tatters. He looked at a little Welsh church but did not think it ugly, although it had no tower and was made of wood and the bell hung from a wooden frame. Merlin's feet splashed through bog and marsh and stumbled over hillocks of heather; bracken fires had already scarred the hillsides; patches of young oats were like squares of silk in a coarse green gown; save where the forest showed in dark patches on the lower slopes there was scarcely a tree bigger than a thorn; even the homesteads looked pinched, with not a tiled roof among them. But Simon saw none of these things. To him this stark land had become a paradise. He saw only the lovely curve of the mountains and their nearness to the sky and the ring of stones placed there long ago by the Giant Argros who had lived on this mountain. As a child creeps to the knee of a fascinating stranger, so Simon Beaumont crept into the commote of Pwll-du.

They reached the lord's mansion just as the rain came down. It was a big house, as befitted the lord's importance. It was stone-built with tidy thatch and had a huge courtyard ringed with stables, byres, brew-house, kitchen, kiln, pigstyes, granary, smithy—all the signs of a powerful and prosperous household. Here lived and held court the lord of the commote, the chief of the chief kindred of Rhys. It was he who lent his house once a quarter for the holding of the baron's court. It was he who gathered the ten cows, two in calf and two with calf at foot, that were the annual tribute of this commote. He was the chief man of the commote and received tribute from all the kindreds in Pwll-du. He had as his clerk and steward Llewellyn ap Thomas.

He was a big man, was Caraddoc ap Rhys, huge for a Welshman, with the short black beard of a chief and liquorice eyes, and he came forward from the high table to greet the Englishmen with all the pride and courtesy of his race. He grasped Seneschal's hand in greeting, then noticed the lord Simon behind him and hastened forward to bend the knee to his lord's son. He inclined his head to Thomas, stared at Huw without liking and led the visitors to the top of the hall. Ceremonial ale and oat-cake were offered. The English soldiers ranged themselves along the wall, their fair heads a span above the Welshmen; John Upton and the two clerks arranged the parchments and quills on a side table; Thomas seated himself behind his great Bible; the bailiff sidled up to the dais; Llewellyn ap Thomas quietly took his place. The business of the day had begun.

Gruffydd ap Kenwick was the bailiff's name, a Welshman with an English mother whom the Welsh had charmed to her death over the top of Blaen-Dyar quarry. He was a man full of fear, because for many years he had been cheating his master the baron; he was afraid of violence, afraid of spells, afraid lest his dishonesty be discovered. He lay like a terrified bird in the hollow of Llewellyn's hand. They all took their places, Llewellyn and Gruffydd at a separate table where the parchments lay like peeled sticks, brittle to the touch. Simon sat down in his chair and for the first time in seventeen years did not turn it so that his withered leg should be hidden from the hall.

Time passed and the court proceeded as usual, now in Welsh and now in English according to the acquaintance of the parties with the English tongue. First came the forester who watched the interests of the baron in the forests of the commote and was a Welshman by birth but a forester by nature, so that in the manner of all foresters he could see no further than his own duty. He poured forth in good English the usual tale, common to foresters the world over, of hawks' nests robbed, honey stolen, poaching and illicit hunting and reluctance to give up the lambs' tongues as a delicacy for the falcons. Some offenders were forthcoming, some not, and he went away grumbling, but as satisfied as a forester ever is with the promise of six pairs of cropped ears and eight fines. There were murmurs among the Welshmen along the walls but Seneschal could not understand them, nor Simon, and to Huw they were no more than the grumbles of soldiers over their mess-tins. Thomas had long forgotten his Welsh. Yet these were murmurs that had not been heard for many years. They murmured that if their English masters did not hunt in the Welshry why should they not have the sport? They murmured that in the days when Wales was free the old princes had always allowed free hunting in the forests after the opening of the hunting season. Under Llewellyn's influence their minds had suddenly travelled back three centuries.

The English clerks scribbled industriously, their quills squeaking on the parchment, and the bailiff unrolled another tube.

'Kenvin ap Evans,' he cried in his weak voice and a little gnome stepped forward, not five foot high.

' *'Rwyf wedi dod i gwyno,*' he said, and Llewellyn stirred and rose.

'He says, my lord Seneschal——' But Huw had already stepped forward and Llewellyn, at a motion of Seneschal's hand, sat slowly down. He looked, as Simon afterwards remembered, not at Huw but at Simon, and for an instant Simon could not see Huw at all.

Huw translating, the routine Welsh complaint poured over them from the gnome's huge mouth. It was that rascally Dewi ap Wledig, look you, letting his swine trample Kenvin's standing hay when he was on his knees in church like a good Christian. Drove his old pigs, he shouldn't wonder. Here was something to cry for indeed, flat to the ground it was, no scythe could come near it. . . . The accusation brought the lanky Dewi from the wall and furious argument ensued, the clash not of men but of kindreds. A dozen gnomes shook fists at a dozen giants, while Thomas stood helplessly with his great Bible in his hands appealing in inaudible English for them to take the oath. Huw grinned, Llewellyn folded his arms, bailiff dabbed ineffectually at the air with weak cries and Simon watched, thinking how these Welsh people were indeed foreign, other, as their name implied. What Englishman could support his claim with such passionate argument? What Englishman had this liquid beauty of speech? What Englishman's eyes shone with this fervour?

At length order was restored, oaths taken, witnesses called, and the long rigmarole of investigation proceeded. Simon marvelled at Seneschal's patience. He never seemed to tire. No yawn gathered in *his* throat, making his eyes water. Question, translation, answer, translation, while bailiff fluttered and Llewellyn ap Thomas looked silently under his long white eyelids and the kindred on the wall muttered their partisan comments.

'One shilling fine, to be paid by Dewi ap Wledig on the fourth day of next month in that he did . . .' Llewellyn flicked his quill; the gnome and the giant exchanged grimaces strangely lacking in hatred and retreated to the wall. The scribes scribbled. Seneschal allowed himself a minute sigh and Simon shifted to a more comfortable position. The Welsh chief Caraddoc produced courtesies at the high table and bailiff mopped his forehead. A scurry of rain came through the south window and half a dozen hands grabbed for the shutters. Suddenly it was very quiet and Simon heard a cuckoo, a Welsh cuckoo with its eggs perhaps in an English nest.

'Meirion ap Morcan,' quavered bailiff and the morning wore on.

An outlaw's land to be awarded, complaints that the men of Carn-y-cefn ran their cattle on an acre of Pwll-du pasture, two hens stolen, three noses blooded, four fines not paid from the last court with the customary fluent Welsh excuses, question, translation, answer, translation, occasionally a pleader in the English tongue. Hywel ap Urien wished his son to be trained for a priest and to study the Latin tongue. Had Hywel other sons? Aye, my lord, three. Permission given. Iago ap Cynan wished his son to learn the smith's craft. Had they not smiths enough then? Only three working, my lord. Davydd burnt his arm on the forge, see, and the muscles did wither like an old root. Davydd was produced with his arm hanging limply in dirty bandages. Permission granted, nothing being known against the family of Iago ap Cynan. The air grew heavy and hot with the smell of bodies. In the open doorway the rain fell like a curtain. Men came and went with dripping garments, old sacks over their heads. Question and answer, the scribbling of quills.

It was a court like other Welsh courts but Seneschal smelt trouble. As a man with a hurt likes to put his finger on the pain, so Seneschal slowly explored the scene with his eyes, searching for danger. Something was different and it was not simply that Huw was translating. There was trouble simmering. He had not sat for ten years at commote courts without being able to smell unrest. Did bailiff babble more than usual? Was Llewellyn ap Thomas more silent? Were the Welshmen more quarrelsome, their gestures larger than life? John Upton seemed unperturbed, his men phlegmatic. Thomas was afraid, but then he was always afraid in the Welshry. He had been up gabbling prayers half the night, to build up a resistance to the Welsh spells, so he said. Young Simon was sitting quietly, rapt, staring at Llewellyn. Seneschal noticed with surprise that his withered hand lay openly on his knee, as if he had forgotten it. A queer one, that, always queer about the Welsh. He would be smelling no danger. Everything he smelt over the boundary was sweet in his nostrils.

At noon Caraddoc rose. The heavy tables were dragged forth and set on their trestles and long-haired Welsh dogs appeared from nowhere, already sniffing for bits. The crowd thinned. The English soldiers eased their shoulders away from the wall and began practising their few words of Welsh, saying '*vach, vach*' to the serving women and poking their sides with grins. Thomas said an English grace and the knives came out for meat. Perched at the high table with the tip of his knife between his teeth and Huw behind his chair, Simon closed his ears to the English courtesies on either side of him and let the tide of Welsh flow over him. He had heard it many times but never in this warm tide that sucked at him like the ebb and drowned him like the flow. It was like the babel of tongues. It spoke to him things that he could understand, although he knew scarcely a word of the language. It spoke, this Welsh tongue, of a beautiful land and a proud people, of men who scorned the peasant's lot, quick to revenge and nursing ancient glories; it spoke of a people easily roused to enthusiasm, workers in magic and witchcraft; it spoke of a musical race, part singers and players of harps who listened to the bards as to soothsayers. Simon listened and let his sauce grow cool and watched Llewellyn's dark head below him and thought many times of Eva Win.

After meat Simon limped out into the threshing rain to relieve himself and collided with a tiny Welshman in the doorway.

'My pardon,' he said in his courteous way, and the Welshman answered:

'A thousand pardons, my lord. There is clumsy I am to be pushing a man, so careless.'

Simon limped on and straddled his legs while the rain beat his shoulders but he scarcely felt the wet for he suddenly remembered who the little Welshman was: Kenvin ap Evans who had pleaded in Welsh because he did not have the English tongue. Simon frowned, his frown like a scar between his eyebrows, and thought that he would tell Seneschal. Then he felt a hand on his shoulder. He turned and looked into the hot eyes of Llewellyn and straightway forgot Kenvin and the teaming rain in his pleasure that this man was his friend.

'Dirty weather, my lord,' said Llewellyn and Simon suddenly realized that these were the first words Llewellyn had ever spoken to him. Yet he knew him for a friend and felt the place on his lame knee where Llewellyn's fingers had rested.

'The Welsh sky weeps to see us perhaps,' he answered with a smile.

'No, there is untrue, my lord. The Welsh sky will never weep to see *you*,' and the emphasis placed Seneschal, Thomas, John Upton and even Huw in a storm of Welsh tears and himself in a shaft of Welsh sunshine. 'There is proud we are indeed to be having you at our court,' said Llewellyn, drawing him with a light hand under the shelter of the overhanging thatch. A group of Welshmen were gathered in the open doorway of the smithy opposite, rubbing the warmth into their arses and watching the rain. There was a push from behind and a man fell face downwards in a puddle. There were roars of good-natured laughter and the group parted to show an arm uplifted, ale mug in hand, a dirty arm swathed in dirty bandages, the arm of the smith whom the fire had burnt, so they said, like an old root. They wanted an extra smith, thought Simon, why should they want an extra smith? But at that moment Llewellyn said, 'Come you now, my lord,' and laid his hand on his arm and the matter passed from his mind.

By this time the rushes of the hall squelched underfoot. Only the dais was dry. The rain fell as if the giant Argros stood in the sky with a pail and laughed to see the hay flattened and the young corn drowned at the roots. We are all in God's mercy, thought Simon sorrowfully with a last look at the rain jumping in the runnels, but it was the Welsh corn that he mourned. Even when he met Seneschal's worried eyes he did not think of the Englishry, the arable valley that, if it lost its crops, lost three-quarters of its livelihood. 'Another hour of this,' said Seneschal, 'and the track will be a river,' and Simon's heart leapt at the thought of sleeping under a Welsh roof. He was excited, expectant. He no longer cared if Llewellyn saw his deformity. Here was a man who wanted him for a friend, who did not care if God had marked him for his mother's sin, who did not hold it odd that he should prefer the Welshry to the fat English fields. It occurred to Simon as he took his place at the high table and shook the wet out of his hair that Eva Win had looked at him with that same acceptance. He had seen the same friendship in her eyes.

So the magic thickened about him.

Anxious to be gone, Seneschal asked if there were any more cases and being told no by the bailiff asked for the list of dead to be read. Bailiff rose, for he acted as coroner for the commote, and unrolled the last of the parchments. The clerks waited, quills poised. John Upton let his belt out a notch and prepared to listen, since it was his duty to check the graves and search the churchyards for unmarked mounds. 'Come on, man,' said Seneschal with his first impatience of the day. Simon looked at the man, who was sweating with fear. Sweat stood in great drops on his pasty forehead and he rubbed the palm of his left hand on his thigh. Llewellyn ap Thomas shifted beside him and said something in a low tone and bailiff jumped as if he had been stung.

'Tastogel verch Tewdwr,' he squeaked. 'Widow, kindred of Tewdwr, died of natural causes, aged about fifty years, fortified by the last rites of the Church, buried in the church of Wainwen.' He paused breathless and the quills squeaked in protest at his haste.

'Iwan ap Aynon, kindred of Meiron, boy child, died of natural causes, aged three days, baptized in the holy Church, buried in the church of Tyla. . . .'

So the roll proceeded. Man, woman and child gathered to God's bosom and freed from the toils and pains of this life. Of them all the last only had died with his sins heavy upon him, dead when the priest reached him to hear his last confession. This was Ithel ap Pengres.

'Ithel ap Pengres,' croaked Bailiff, wetting his dry lips. 'Kindred of Bwlch, aged about thirty years, died without the consolations of his religion, killed by a fall at the quarry of Blaen-Dyar, buried outside the churchyard of the church of Garndyrrys.'

Bailiff repeated the obituary in both Welsh and English and sat down abruptly. Seneschal hesitated. If they left now they might still make their way through the forest and reach the castle before the road became impassable. He was needed in the Englishry, he knew, and the soldiers would be needed for ditch digging at first light in an attempt to carry away the flood-water. The baron was powerless without him, for Richard had not a brain in his head and the castle yard would be filled at dawn with frantic peasants begging for aid. What if a man did fall over the quarry? Went too near the edge, most like, and felt the ground give way under his feet. Bailiff sat down and there was sudden quiet, the rain on the shutters like a roll of drums. There was a whinny from an English horse and Seneschal had already felt the muscles of his legs contract for departure when a voice cried, '*Ni chwympodd, fe'i taflwyd i lawr.*' It was a woman's voice from the back of the hall and it came again. '*Ni chwympodd, fe'i taflwyd i lawr.*'

'What is it?' asked Seneschal amidst a buzz of talk, and Huw replied with a startled look:

'She says he did not fall, but was pushed.'

Seneschal sighed, the deep sigh of a just man who sees weary hours ahead of him, and sank back in his chair. Llewellyn's eyes, startling in their dark brilliance, turned towards the high table and bailiff frankly shook in his dirty shoes. The hall hummed with talk. The woman was brought forward and sworn on Thomas's Bible and the investigation began. There followed three hours of unwilling witnesses and tedious translation, three hours of lagging steps and downcast eyes and transparent reluctance, but none dared commit perjury with their hands on the sacred Book and by the hour of Vespers a man stood accused on oath of having pushed Ithel ap Pengres over the lip of the quarry so that he died with his sins heavy upon him.

He was a good-looking fellow, the accused. Gronow ap Bol his name was, of a neighbouring kindred, fair for a Welshman, with red in his cheeks and his hair cut short to his ears. A good neck for hanging, thought John Upton, thinking of the stout English rope on his pommel. Now by Welsh custom, long tolerated by the baron, a man of the Welshry accused of murder could be declared guilty or innocent by the men of the commote, so many from each kindred giving voice in the ccmmunal oath. It took an hour to assemble them, a hundred men of Pwll-du standing bareheaded in the pouring rain while Thomas stood Bible in hand before them like a bedraggled crow, with water streaming down his cloak and making pools at his feet. Cursing the wet Seneschal climbed on to a tree-stump and Gronow ap Bol, his hands tied behind his back, was placed before him. Simon stood in the doorway watching, smelling death. Bailiff put the question, Thomas raised the Bible, and three times came the answer, a hundred voices become one. '*Dieuog!*' they shouted, and Simon breathed a great sigh of relief. The Welshman would not hang. But Seneschal had noticed a curious thing. He noticed that the hundred pairs of eyes, dark eyes in dark faces, were turned not on Thomas but on Llewellyn ap Thomas, who stood on a little prominence to the south of the house. He is playing them, thought Seneschal. When he lifts his finger, the tune changes.

Seneschal heaved another sigh. It would be the night now, he knew. Calling Huw to his side he gave him his instructions. Huw mounted the tree-trunk, raised both hands and gave a shout that could be heard in Careg-Maen. 'Wait! The trial is not yet over,' he cried in Welsh. Gronow paused in rubbing his wrists and his smile faded. Bailiff plucked at Llewellyn's coat and was ignored. 'My lord Seneschal is not satisfied with the oath,' shouted Huw in Welsh, putting up one hand to make a dam over his eyebrows. 'Each man will make separate oath with his hand on the sacred Book.' There was a shocked silence and eyes turned on Llewellyn, who nodded once, twice, three times and turned away.

So they hanged Gronow ap Bol after all, for none dare imperil his immortal soul by telling a lie with his hand on the sacred Book. Communal perjury now, that was one thing, but to do it with one's fingers actually on the Book, that was quite another. Not even Llewellyn's magic could make them do that. So *Dieuog!* turned to *Euog!* and John Upton fetched his rope. The noose was made ready, the rope thrown over the branch of a solitary oak and the murdered man's brother climbed up among the young leaves. The cart was brought and the doomed man placed upon it. The horse was harnessed and placed between the shafts. Gronow made his last confession with all the courage of his race and his head was placed in the noose. The driver took his seat and raised his whip. He brought it down smartly on the horse's rump and the cart rushed from under the murderer's feet at the same instant as the dead man's brother leapt for his shoulders. The neck snapped like a bow-string and soon there was nothing but a pair of dangling feet and the pounding rain and Simon crouched in the mud with Huw bending over him.

6

WHEN Simon felt Huw's hand on his shoulder and looked up, he looked up into darkness. A strange blackness had come over the sky, like the darkness on the day of the Crucifixion. The rain had stopped, leaving a breathless void. Below them the tops of the trees writhed like snakes, although there was no wind to move them. The sky was like lead, dark and heavy, and thunder growled like a wild beast in a thicket. All round him men stared at the sky and fell on their knees and crossed themselves, muttering that here was a sign of God's anger for the hanging of Gronow ap Bol.

Simon heard the murmurings through the growl of thunder but did not understand them. Nor did he fear the storm. A storm was God's anger, he knew, but God could not be angry about the hanging. The man had murdered. If he was condemned, he should pay the price. Simon's acute mind was not yet so shrouded in magic that he could not see that his own loathing for cruelty and death did not mean that no man should ever be hanged. His compassion reached out also to the murdered man and his wife and children, to the crushed body and the soul in mortal sin, gone to the everlasting torments of hell before the priest could reach him. The sufferings of perdition were worse than the sufferings of a broken neck. 'No,' he thought, wiping the vomit from his mouth, 'the sufferings of Ithel ap Pengres will never end. God cannot be angry at the hanging. I am sick not because the man should not die but because suffering always makes me sick. It is a measure of my difference that I cannot watch any suffering without this terrible faintness coming over me. Even here, in the Welshry, it is the same. I am still different. I was the only man who turned away his head, unable to witness the murderer's death.'

He got shakily to his feet, pressing on his one strong knee.

'Church now, is it?' asked Huw, wise from long experience and knowing they must sleep at the mansion overnight. The track to the ironworkings was a rushing stream. Although it was but six hours from noon it was as dark as a summer night and flickers of light behind Pen-y-val showed that the lightning was coming. 'God's anger,' said Huw, pointing and crossing himself. 'There is terrible to see God's anger. Strike a sinner it will, hide he never so deep.'

Simon hastily thought of his sins and was reassured. The lightning would not strike him. He saw that they were alone now, save for the corpse slowly turning on its rope. Everyone had crept away, some to the hall, some to the outbuildings, many to their homesteads to milk their terrified cattle or view their flattened hay. Seneschal was stripping off his wet things in Caraddoc's solar, Thomas was wringing out his gown and repeating Ave Marias, one to every wring. The soldiers were steaming in front of a new-kindled fire, determined not to show the Welshmen their unease. Simon and Huw stood alone in the eerie half-light, watching the trees below them tossing without a wind.

'Church now, is it?' asked Huw again and a voice answered him in English from behind his back.

'Show you a church, my lord? The church of Garndyrrys. There is time before meat.'

It was Llewellyn ap Thomas. He had come upon them like a fairy, out of nothing. 'The priest is my cousin, my lord. If you wish to have the Mass he will serve you indeed. A lovely man. Deem it an honour he will to have you set foot in his church. Come you now, my lord, and I will show you.'

They walked, the two of them, towards the stables, the Welshman upright and dark, the Englishman lopsided and fair, and Huw watched them go. For the first time in eight years his master had not invited him to follow. He waited until the horses were saddled and the riders abreast of him, then he stepped forward and laid his hand on Merlin's bridle. 'I am to bide, is it?' he asked, looking at his master. But Simon did not return his look. He looked instead over Merlin's ears and slowly nodded his head, once, twice, three times, as Llewellyn had done on the mound. The horses moved on and Huw gazed after them, then deliberately he bent his head and spat into his bosom. He did not want to be charmed like his master.

On their way Llewellyn spoke of love. It was as if he had seized this opportunity to tell the lord Simon something that he wished him to know. No one before had ever spoken to Simon of love. Marriage, yes, appetite, yes, his father had mentioned both, and there had been that conversation with Huw among the apple trees. But Llewellyn now spoke of a different kind of love, of a love unsung in England, the romantic love of the Welsh poets; he spoke of loving a woman with the heart as well as the bowels; he spoke of woman neither as a goddess on a pedestal nor as a body in a bed but as a wine which, when once tasted, man cannot do without. A magic wine that few are destined to drink.

'Have you drunk this wine, Master Llewellyn?' asked Simon. 'Have you tasted this magic wine of love?'

Llewellyn slowly shook his head with his eyes on the mansion snugly settled in the crook of the hill. 'There is no room in me for such love,' he replied. 'God is wanting other things of me, look you. It is like a fire with me, this land, hotter than the fire of women.' He turned to look into Simon's grey eyes, with the frown between them like a scar. 'But you shall have your wine, my lord. There is waiting it is, the cup to your lips.'

Simon smiled and the scar vanished. He did not think it strange that Llewellyn should already know of his love for Eva Win and of his eagerness to take the cup and taste its sweets. He knew so many things, did Llewellyn. Already the little fair English bird perched on his shoulder, eyeing his outstretched hand. Only one other thing of moment did Llewellyn say on their return from the church. He drew rein short of the house and turned his horse to stand between Simon and the waiting figure of Huw. 'There is peaceful you are here, my lord. You should have been a Welshman, I am thinking,' he said. When Huw came to meet them and take Merlin's bridle Simon saw the spittle shining on his coat but he did not recognize it for what it was because Llewellyn had charmed him.

He found Seneschal in the solar, shivering. He sat on the

edge of Caraddoc's bed with a blanket round his shoulders and a bowl of hot spiced ale in his hands, his teeth chattering against the rim like dice. The cursed Welsh rain had got into his bones, he grumbled, and he sank back under the covers. So Simon alone saw the Welshmen vying with the English at the butts, splitting the English arrows at a distance of two hundred paces and skewering dead rabbits tossed into the air. He alone saw the Welsh lances lobbed into the exact centre of a penny, making a click of metal on metal. Where Seneschal might have felt fear Simon felt only wonder and did not feel surprise that so many lances should be needed for hunting polecats.

That night he alone sat with Caraddoc ap Rhys at the high table, while Seneschal sweated and worried under the blankets and Thomas bit his nails beside him and bailiff breathed a little more freely. A hot, still night followed the storm, with a thin slice of moon, and when the soldiers had steamed themselves dry the fire was doused. It was a magic night. In the lulls of talk and music Simon could hear the drip-drip of the thatch and the rush of streams that had not been there in the morning. The great door of the hall stood open and from where he sat with Huw at his feet he could see a sharp shoulder of mountain and five stars in the shape of a cross. After meat, eaten Welsh fashion three to a platter, the English soldiers retired into shadowy corners to enjoy themselves but the Welshmen drew their benches forward to the rushlights and picked their teeth, waiting. Simon sat bright-eyed and expectant as they, but Huw, tired and heavy-hearted, laid his head down at his master's feet and slept.

First came the notes of the harp, plucked by invisible fingers, charming Simon's soul out of his body. Used only to the wailing of bagpipes or the scraping of an English fiddle, at best to the simple chirrup of a shepherd's pipe, he listened enthralled to the triple melody, captivated by the blunt chords and the thin tinklings that sounded like the voice of a Welsh stream. This was music such as he had never heard. He could not see who played but he placed Eva Win at the harp with bare white arms and thin fingers, and each time the music stopped he willed it to go on. It was an unearthly scene, the dim lights and dark heads and the cross of stars framed in the doorway. It was a scene Simon was to remember to the end of his days, not a picture painted on glass but a picture in a dream with no sharp outlines, no clear gold or black or blue or red, only the music, each note as distinct as a drop of crystal water, as the drip-drip of the thatch. Below him at a lower table sat Llewellyn with his dog's head on his knee. They sat like statues, man and dog, listening to the music.

Presently the harp stopped and into the rushlight stepped a woman. An old woman, Simon thought, for her face was like a walnut, but when she opened her mouth to sing youth rushed out. It was a strange song, almost as if the voice and the harp were at variance. Harp and voice wandered each in its own sweet direction, then, just as he felt they had lost each other, they came together with a harmony of such perfection that he felt he could not support it. Then while he held his breath they wandered off again, only to come triumphantly together as before.

There was applause along the benches but softly lest it should break the spell. Even the English soldiers in the shadows stopped fumbling at Welsh bodices and began to listen. There was another song and another. Simon had no idea what she sang but the marriage of the tongue and the throat, the words and the music, was so lovely that he could have listened for ever. For an instant only, when the singer paused and Simon idly traced the sign of the cross on his body as a man scratches his ear or wrinkles his nose, for that instant he wondered that Huw did not wake up and nudged him with his sound foot. But Huw did not wake.

There was a stir in the hall. Lights were blown out. A single candle as big as an altar stick was stood on a pole in the centre of the hall. The dais, the walls, the benches, all retreated into shadow and all eyes were held by the circle of light. Suddenly, in this circle of light appeared an old old man. He neither shuffled nor crept, he simply appeared. He was as old as a man can well be but he held his back straight and his long white hair mingled with his beard. He wore a long white robe that showed his gnarled toes and over his shoulders a red cloak, as red as the red dragon of Wales. 'Iolo! Iolo!' went the whispers round the hall. 'Iolo Goch! Iolo of the Red Mantle!' The old man struck three notes on his lyre with his gnarled fingers and instantly, without a word sung, time for Simon lost all meaning. Hypnotized by the light, his pupils dilated until his grey eyes turned to black. The man sleeping at his feet, the man shivering under the covers, even the man with the dog, all lost their reality under the spell of the old man's magic. Castle, town, fields, father, Merlin, even Eva, even the holy sacrament itself, all slipped away into the darkness leaving only the old man and the lyre and the golden light.

He sang. He sang in a voice like a whisper of wind, with no power but with great sweetness, and every syllable was as clear and crisp as an icicle. What the words meant only God and the Welshmen knew, but Simon understood, he did not question how, that these were no ordinary songs. In some queer way he seemed to grasp their message. Now the old man sang of love, celebrating in short rhyming lines the love of man for woman; not the courtly worship of a knight for his lady nor the desire of a beast for a mate, but the love of which Llewellyn had spoken, the love such as he felt for Eva. The mood changed and he saw the ageless beauty of the Welsh mountains, the charms of nature that no Englishman thought to praise. Without understanding a single word that was sung he smelt the heat of Welsh hay, the sweet smell of the cattle. In that old voice he could hear the chant of the Welshmen to their oxen and the rushing of their many streams. Again the mood changed. A harsh note was struck and he heard a war song. A history? A prophecy? He did not know nor care. Gone were the pretty rhymes, this was stern stuff, a song to make Welsh eyes shine brightly and link arm to arm. Here was blood and ancient glory and praise of the Welsh princes and who knows what future defiance. As the gnarled hand plucked faster and the ancient voice rose higher, men began to stir on the benches. Gnome embraced giant, the trampled hay forgotten in a wave of patriotic fervour. Feet began to rustle in the rushes. More than one English soldier laid his hand on his knife. But it was only a song after all. The song ended, the old man drooped and crept away and fresh lights dazzled the eyes. Life returned.

Only now did Huw wake. He woke suddenly, leaping up with his hand on his knife as if he expected danger. 'What is it? What is it?' he cried, alarm looking out of his sleepy eyes. Simon told him it was nothing, nothing, but Huw looked at his master's rapt face and saw danger round him like a mist.

Later, they all slept. Caraddoc ap Rhys lay in his solar listening to Seneschal's teeth chattering and the rattle of Thomas's beads. Simon lay on a mattress under the high table with Huw on the boards at his side. The soldiers huddled in the wet rushes and there were many whimpers of pleasure. At first light Simon opened his eyes and saw against the delicate morning sky of the doorway three figures. Everyone slept but these three; even the humps in the rushes were still, worn out with their pleasure. There was Llewellyn ap Thomas, there was a strange man with a brown beard and a brown gown that reached to his feet, and there was a young boy. The strange man looked like a monk, except that his hair was long. The boy looked like a king, except that there were no Welsh kings. He was slim and straight with a proud neck and dark hair hanging in curls on his shoulders and a curious crescent-shaped mark over his left eyebrow. He stood close to Llewellyn as if he liked to feel his hand on his shoulder. He was about six years old.

The three stood enclosed by the morning, tied by invisible threads. Then someone stirred, the boy and the brown man vanished and Llewellyn, with a last look at the milky sky, entered the hall.

At the hour of Prime they left. Seneschal had stopped shaking but his forehead burned like a griddle and he was obsessed with the loss of his St Christopher medal that had hung round his neck on a string since he had run barefoot as a boy in the Herefordshire meadows. He imagined it had fallen in the rushes and had spent some time on his hands and knees in the solar peering and shaking, but he had not found it. He could not imagine the Welsh would steal it. It was made out of Cornish tin, of no value save to himself. The ground steamed in the early sun and their horses sank up to the fetlocks. The torrent on the track had dwindled to a double stream so that each rut ran with brown water, but there was foothold in between for the horses, who walked stiffly and stepped delicately over fallen branches and managed to reach the highway without hurt. Here they found destruction. The torrent had flowed straight into the mouth of the ironworkings, which were flooded to the height of a man's waist. There was nothing to be done but divert the stream with stones and wait for the water to fall. One man had already been down and barely dragged out his life by the heels. Even at the mouth they could hear through the gurgle of water the gentle sigh of clay walls subsiding. The fires were already relit, spitting with wet sticks, but they would not be working for long. The pile of iron ore at the side of the road was alarmingly low.

The storm had after all spared the English fields. The river was still within its banks. The fields of young wheat still bristled with green. The ditches were full, but with water not with earth. The puddles in the highway mirrored the pink and blue of the early sky, but there was more road than water. The storm had evidently passed over lightly. God's anger had lain with the Welsh.

They reached the castle in time for breakfast.

'Well,' said the baron, 'what news of the Welshry?'

Seneschal opened his mouth to speak but no sound came. The fever had him in its grip. He pressed his fingers to his aching eyes which felt hot and bald. Even Simon, with Eva Win in his mind, noticed his distress. Seneschal longed to shout warnings but although the arguments were ready in his head he could not get his tongue to move. He mumbled, swaying his head from side to side as if it were too heavy for his neck. Sweat ran down his heavy face into the corners of his mouth while he gasped and mumbled and Simon bent forward to receive the scalding breath on his cheek. At length he managed to shape one faint word. 'Trouble,' he whispered, and then, more faintly, 'Trouble.'

'Trouble?' said the baron. 'What trouble? Speak, man.'

But Seneschal was past speech. He stumbled away on Huw's arm and it was many weary burning days before the fever loosed his tongue. The baron sat in thought, gazing absently at his preoccupied son. Trouble? Sick fancies? The babblings of fever?

'Simon,' he said quietly and spoke three times before his son turned. 'Simon, did you see trouble in the Welshry?'

Simon considered.

'Trouble, Father?' he said at length. 'No, I saw no trouble.' And his father grunted, happy to think that Seneschal's doubts were feverish imaginings and that he could give his undivided attention to the draining of Penperlenni. Even when he heard later from Thomas about the haymaking and the hanging he saw no particular danger. Danger lurked, he knew, but had it not always lurked? He heard its growlings and grumblings from time to time, as now, but he saw no sudden sign of its bursting from the thicket. And of late years the growls, he was convinced, grew less. The Welshmen did but prick with pins, as old women pricked for a witch. There had been seven years of peace in the lordship and please God there would be seventy more. He saw no need of extraordinary measures. If the Welshmen made no secret arms and found no leader and Glendower's seed dwelt meekly in England under the king's eye, fettered with silken fetters, there could be no cause for alarm. King Henry IV was secure on his throne these four years, the pretender Mortimer was fast in prison, Hotspur long since dead, struck down by young Harry of Monmouth in the meadows of Shrewsbury. Glendower too was dead, a ghost some said, still marked by a crescent on the forehead where a horse's hoof had struck him as a youth. But a ghost cannot lead an army and there wanted but a short space before the old king would die and the glorious Harry of Monmouth would take his father's crown. Already the king was said to be dying. A leper, by all accounts. His hair fell in handfuls and he left a layer of skin in every bed. Soon he would die. Then indeed the baron trusted the Welsh rumblings would fade, for did he not call himself a Welshman, this Prince of Wales? Was he not born in Monmouth Castle? Had not the Welshmen come to love him, the same men who hated his father? Had he not promised them tuppence a day to fight the French dogs within a twelvemonth of his crowning?

So the baron fell happily to planning the draining of Penperlenni while Seneschal sweated and shook on his mattress, with leeches sucking at both arms, and was ridden by nightmares, moaning for his St Christopher medal and dreaming that a traitor had opened the town gates and that the streets ran with blood.

And Simon? Simon slowly spooned his sops with his eyes on the sunny doorway, so deep in his thoughts that, when Old Peter came hobbling to tell him that Eva Win had brought the livery, it needed the touch of an arm to rouse him. He spoke to her in the courtyard and had a man take the bundle and gave her money for her father. When he looked, he saw nothing but her and Blorys behind her head. He was drowned in her dark eyes. He took her hand and felt it frozen to his, like the thieving boy whose hand had been frozen to the wall of the church and whose imprint was there to this day for all to see.

When eventually he let her go he looked at his hand to see if her fingers had left their mark on his skin. 'I may come?' he asked, and she answered:

'Aye, my lord, tomorrow at the closing of the gates.'

When she left him he felt as if she had taken his bowels with her.

Later in the day he took his mother for her walk on the rampart and from the height looked down upon the street that ran from the castle to the north gate and out into the way to the Welshry. He noticed a man like a monk, except that his hair was long and mingled with his beard, a man in a long brown gown whom he had last seen framed in the door of the hall in Pwll-du, with Llewellyn and the noble boy. When he saw Martin later he asked him the man's name.

'Blenith ap Penros from Pwll-du and it's the same man, I think. A thin old man, is it? With blue eyes, strange in a Welshman?'

'I could not see his eyes. He wears a brown gown to his ankles and has grown his hair like a bard.'

'Ah, it is the same. A Lollard, I am thinking.'

7

'A LOLLARD?' said Simon, frowning. 'A Lollard, Martin? What is a Lollard?'

Martin stared at him in surprise. To live for seventeen summers and not know a Lollard? But what could be expected when his father kept him in the lordship like a beetle in a box and the boy had seen nothing of the world, nothing even of England save shrines and the tombs of martyrs? As a young child he had peeped at England through the silk curtains of a litter as he was jolted along the high roads in search of miracles, but since he was ten years old he had scarcely ever left the lordship. The journey to Usk to take his sister Blanche to the nunnery was as far as he had gone outside the lordship in seven years. Ten miles along the flat river road, what adventure was that? Where indeed would he be learning about Lollards if Martin did not tell him?

'You have heard tell of John Wycliffe, now?' he began. 'Him who was twice tried for heresy by the archbishop's court and lived to die in his bed?'

Aye, Simon had heard tell of him, although he had died more than a generation before.

'Well now, he said all was not well with the Holy Church, that one. Said that the Church had dirt on the hem of her garment and should make herself clean. He said the Church had given herself over to riches and worldly cares and lost sight of Christ's poverty. Said the bishops lived like lords, too, and the abbots like barons, and that they spent more time at court or hunt than in church. He wanted to have the Church stripped of her lands and possessions, he did, wanted to see all priests of the Church dressed like me, devoted only to the care of souls.'

He touched his coarse black robe as he spoke and moved his toes in his broken sandals. Simon noticed that he did not speak with disapproval. Simon thought of the prior, his rings, his hunting dogs, his sleek hunters and his fine dinners and the thousand acres of pasture and forest that he owned in the lordship and he felt a rush of sympathy for this John Wycliffe.

Martin went on to tell him how John Wycliffe had wanted the services of the Church said in the mother tongue, so that the people could understand. He even wanted the Holy Bible written into the mother tongue so that those who could read could read it for themselves.

'In Welsh?' asked Simon, thinking of the old women kneeling in Garndyrrys Church with the incomprehensible Latin in their ears.

'Aye, in Welsh too for aught I know, but Wycliffe did not have the Welsh. From Leicestershire, so they tell me. He did translate the Gospels with his own hand and his Lollards copied them. Banned by the bishop, too. Four copies burned at the bishop's palace at Mathern last Yuletide.'

Once again Simon noticed Martin's curious tone and remembered how Thomas had told him that Martin was not in the bishop's favour.

'He saw evil in the Church, so he said. He wanted to pick it out as a man picks dirt from between his toes. Pardoners now, he was mighty hard on pardoners and all those who make a traffic of God's pardon. False relics and the like, they were gall to Wycliffe . . .' Here Martin paused, then added, 'As to all good men.'

Wycliffe too? thought Simon with a sudden leap of the heart. They were not alone then, he and Martin, in their loathing of the Pardoner.

'And summoners?' he asked hopefully.

'I do not know about summoners. A bishop must have his officer, I suppose, as long as he does not turn over a stone to find him.'

Simon smiled, pleased to find his opinion of the Summoner shared and more than ever thankful that he had saved Stephen Oxted from a gelding.

'But he went too far in the end,' said Martin. 'He stepped beyond, did Wycliffe.'

He hesitated and Simon waited to be told what Wycliffe had done. 'Yes?' he said. 'Yes?'

At length Martin said, with his eyes on the simmering pot. 'He denied the power of the Pope.'

Simon was shocked—who would not be?—but curiously he had for an instant the impression that Martin had been going to say something worse. Yet what else could he say? What worse thing could a man do than to deny the power of the Pope? Aye, Simon was shocked, but not so shocked as he might have supposed. He thought of the Papacy as it was now, in the year of grace 1411, with a Pope at Rome and a Pope at Avignon. There could only be one Pope, elected by the cardinals' unanimous vote; therefore it followed there was no true Pope at this time, no infallible voice to guide and direct. Yet the Holy Church still stood, priests still absolved, still put God into men's mouths, still baptized into the true faith.

'Is this heresy,' he asked, 'to want to pick dirt from the toes of the Church?'

'His sayings have been condemned by the archbishop's council,' replied Martin, making a prim line of his mouth. 'His followers, these Lollards here like Blenith ap Penros, they can be brought before the bishop's court for questioning any time, if the Summoner can catch them.'

'And what will the bishop do with them?' asked Simon, thanking God the bishop was an old man and had but one Summoner in the lordship.

'If the Lollard does not repent, he will burn.'

Burn? Burn like the man who was caught in the bracken fire on Pen-y-val and roasted so slowly that they heard his screams in Lwyndy?

'Aye, one has burnt already.'

'Burn for no worse than wishing the Church pure and clean?'

Again Martin hesitated. Why should he be so loath to tell Simon the truth? Why not tell him the final error into which Wycliffe lapsed and for which they burnt William Sautre? Why did he hear God's voice whispering in his ear, not to tell Simon of the final heresy? Surely it could not be that Simon would believe it? He hesitated, but he was used to obey God's voice so he simply answered: 'Archbishop Arundel fears the Lollards, what they may say. But if this Lollard wants nothing worse than to pick dirt from the Church's toes he shall have the freedom of my churchyard.'

'Worse?' echoed Simon. 'What could be worse?' but Martin did not reply.

The Lollard preached at sundown, standing on a tombstone for all to see him.

'There is evil I am seeing in the Church,' he cried, raising his thin arms, his eyes blazing. 'Awful indeed it is to see a man of God lapped in fur and ringed with gold, nibbling dainties from a jewelled knife. There is a thing for you, a man of God turned counsellor, bending the knee at court instead of shepherding his flock. There is disgrace now for a priest to wear out his arse in the saddle instead of his knees in the chancel.' There were sideways glances here as the audience to a man thought of the prior. 'Here is something to cry for indeed that God's holy words should be forgotten.

'And He said: "Go you. I send you as lambs among the wolves. Therefore do not carry a satchel nor a script nor shoes and greet no man on the way. . . ." '

Listening to that sweet-strong old voice, Simon felt that here was a man after his own heart, a man who thought as he did, a man to be trusted. He smelt no heresy here and already Martin's fingers had relaxed on the besom, and presently he leant it against a tree and folded his arms, like a man who does not disapprove of what he hears. Simon rested on his sound hip and reflected that here was a man who would not stare at his deformity, nor wonder why God had marked him so. He looked at the Lollard's noble head and at the dark mountain of Blorys rising behind him, black against the dying sun. So this man knew Llewellyn ap Thomas and was, he was convinced, his friend. Were they not of the same commote? Had he not seen them together talking in the dawn? Llewellyn would favour this Lollard, he was certain, for the Welsh churches were poor and looked with disdain at the fat priories and palaces of England. There were no rich churches in the Welshry, no wealthy priories. In fact, no priories at all. The Welsh monks lived singly as hermits beside holy wells or streams, eating only the charitable crust. Each Welsh priest dwelt in an annexe of his own plain church, with wooden walls around him and thatch above him and his bell hanging outside on a wooden frame. Simon could imagine the Welshmen giving the Lollard great welcome. He determined to speak with him further, if he was staying in the town.

The Lollard finished speaking and began to sing. It was a Welsh hymn, but he sang in English so that the people could understand him, and soon the crowded churchyard echoed with English voices, bashful at singing a holy song, Welsh fashion, on consecrated ground. Simon heard Huw's voice booming in his ear. The song ended, the Lollard stepped down and Simon saw two things. He saw Brother Gregory on the edge of the crowd, scowling, and he saw Philip Win standing with his back to the porch, smiling with such happiness that for an instant he did not recognize him. He moved forward but people surged between them and when next he looked he was gone. He caught a man by the sleeve. 'Where does the Lollard sleep?' he asked.

'With the tailor, my lord.'

'Ah,' said Simon Beaumont.

At curfew he left the castle and went, with Old Peter hobbling behind him, down the cobbled streets to the tailor's wishbone house. Huw had wished to go with him but he had told him no and had left him binding wet rags on Seneschal's burning forehead, blind to his devotion. He left his mother in the solar with Alice, playing with her squirrel and smearing its droppings on her dress. Richard was rasping his mitts in the sand-tray again, as if they were not shining already. His father had got John Upton on the dais beside him, his head over the map. He had asked Simon about the Lollard and seemed satisfied to hear that Martin was not uneasy. If he carried no arms and preached nothing against the doctrines of the Church, he could bide within the walls. As his son limped from the hall, dragging his lame foot in the rushes, William Beaumont looked at him from beneath his shaggy eyebrows and shouted after him: 'Mind my words, boy. You have yet to prove Brother Gregory right. Sound and strong, eh, Simon? Sound and strong.' Simon waved his left hand, pleased to think that tonight he would make his father happy.

They skirted the market-place, lame master and lame servant, and came to the tailor's house from the direction of the priory because Simon wished to avoid the gallows where John Fletcher still hung, caught yesterday in robbery on the highway and strung up by the Constable at the same hour as Gronow ap Bol. The tailor's door stood open and Philip Win came forth to greet him as if he were expected. Simon stepped across the threshold and stepped into another world. A rush-light burnt on the table and another in a bracket on the wall, and in their dim light he saw the lovely Eva, his heart's desire, standing with her dark hair falling about her shoulders and the light on her face. She seemed to swim out of the shadows towards him like an angel. But she was not alone. At the table sat the Lollard with a book between his hands. For a moment no one spoke. The only sounds were the breathing of the cow behind the laths and the murmur of hens over their heads and the stiff sound of the turning leaves under the Lollard's thin fingers. Then Old Peter broke wind and Philip showed him a corner where he could squat with his behind on the earth and his back against the plaster. So he sat, as he was to sit for many such evenings, looking at the clever ones; the funny thin man so like the wooden statue in the church, the one in which God lived; the fair, apple-cheeked tailor whom he liked; the white and black daughter whom he hated; and the lopsided lord for whom he would have laid down his life.

'You will not be knowing this, my lord, I dare say,' said the Lollard, pushing forward the book. Simon sank down on to the bench, eager to have speech with this man but wondering none the less when he could be alone with Eva. It was a beautiful book, leather the colour of rubies and every page illuminated with birds and beasts in silver and gold. The frontispiece bore the inscription, in italic script, *'Godde's Lawe', the four gospels translated into the English tongue by John Wycliffe.*

'A dangerous book, I'll warrant,' said Philip, taking his seat.

'A costly book,' said Simon, feeling the softness of the leather and the thick parchment.

'Costly indeed,' said the Lollard, 'my only possession, look you, save my gown and my sandals and my staff. Scruples I had about taking it. There's funny, I said, for a poor Lollard to have such a noble book, but he did say it was for God's work, see, to give chapter and verse to my arguments.'

'He?' said Simon. 'Who?'

'Why, Llewellyn ap Thomas, see. Come into Herefordshire, he did, last Shrove Tuesday with money in a bag from Caraddoc ap Rhys. For a Bible, look you. Come speak to your kindred, he says, there is need of you indeed in the lordship of Abercibbi. So I bought the Bible from a scribe who works in secret and came into the land of my boyhood. It is a good thing indeed to feel oneself needed.' And he sighed to think of twenty years of running and dodging and the besoms of hostile friars.

'And you are to stay?' asked Simon, ever conscious of Eva's white face, but eager none the less to know more of this man whose thoughts tallied with his own.

'If God wills it,' said the Lollard. 'There is a good man is the priest Martin but not all are as good as he. The priest of Llanfoist now, a whore to his bed every Sabbath eve and marked with the pox for all to see. Yet curse for his tithes he will, see, like he was a true man of God. Filth! Filth!' And he beat his thin fist on the table, making the mugs jump. 'There is having it I will out of God's Church now and leave it clean and pure.' He looked at Simon with his blazing blue eyes. 'Believe me, my lord, believe me now, there is no purity you will be having in the Church until filth and riches be rooted out. See God's punishment every day you can, plague, sickness and storm, the punishment for an impure Church. "Do not carry a satchel nor a script nor shoes . . ." '

'But you carry script,' said Simon, looking at the book, 'and shoes,' looking at the stout sandals.

'Aye, there is truth you speak,' said the Lollard, suddenly quiet. 'There is but a poor thing I am after all——'

'Poor be damned,' burst out Philip. 'You be rich, man, rich in holiness. There's truth in your mouth. The Church do wallow in riches like a sow in the muck. Take the prior, now, a fine lord for you. He got furs and velvets and he do heat his parlour with coals and he got two rings to every finger and he don't know a cabbage when he got one in front of his piggy eyes. Strip him, I says, and what you got? A fat old buzzard with a hanging belly and an eye for the women. What right do he have to lord it over the priest? Strip him, I says, and all others like him.'

'It's true,' cried the Lollard. 'Come it will, in God's time. Wait you, daio, only wait. Here is our talisman, here is our guide.' And he struck the Bible with the flat of his hand. 'Here is God's true word, for all who reads the English tongue. There is nothing here of no cathedrals, no fat priories, no fawning bishops. There's no pardoners here, look you, no penny penances, no graven images, no——' He stopped suddenly and lowered his eyelids, as if he feared to say too much. Simon was astounded. He gazed across the faint light at Philip Win, a dumpling man transformed into a burning bush. His eyes shone with fervour, his cheeks glowed.

'I seen it in a dream,' he cried. 'The messenger of God come and tell me I weren't the only one what thought so about the prior and all them riches. 'Tisn't right now, 'tisn't as it says in the Book.'

'You can read?' asked Simon in surprise.

But Philip shook his head. 'Where would I be learnt to read, my lord? Nay, but I do listen to what this good Lollard reads from his holy Book and there's nothing there about no priors being lords of lands and hiring stud stallions for silver nor about no pardoners neither, I reckon. It's my belief there's many errors in that there Latin. Fair pulled the wool over our eyes, those churchmen have. Hoodwinked now . . .'

He grumbled on and Simon shifted his gaze to the Lollard who was looking at him intently over the flickering light as a man looks at another whom he wishes for his friend. 'Do you believe, my lord?' he asked at length. 'Do you believe the time will come when God's Church shall return to its true holiness and purity? Look into your mind now, and tell me. Do you believe?'

'I wish,' replied Simon slowly; 'but I cannot believe. The Church has been rich for so long, the priory has been here these three hundred years, pardoners are as old as the Papacy. How can you hope to clean the Church of all that stands between her and God?'

The Lollard leant forward, his knuckles gleaming white on the Book. 'There is support we have, my lord,' he whispered. 'A hundred Lollards in Herefordshire alone. Twice the number in Leicestershire. As many more in Bristol. The Welsh too, there are good Lollards for you. In parliament too.

Before I left Herefordshire I was hearing of the petition. A hundred knights of the Commons, my lord, marched up to the old king they did. There is a thing for you now indeed. Asked that he took away the temporal possessions of the Church and reduced her to the apostolic poverty desired by Christ.'

Simon had a vision of the prior cooking his own bacon and cabbage as Martin did, and he smiled. 'The Welsh, said you? Are there indeed Lollards among the Welsh?'

'Cut a Welshman open, look you, and you will be finding a Lollard. There is nearer a man is to God on Welsh soil than ever he be in England, I do believe indeed.'

'And Llewellyn ap Thomas?' Simon persisted. 'He believes as you? He wishes to purify the Holy Church?'

The Lollard raised his hands from the Book and the light of true conviction blazed in his eyes. 'There is no man in the Welshry more fervent than he, believe you. Did he not come all the way into Herefordshire to find me and beg me to bring the word to the lordship? Was he not bringing me money for God's Law? Did he not say to me: "Go you now, daio, into the Englishry and tell them the words of truth. Go you to the town. Lodge you with Master Win, whose daughter has the Welsh. There is welcome you will be there. You speak with the lord Simon, he says, there is a man now that loves the truth above all things. When the time comes for a blow to be struck at the riches of the Church, there is a man indeed that will help to strike".'

'Images now,' said Philip suddenly, 'graven images the Book says. Thou shalt not worship graven images, thou shalt not bow down and worship graven images, that what it says, eh? Eh dear, but you should see the people at it. Flop, flop, down on their knees before wooden gods and stone dolls. 'Tain't right, I tell you, 'tain't right. I'll swear they think God's inside them. Even Martin now——'

'Here is something to cry for indeed,' said the Lollard. 'Seeing God, they are, where God is not. And not only images neither. Seeing God, they are, in . . .' Again he stopped, drawn up short of the final heresy, remembering Llewellyn's words of caution. He did not want to be whipped from the town, the more so as he had the young lord's interest. He looked into those unhappy grey eyes, a pace from his own, and said: 'There is nothing like statues, now, for coming between a man and God. A grand chopping there will be, mind, when the blow falls.'

Simon looked dreamily past his head into the deep eyes of Eva Win. 'Aye,' he murmured, 'there will be a great chopping, chopping of rotten branches, chopping of old wood.'

'The sooner the better, I says,' said Philip Win, rising and giving Old Peter a kick. 'Come on, Old Peter. Chop, chop, chop,' with a friendly kick for each chop. 'You can wield an axe, eh, Peter? You got a strong arm for chopping up statues, eh?'

Old Peter blinked and yawned and spat between his feet. 'Chop, chop?' he asked, looking at his master.

'Aye, Old Peter,' said his master, smiling. 'Chop, chop, chop.' And he chopped an imaginary statue with his left hand.

Soon after they left the house. They stepped out into a radiant and still night, with the moon hanging hotly in a cloudless sky. Simon stood with Old Peter beside him gazing at the black outline of Blory and heard the bolt shot behind him. There was a fire in his blood and a trembling in his belly. 'Come you now,' said Eva in his ear, and he knew he would follow wherever she led. She carried a rushlight in her hand and he followed the flame round the side of the house to where stood a ladder that was the only entry to the upper room. Eva climbed up before him, the light in her hand, and he heard the creak of hinges as the door swung back. A hen clucked once and was still. 'Come you,' she whispered again, and he began to climb the ladder, in difficulty with his weak leg. At the top he caught hold of the frame with his sound hand and pulled himself into the room and Eva bolted the door behind him.

It was a low room, scarcely high enough in the middle for his head. Light from below gleamed faintly through the cracks in the floor. He could hear the hens rustling among the beams at one end and caught the dull gleam of an eye. The heat was stifling. Already the sweat was running down his back and he pulled off his surcoat so that he stood in his white shirt and tight green hose, one leg so much thinner than the other. He watched Eva fit the frame into the solitary window and set the rushlight before it so that the flame sent fantastic shadows dancing on the oiled linen. His heart hammered. He was afraid. What if Brother Gregory were wrong? What if, after all, he needed a magic mitten? What if he failed in the doing, gave the wrong responses, as in his hideous dream? He wiped his forehead with his sleeve and watched Eva combing her hair, singing under her breath but not speaking. Quietly she poured milk into a saucer from a little jug and went down on her knees beside the chest. '*Llyffant bach,*' she called softly. '*Llyffant bach annwyl.*' And presently into the flickering light crawled a great green toad. He looked at Simon without interest and thrust his toothless mouth into the milk.

'*Cariad bach,*' crooned Eva, crouching over him and running her finger down his warty back. Not until the toad had drunk his fill and crawled, bloated, back under the chest did she rise from her knees.

Simon looked at her in the weird light. He had never seen a woman so lovely. His love for her was indeed the love of which Llewellyn had spoken, the love lauded by the Welsh poets. It was neither the love of a knight for his lady nor the lust of an animal for its mate. He loved this woman with all the passion of a sensitive man burdened with a crushing sense of difference, a man hideously marked by his mother's sin, whose only moments of real peace hitherto had been at the Mass. She had but to look at him for his bones to turn to jelly. She looked at him now as she slowly untied her laces and he was powerless. He could neither move nor speak. Slowly, with her eyes upon him, she let her gown fall about her feet and stepped naked into the light. She was tall, taller than he, and white. He had never seen skin so white. Her hair hung about her like a cloak and she drew it aside so that he might look at her. She stood there without shame or shyness, with unearthly beauty, and Simon was lost. Lost in love, lost in magic. Everything was forgotten, his deformity, his bitter sense of difference, his father, Huw, Old Peter, even Llewellyn. Here was peace and forgetfulness. Here indeed would his manhood be proved. Here was his Welshry, his sanctuary, here was—ah no, not his Mass. This woman took away his melancholy as surely as the blessed sacrament, but Simon was not sunk so deep that he saw in her a substitute for God and Holy Church.

Even when he pressed his mouth between her white breasts, each stained with its dark aureole; even when he laid his unequal thighs upon her and felt no difference between them;

even when the flaming arrow pierced him, sending its sweet fire through every vein of his body—even then he never quite lost his consciousness of God. Even when he called her his miracle, deep in his heart he did not believe it. He knew that God's true miracle did not lie in her. She was not the miracle of healing for which he prayed.

Yet he loved her with passion, was bewitched, everywhere aware of her even when he had left her, consumed with desire. The instant she touched him his fears fell away. She never spoke of his deformities. She did not seem to see them. She let her long white hands go over him, right side as left, as if there were no difference. With her he felt whole. He was a man like other men, a breathing, potent man fit to take a woman and not fear her laughter.

So he took her, in the stifling heat of the upper room with maybugs crashing against the window and hens rustling among the beams, and Brother Gregory's words were proved. He took her and lost in her body another of the many dreads that had weighted him.

Many hours later he lay sleepily in the dawn with his withered hand between Eva's thighs and looked at the crimson mark beside her nipple, on the edge of the dark circle. It was the length of his finger and had the shape of a red new moon. He touched it lightly with his lips but she did not seem to feel his touch, yet the instant his lips moved and clung she awoke and caught his head between her white hands and desire leapt in his blood again.

When the first sun shone through the cracks in the far wall, making the hens restless, Eva rose and opened the door, letting the birds go flapping over Old Peter's head to the ground. Then before she dressed she poured milk into the saucer and called '*Llyffant bach,*' as before. When the toad crawled out she crouched over him, her body like milk in the soft morning light of the doorway, and stroked his back. Simon pushed his legs into his hose and thought there was really no need for Huw to help him. He could manage very well. But Eva had to tie the strings of his shirt, standing close to him so that he could see the crimson mark quite clearly. That done, she kissed him long between the lips, pressed his mouth to each breast, and sent him away.

'I may come again?' he asked, letting his eyes go over her, loath to let her go.

'There is a thing for you,' she smiled. 'Wanting when he has but done. Yes, *f'anwylyd*, I'll not be keeping you away. But you must come to the house mind, proper, and talk with my da first of an evening.'

So it was made certain that Simon would talk with the Lollard as the price of a night with his love. Not that he was loath, far from it. He was eager to speak of the cleansing of the Church and to hear the Gospels read in the English tongue. Huw had receded far into the mists of his mind. He never once thought that until this night Huw had never slept but at his side for eight long years, nor had he at this time the power to picture Huw's unease. Llewellyn's long fingers had stretched even into Eva's bed. When they lay with their legs entwined and Eva's hair over them like a coverlet, watching the sunlight creep under the door, Simon asked her sleepily if she pined for the Welshry and wished herself back in Pwll-du instead of in the cramped English town. She pondered, then answered that she carried the Welshry with her in the blood her Welsh mother had given her.

'But there is missing Llewellyn ap Thomas I am,' she said with her mouth on his ear. 'There is much liking between us.' She turned his face to look at her and for an instant he had the curious impression that she looked at him with Llewellyn's eyes.

'And your mother?' asked Simon, dreamily surprised that he should feel no jealousy.

At once he felt a shutter fall between them. She lowered her eyelids. 'My mother?' she said. 'Drowned she was. They found her eighteen years this midsummer, in the weir at Nant-oer with her back against the fish-traps.'

8

THE first thing Simon did when he came down Eva Win's ladder was to go to Martin for absolution. The second thing he did was to go in to his father. He found him perched on the edge of his bed trying to inch his back a little straighter. He was bent like a bow and his knees were locked in a crook. When he stood he was curved like a question, peering up at his son from beneath his bushy eyebrows. Simon was struck afresh by his smallness. Such a tiny man, with such a big voice! His wife towered over him like a dead statue with a dead face. Yet he never complained, save that he could no longer get his legs round a horse. He would suffer any jolting to visit the furthest manor of lordship, although he could no longer bear the long pull into the Welshry. Now, with Seneschal raving on his mattress and Richard so stupid and Simon so queer, he was flogging his frail strength to do the work of a healthy man. God had certainly not blessed him in his children, he sighed, although he could not but love this son, for all his oddity.

When the baron was dressed and settled with his sops in his chair Simon approached him, suddenly shy. 'Father,' he said at length, 'I have done.'

The baron looked at him sharply. 'Done, boy? Done, indeed? So Brother Gregory spoke truth, eh?'

'Aye, Father, I have lain with a woman.'

'Like to get her with child?'

'Aye, Father,' said Simon, but surprised. He could not imagine Eva with child. Children did not love her, so he had heard.

His father smiled into his sops, thinking of the day he first lay with a woman, and Simon watched him in the manner of all sons who think their fathers old. At length the baron laid his bowl across his knees and waggled his spoon stiffly between his fingers. 'Good, boy, good,' he said. 'Now we shall have the lady Eleanor here. I did but wait for this.'

Across the harmonics of Simon's brain a false note was struck. 'Eleanor, Father?'

'Aye, Eleanor. Sister to the heir of Wentloog. Thirteen summers and big breasts already, so they say. You will mind her father, Simon. Edmund Audley, a gross man with red hair and a swelling in the throat. His son is only three years of age and they do say the hand of death is on the father already. If he dies before Humphrey is of age the lordship will lie in the wardship of the crown. If you marry the sister, I shall petition the king that you administer Wentloog for the period of the heir's minority. He owes me as much for my support against his enemies. A happy plot, do you not think, Simon? If the boy comes of age, you are to have as your wife's dowry two thousand acres between Cwm-y-Glyn and Nant-Carn, to march with our southern boundary. If the boy dies, you shall be the baron of Wentloog in the right of your wife's inheritance. I have had this for long in my mind's eye.' He scraped his empty bowl, not looking at his son. 'I have seen the girl, a strapping wench with good thighs, so her mother tells me, and a broad belly for child-bearing. Freckled, mark you, but without hot humours. There is nothing more perilous than hot humour in a wife, Simon. At best it leads a man into indulgence, at worst——' He stopped, his face suddenly darkened with bitter memories. 'At worst,' he said slowly, 'it leads a woman into deadly sin.'

There was silence. The father saw once again his wife's face filled with guilty terror, her uncle's whiteness. The son struggled like a blind man for the light.

'Eleanor?' he said stupidly. 'You would have me wed?'

His father burst into a shout of laughter. 'What did you expect, boy? What is the tool if not for use? You must have sons, Simon, many fine sons. If Richard's woman does not whelp, your eldest son shall follow Richard as Baron Abercibbi. Marry, boy? What is a man's seed for but to be planted in his wife's womb?' But still he scraped his bowl and still Simon stared.

'Marry, Father?' he stammered at last. 'How can I marry if I do not love?'

The bowl dropped with a clatter. William Beaumont turned upon his son a face wiped clean by astonishment and disbelief. The traditions of centuries, nay, the whole teaching of the Church, had been shaken by that one shattering question. 'How can I marry if I do not love?'

'Love? Love?' he repeated, peering at this son, this stranger. 'What has marriage to do with love?'

Seeing his son bewildered he motioned him to draw a stool to his side that he might tell him about marriage. Richard had given him no trouble, but this boy—in marriage as in everything he brought the wrong mind to bear. He had never seen life through the eyes of a normal man, this queer son of his. He was like a stranger in his own land, that he needed telling even in such a matter as this.

'Simon,' he said at length, loath to begin. 'Now you have lain with a woman you have known appetite and gratified it. You have filled your belly—or rather a woman's belly'—and he chuckled at his own joke—'now you know what appetite is.'

'I know what love is,' said Simon quickly.

'Love? Love?' cried his father. 'Who are you to talk of love? A boy of seventeen summers? There is only one true love, Simon, blessed by the Church and the saints of all ages, and that is the love of man for man. True comradeship, that is the only true love. I knew it as a boy with my cousin Adam, when we were together at Warwick's Court.'

I could know it, thought Simon suddenly, I could feel such a love for Llewellyn ap Thomas.

'The love of David for Jonathan,' his father explained, 'that is the only true love.' He plaited his gouty fingers round his spoon and said with heavy emphasis. 'That is the only love blessed by Holy Church. All other love, save the love of a mother for her child, carries with it the seed of sin.'

'But a wife, Father,' burst out Simon. 'There can be no sin to love your wife.'

'You are mistaken, my son, as Martin will tell you. Every sexual act carries the seed of sin. Marriage does not sanctify passion. Every time a man lies with his wife he commits a sin; a small sin if he wishes only to get her with child; a bigger sin if he but gratifies his animal instinct; a mortal sin if he lies with her in passion and gives her pleasure in love-making more than is necessary for the erection. When you speak of love, Simon, and say you cannot marry without love, you mean that you cannot marry without passion. I tell you, if you marry your wife with passion and lie with her with passion, you imperil your immortal soul.'

Simon stared at him, wide-eyed with incomprehension. 'What if you lie with a woman who is not your wife, what then?' he asked.

'If you are married it is adultery. If you are single it is fornication and the priest will give mild penance, if it is for appetite.'

Simon thought of the mild penance Martin had given him. Had he but known! 'But with passion, Father? What if you be single and you lie with a woman in passion?'

His father looked at him intently for a long time and nodded once or twice to himself. 'You have tasted passion then?' he said at length. 'And you find it sweet? You are not the first man to have done so nor the last, but you must root it out, Simon. It has no honourable place in a man's life. It comes between a man and his duty. Lust now, the appetite of the moment, man being what he is, the Church recognizes his need and does not give severe penance. When a man's wife is with child and continence is damaging his organs then he may take a serving-maid to his bed and the Church not look on him with anger, if he does penance. His lust is a sin but a small sin. Boys and girls tumble in the heather, the work of a moment, and it is but a small sin. A soldier takes a wench in the rushes and gets her with child, the work of an instant, and it is not a great sin. But if a man makes love to a woman with passion and lies with her for pleasure, then he sins indeed.'

'Not all think as you,' cried Simon and stopped short when his father turned his eyes on him.

'The Church thinks as I,' he answered. 'I do but tell you the teaching of the Church.'

'But the poets! They speak of passion and not condemn it.'

'The poets! French romances of dying knights and languishing ladies, there is no passion there.'

'Nay, Father, I did not speak of the French but the Welsh.

Davyd ap Gwylim now, he praises passion and the love of man for woman.'

'Oh, so you read the Welsh now, boy? Has Huw learned to read so sudden?'

'It was not Huw told me, Father, but Llewellyn ap Thomas. The Welsh are full of passion, great lovers, so he says.'

The baron blew down his nose. 'The Welsh!' he cried. 'And when has the Welshry been the yardstick for our measuring? Your head is stuffed full of Welsh nonsense, boy, and has been from a child. Listen not to the Welsh but to Mother Church. I tell you marriage has nothing to do with love. Can you not see, Simon? It is putting a man in danger of mortal sin for him to feel passion for his wife. If he lies beside her night after night and desires her not for the seizing of a moment but for the enjoyment of hours, how can he keep his soul free from sin? How can he kiss her if not between the lips? How can he top her and not like to gaze on her? Believe me, Simon, it is far better for your soul that you should not love your wife.'

Simon sat silent, seeing before him only many nights of mortal sin with Eva, and many days of heavy penance. It did not occur to him that he could step out of danger by stepping out of her bed. He could not leave her, he had not the power to tear himself away. He was drawn to her bed as iron to a magnet. And Eleanor? Thirteen summers, big breasts and a broad belly—and freckles. Red hair, like as not, a triangle of red hair. He closed his eyes to keep out the picture. He did not disbelieve his father. Things were as they had always been. Always he wanted what it was not right for him to have. He wanted Eva, to lie with her every night and be made whole; now they said he should be wanting a red-headed girl with fat thighs and glad to get her to save his soul.

'And what if I do not marry?' he asked, but without hope.

'Not marry?' the baron looked at him as if he had asked him what if streams ran uphill or what if the earth were round. 'Not marry, boy? But it is your duty to marry. By the law of the Church all men must marry if they do not take holy vows. To say nothing of your duty to your family and your obligation to enrich the March with lands.'

Duty! Duty! Simon felt the net of duty closing him in. Duty to his station, duty to fit the niche prepared for him, duty to accept all the evils and cruelties of life and not kick against them. Duty, duty, shrieked his mind, but he said nothing.

Encouraged by his quietness the baron said: 'Lammas Eve, that is a good time for a wedding. Between hay harvest and corn harvest, two months from now. I will write to Audley and have John Upton take the letter to Newport, with presents. You shall be wed here. Audley may have the hand of death on him but he can still sit on a horse.' When his son still did not speak he laid a crooked hand on his shoulder and said: 'Trust me, Simon, it is for the best. Sow your wild oats now, before Lammas.'

Strange days followed, days in which Simon rode the March under his father's instructions and began in Seneschal's absence to see more of the English farms than ever before. He saw them but dimly, as he was seeing Huw. He was not stupid; his reports were accurate, his orders clear; he was a true mouthpiece for his father; what his father told him to do he did. But his daylight hours seemed to him unreal. He felt like a man in purgatory, waiting through long years for the opening of heaven's gates. He used to watch the crawling progress of the sun towards Blorys and listen to the bells ringing the slow day from Matins to Compline. He heard the curfew as a condemned man hears his reprieve. He welcomed the shutting of the gates as a prisoner welcomes the opening. The evening Angelus meant no more than that he could turn Merlin's head towards the town, towards evenings of talk and nights of love.

They began to murmur, these sturdy English peasants, that the lord Simon was a queer one indeed. The farmers of the English manors, silent yeomen who had known him from his birth, looked at him and shook their heads. The draining of Penperlenni, the grinding of shears, the clearing of fish-traps, hoeing, thatching, the sharpening of sickles, the hounding of death duties, the obsession with rents, the progress of an English May passed before his eyes, usual, without inspiration.

He seemed to move in a dream world. His nightly conversations with Philip and the Lollard had the qualities of dreams. Even in Eva's bed with his withered hand betweeen her thighs he could not say, 'This is real, this is usual.' Passion beset him, was satisfied, beset again, but Eva's caressing fingers were not as other women's fingers. They held him body and soul. Sometimes he felt he could scarcely breathe save in her breath. At Mamhilad the miller's daughter, a fine woman much given to lusting, drew him into the granary and undid her bodice but he started back as if there were a viper at her breast. When the wise woman brought him the juice of burdock mixed with box and made into an ointment, he asked her did she take him for a leper and told her to take it to the lepers at the priory.

He was not happy. Each night in Eva's arms he forgot his deformed body but forgetfulness did not bring him the peace he had expected. His love was like the fever that burnt Seneschal, something that possessed him and drove him night after night into deeper passion. Each night he seemed to sink deeper into Eva's body. Eager for love, she awoke to his lightest touch, save on the crimson mark. It was a curious mark, such a perfect curve. Night and morning the toad drank his milk, the hens rustled and flapped, Old Peter snored at the foot of the ladder and Simon sank deeper and deeper under Eva's spell. He began to dream of her even when he lay asleep in her arms. One hot night he fell away from her side and dreamed that he awoke to find the toad sucking at her breast, not at the nipple but at the crimson mark, while she crooned over him and stroked his foul back. When he covered her she took the crucifix from around his neck, saying that it hurt her skin.

He saw her everywhere, was everywhere aware of her, save at the Mass. As the days wore on the Mass became his only moment of true peace. With God in his mouth the mists were for an instant held back as if by a divine hand. Daily he confessed lest he die during the day in mortal sin. Daily his penances became heavier, while Martin waited anxiously for this sickness to pass. Such fever could surely not last. Yet Seneschal still raved on his mattress, crying for his St Christopher medal and shouting, 'Trouble, trouble,' and Simon still went nightly to the tailor's house.

He listened to the Lollard telling how kindly he had been received in the parishes of the Englishry; how the priests had let him preach against the riches of the Church in the churchyards and how there was much feeling against the priory in the lordship. He told them how at Llanellen the people had straight gone and taken the images from their church and thrown them into the river. At Llanfoist a man had split a wooden statue with an axe to boil cabbages.

'The people are with us,' he cried. 'Fought they did for a sight of the Bible in their own tongue. Not a priest there is save at Llanfoist but hates the prior and his riches. Here is something to praise God for indeed. Listen you now and mind what I say. If a blow for Mother Church were struck in this valley, there is no knowing what would follow. The Welsh are Lollards almost to a man, I am thinking. The Lollards from Bristol likewise, here in two days, mind, by the ferry at Mathern. There is but a day's ride it is from Hereford where they number many. London is with us, and Leicester. Four shires and a March. No knowing now what we can do.'

'Do?' said Simon with his eyes on Eva. 'What can we do?' And Eva smiled to hear the word 'we'.

'Open the gates, my lord, early, and let those that want to do God's holy will take the images from the priory church and burn them, smash them. Ah, there will be the day indeed, a holy shambles. No harm to come to the monks, but to give their jewels to the poor and share their rich lands and fat-stock among the people. "Take you neither staff nor script," the Lord said, but there is not carrying out his words we are. Sweep out the dirt, daio, a grand sweeping, like. Lechery, simony, the whoring of monks, the sale of God's pardon, give them a clean sweep, boy. There is copying the Bible for you too so that men may read the truth of God's Law. There is saving the people we shall be from the sins of idolatry and the sins . . .' He stopped once more and once more Simon had the impression that there was more to be said.

Simon was silent, his heart hammering. He thought of the prior, his paunch, his fat fingers loaded with rings, his scent and his dogs. He thought of the priory scarcely a stone's-throw from where he sat. It was true what Philip said. The prior lived like a lord. Riches came in between the monks and God. There was scarce room in the crowded round of the estates to gabble the services. There was not a man there put fewer than five courses under his belt. The Church glowed with rich glass and fine embroideries and costly gold and silver. Even the greyhounds wore silver collars. How much better indeed that these riches should benefit the poor. And the images! Not an inch of wall without its statue, Christ, the Virgin, saints without number with jewels in their very toes. He thought of these things; then he remembered how the prior had cried at the miracle of the glow-worm and doubt pricked him. The Lollard wanted him to open the gates and let the people despoil the prior. It was God's will, he said. There were Lollards in plenty in the Englishry and the Welsh were Lollards to a man, he said. He was a holy man and he said this was God's will. Yet Simon hesitated. He thought of the Pardoner and his filthy scraps of parchment, of the Summoner and how he rolled Stephen Oxted's gelding round his tongue like a sweetmeat, and he thought how he would like to sweep them away. He felt like a man in the ordeal, who has to pick the stone without scald from the bottom of the boiling pot, only it was truth for which he fished. He turned over the Lollard's words while he looked at Eva, and Philip sat silently, staring unseeing into Old Peter's open eyes.

He had been quiet all along, no longer the firebrand. It was as if he were not listening but thought of other, more important things. He had not once spoken since Simon took his place at the table. His bitterness and violence were suddenly gone. Simon was puzzled by his look, which showed fear and wonder and above all a sudden illumination, as if he would say, 'Of course, that is how it is, that is the truth.'

Presently Eva went out and Philip roused himself. They all rose. Philip had his usual joke with Old Peter. 'Chop, chop?' he laughed, and Old Peter asked his master, 'Chop, chop?' and Simon smiled and said, 'Aye, Old Peter, chop, chop, chop.'

Simon remembered that night for many things. As he stood in the moonlight at the bottom of the ladder, with Eva already naked in the shadows above him, he heard the priory postern gate creak and saw a hooded figure slip within. Later when the toad was fed he lay with Eva in the light of the moon and she took the crucifix from his neck, as was her custom, but before she pressed her lips where it had rested she said, 'A good thing it is indeed to have a man's love.' When he did not answer she put her hands, protesting, against her breasts. 'No, speak you,' she said. 'Doing is for after. Answer me now. There is nothing indeed you will not be doing for me, *cariad bach*. Nothing, is it?' And she made him look at her.

'Nothing,' whispered Simon, trying to move her hands.

'I have but to ask, is it, and you will be doing it?'

'Yes, yes, you have but to ask.'

'Wait you. There is impatient you are. Believe you what I tell you?'

'Anything, anything.'

'Say I a thing is so, it is true, is it?'

'Yes, yes.' And he plucked again at her hands.

She brought her face forward and flicked him with her tongue, once, twice, on the mouth like a snake. 'Look you now,' she whispered, 'there is a time coming and soon when I shall be telling you what to believe.'

Only then did she take away her hands but of all her beauty he could at first see nothing but the crimson mark.

The days and nights passed. Midsummer drew near. The Welsh salvaged what they could of their beaten hay, the English reaped a fine hay harvest. The baron's hay was stacked as well as might be without Seneschal's eagle eye and the wheat grew well, already up to a man's knee. Rain fell softly. The auguries were good. The English apples clung to their trees. Two more acres were converted from the waste and ploughed for autumn sowing. The clip yielded well and of good quality; ten loads of fleeces left the lordship for the ports. The ironworkings dried out at last, the walls were shored up and diggings began again. The forge fires were relit and the puddling poles no longer stood against the walls. Simon rode hither and thither on Merlin with Old Peter hobbling behind him. Richard brightened up his wits. Huw was everywhere, doing the work of two men, for Seneschal still raved on his mattress, weaker now, and Brother Gregory shook his head. The baron pored early and late over his map and his accounts and one night, before the feast of St John, Simon had a revelation.

For an instant of time he saw his father as he really was, as he had never seen him before. He saw them all, ranged along the high table like wax figures. His mother white and dead, with her dark hair looped over her ears and squirrel droppings on her dress, possessed, damned. Alice, giggling and unsure, her hopes of a child fading from month to month, seeing perhaps shades of the cloister creeping. Richard with his drooping moustache, his scar from eye to mouth and his friendly, empty eyes. Huw standing behind them, worried, loyal, loving him with the love of which his father had spoken, breathing his breath. His father, tired, old, worn, with pain and worry and his wife's sin, struggling to repair the damages of Glendower's army and keep the peace of the March, living on the rents from Herefordshire and Warwickshire. For that instant, for as long as it takes a man to say Ave Maria, he saw his father as a soul in need and himself as the man to help him. Then, as suddenly, the shutter fell, the door closed, and they became but wax figures.

His father was indeed tired. He had a premonition of death. His greatest hope was that he should live to see Simon safely married and his wife with child. He would not live to see her give birth, that he knew. He had dreamed so seven times and twice the bread had sunk in the wine cup. He was anxious that his tomb should be made ready in the priory church and a likeness taken for his wax image. Now the cattle were safely in he would send John Upton into Herefordshire for a worker in wax.

To see after his tomb he chose Simon for even the journey of five hundred paces to the priory gave him more pain than he could bear. Simon entered the priory gate reluctantly. It stood open, with a doorkeeper, the only entrance into the priory grounds save the little postern gate through which he had seen a monk slip in the moonlight. The priory lay snugly within the town walls, for they were wild times in the year 1100 when the foundations were laid and the brothers had felt safer within the stout gates of the town. It was the hour after dinner when Simon asked for the prior. The courtyard baked in the heat of noon. Vapours arose from the fishpond. Dogs yawned in the shade of the cloisters. The only sounds were the pounding of a pestle from the kitchen and the sleepy noises of the town.

'The prior, my lord? He is engaged on business. If you will but wait . . .'

Business? Simon could guess what business; sleeping with his hands on his fat belly, clasped over five courses, a kerchief over his baldness to keep off the flies.

'If you will have the kindness but to wait . . .'

Wait? Who was the prior to keep the baron's son waiting?

Indeed the prior was a proud lord to keep Simon Beaumont waiting.

'Tell the prior who awaits him,' he said.

The doorkeeper looked uneasy. 'By my faith, I dare not disturb him, my lord. Always at this hour—I have my instructions. . . .'

Simon flushed, his dislike come to the boil. Only the memory of his father's eyes, full of pain in their wrinkled sockets, kept a tart answer from his lips. 'I will wait,' he said briefly, and began to limp up and down the grass, chafing.

Time passed. The doorkeeper dozed on his stool. A novice passed through the cloisters, rosary swinging. The sweat ran down Simon's back and was sticky in his armpits. Business indeed! he raged. Who would have business with the prior at this hour, the hour of recreation? He stood irresolutely in front of the church door and peered inside. He had never been into the priory church since he was ten years old and had drawn back his head when those scented hands offered him the wafer. Even to think of God's body in those fat fingers made him sick. Yet it was cool within and he stepped inside. A burst of glory met his eyes. It was true what the Lollard had said. There were treasures here to feed a thousand poor. The sun streamed through the rich glass, falling in patterns of blue and red and green and gold on the tombs. Here they all lay, all his ancestors wide-eyed on their stone lids, brilliantly caparisoned. They lay watchfully, staring at the roof with their feet on their dogs. George de Cantelupe, William Hastings, Richard Fitz-Allan, they all lay quietly on their stony beds with their bones beneath them, fully equipped for death in their chain mail and embroidered surcoats and golden spurs. But for their stony eyes they might have been sleeping. Here his father would take his place, in this quiet company, and Richard after him. But not his lady mother. There was no place for her in this sanctified spot among the other stone ladies. If the devil still possessed her she would lie outside the walls in unhallowed ground.

The light from the east window gleamed on the costly gold and silver of the altar, the candlesticks and stoup, the chalice and the pyx. It struck sparks from the gold embroideries. The brasses glowed. Each statue in its niche sparkled with paint and jewels. The floor dazzled with its tiles. There was not one plain surface to be seen, not one oasis for the eye. Words came into Simon's head spoken in the Lollard's voice. 'It is easier for a camel to go through the eye of a needle than for a rich man to enter Heaven . . . Blessed are the poor for theirs is the Kingdom of God . . . sell that you have and give alms . . . for where your treasure is there will your heart also be.'

Simon stood in the brilliant empty church, hearing the Lollard reading God's Law in the mother tongue and pictured the niches without their statues, the altar shorn of its precious metal, the windows stripped of their glass, the horses sold, and the great estates divided among the peasants. He pictured the prior in a hessian cassock, his fingers stained with earth, blowing his own fire and preaching the word of God to the people. This was God's will, he was sure. Absolution, baptism, the blessed Host—the three pillars of the Church, not draped in embroideries nor studded with jewels but soaring towards heaven in all their simple strength. To absolve from sin, to receive into God's Church, to put God into a man's mouth—and he did this, what need had the priest of the trappings of wealth. Nay, wealth brought evil into the Church, for in its fatness foul things bred, feeding on richness.

Dazzled with the splendour Simon limped up the nave towards the altar and climbed the steps one by one. He was filled with a desire to tear down the prior's splendid cope and trample it. He stretched out his sound hand to feel the gold threads and strange little voices seemed to be whispering in his ears. Llewellyn would have rejoiced to see him now. He stood irresolute, a tiny lopsided figure in green and apricot, his yellow head shining in a shaft of sun. It was very quiet. Gradually into his ears crept the sound of voices. He looked round. Behind him was a doorway, so deep in shadow that he had not seen it and from it led a flight of stone steps going upwards in the thickness of the wall. He began to climb, dragging his leg after him. The voices became louder. Soon he became aware of light and found himself in a tiny chamber lit by an unglazed window through which poured the noonday sun. He looked out. Before him rose the south wall of the town. Below was a brilliant patch of green grass and here he saw the prior with two others.

The prior had business then after all. He wore a gown of purple velvet with a gold chain round the waist and he walked in the shadow of the wall, but the others wore coarse white gowns and stood in the full sunlight with their backs to the church and their hoods thrown back. They had hairless heads covered with brown patches and they swayed in a weird way, as if they balanced on their ankle-bones. Their heads moved from side to side as the prior strolled and talked before them. Voices rose in the still air, one rich and deep, the others like the croaking of crows. As Simon stared a cloud came over the sun, the prior stepped away from the wall and the others turned to face the church. They were the lepers.

Simon retched. These were not men but monsters. They were without ears or noses, their blind eyes covered with weeping sores. Their faces seemed twice life-size, swollen into the monstrous proportions of beasts and covered with knobs. And their hands! No nails, no fingers, simply rotting stumps. Simon clung to the sill. These then were the prior's business, these pitiful creatures doomed to rot slowly away until their disease reached their hearts. Every day at this hour, the doorman had said, the golden hour of their rotting, dragging day. Simon stared. This then lay beyond the treasures and the riches. This was the hair shirt under the velvet gown. His brain rocked. He clutched the stone as if he were sinking. For two brothers had appeared to take the lepers away and before he left them the prior kissed first one rotting hand and then the other. Without ostentation, as if he did it every day.

Simon limped past the doorman without a word, his father's tomb forgotten, and an hour later Huw found him still vomiting in the herb garden.

That night Old Peter was missing from the hall. Not since the night he had fallen in the fire had he willingly left his master out of his sight, yet he was missing, gone to the church, the porter said. Simon sat at table and explained to his father how the prior had been engaged and he would go tomorrow. He longed for Eva and oblivion and stretched his ears for curfew. At length it came and he rose, seeing but not noticing that Huw was not in his place. At the castle gate he hesitated, then instead of turning directly to his right, the shortest route to the tailor's house, he limped straight up the cobbled street to the church, Martin's church with neither treasures nor lands. He could never say why he did so. He had been at Mass in the morning and confessed his sin. Yet he went towards the church. He heard the sounds of the axe before he even reached the churchyard. Huw's face swam out of the darkness, Martin's behind him, illuminated by torches. He hurried forward, tripped over the step, did not even wait to dip his finger in the holy water. In the light of the torches he saw Old Peter, industriously chopping up the wooden statue of Christ that stood just inside the door.

'Peter,' he cried, hastening forward.

Old Peter paused, chopper in hand, and said, 'Chop, chop, is it?'

'Peter, what in God's name are you doing?' cried Martin.

Old Peter turned from one to another and in the torchlight they saw the tears pour down his dirty cheeks. He said the longest sentence man had ever heard him speak. He said, 'I am chopping up my Saviour,' and the tears ran down his cheeks.

9

MARTIN stuck it together with fish glue and, if the women noticed it when they came on the feast of St John to pray for their ailing children, they did not say so. Old Peter received no punishment for his sacrilege, for he was a natural and had the young lord's protection and Simon knew well what had led him to it. This alone had penetrated his dim understanding as he squatted night after night in the corner of the tailor's house and watched the clever ones talk and gesture. Chop, chop, they had said. Chop the images, they had counselled, and his master had said the same. Chop, chop, Old Peter, he had said. And if God lived in that statue, the only other solace of Old Peter's weary days, who was he to question what his master said? So he chopped up his Saviour, weeping, and put a naked hobbled foot into the door of Simon's mind. Simon told Huw to take Old Peter back to the castle that he might get into no more mischief, and he left Martin stirring glue over his fire, deep in consultation with the carpenter. He limped out of the churchyard and down the cobbled slope towards the east gate, thirsting for the oblivion Eva could give him. It was a weird night, Midsummer's Eve. The moon was hot and full, like a golden coin, but the air was not still. Little rustlings and breathings came and went like the passage of witches. Outside every house hung a bunch of St John's Wort to ward off the witches, for this was the night of their Sabbath when they flew through the air on queer animals and gathered in the forest to drink babies' blood. This was the night when the wise woman locked her door lest the townspeople should do her harm. A strange night, full of murmurings.

Simon passed the bear-post, dragging his foot in the dust, and came to the tailor's house. The door stood open, the light flickered within, but Philip Win sat alone. The Lollard was missing. Eva was missing. There remained only Philip, the cow and the hens.

Simon stood at the door and gazed at the little dumpling tailor, puzzled by his expression. All his fire was gone. He was looking at the table as if he saw words written there whose message he had just fathomed, as if he were a boy construing a passage whose meaning had just burst upon him.

'The Lollard's gone into the Welshry,' he said in response to Simon's enquiries, 'to Pwll-du.' And his daughter? Philip looked at Simon as if he did not remember who his daughter was. Eva? Where was Eva? 'Ah, gone to Mamhilad with a coat she has. Leave it be, I tell her, and send it on a cart but no, go she would this day at Vespers. Wait you, I says, but she didn't mind me. She gone her own way since a child, has Eva. She'll be back tomorrow, my lord, God willing.'

Simon felt his legs trembling; the blood roared in his ears. Was he to sleep alone then? He looked at Philip and saw that he was speaking.

'Say a rat do eat it now, do he eat God? Say the priest do leave it, careless like, for the rat to nibble, do it change all sudden because the rat come sniffing? 'Tisn't sense now, is it? He never said no such thing, I am thinking. Hoodwinked, like I said. In memory, that's what he said, like the Lollard learned me. In memory, that's what. Is it likely He's be cutting bits off Hisself and letting His blood like a leech? Be there aught in the Holy Book about eating a man's flesh like a heathen? 'Tis not a Christian action even in famine to eat bits off a friend. I seen it all of a sudden like, that what he said was right. I seen it . . .' He murmured on and Simon wondered what it meant, this talk of rats and letting blood. Had the man taken leave of his wits? His eyes shone strangely and he was pale, all the colour drained from his round cheeks. 'If a rat get at it now——'

'What?' cried Simon. 'If a rat get at what?'

'Why, at the sacraments, my lord, at the holy wafer, like the black rat in the church that do bear a charmed life.'

Simon thought of his hideous dream where the rat's whiskers had twitched over the bread while he gave the wrong responses. 'Well, and what then?'

'Why it do go to show, my lord.'

'Show what, man?' cried Simon.

'The truth.'

'And what is the truth?' asked Simon, wishing that Philip could give him an answer.

But Philip did answer.

'I'll tell you the truth, my lord,' he said. 'The bread don't change into flesh nor the wine don't change into blood. It's not God you got in your mouth. There! That's the truth. The Lollard told me.'

Simon sat like a stunned man. His mind groped for understanding. Had Philip hit him? Had a beam fallen? He stared stupidly about the room, while the floor rocked under his feet. Thinking he had not heard, Philip said it again. 'The bread don't change into flesh nor the wine don't change into blood. I always wondered, now I seen it clear. 'Tis not God you swallow. The Lollard tell me.'

Simon clung to the table with his feet on the edge of hell. Slowly, slowly, he moved backwards, away from the yawning pit and the everlasting flames. He breathed fast, like a man all but taken by the hue and cry who leaps in the strength of despair over the churchyard wall and clings to the sanctuary of the cross. This then was the danger. This was what Martin had hesitated to tell him, what the Lollard had been slow to divulge. This was heresy. He knew the smell of it. It stank in his nostrils like brimstone. This was the bootless crime, the final error. Who questioned the miracle of the sacraments questioned the very faith of the Church. This miracle was the rock bottom of the Catholic faith. '*Hoc est corpus meum,*' Christ had said, and for fourteen centuries the Church had taught the miraculous truth of His words. Who was Philip Win, who was the Lollard, who was John Wycliffe, to question the truth of the Holy Church?

'What, what!' he whispered, frightened and appalled, even Eva driven from his mind. Yet he understood at last. This was the path the Lollard would have him tread, the path of heresy. He saw the small beginnings, the dirt between the Church's toes that he would have picked out, the fatness of the Church's wealth that he would have sliced away. He thought, shuddering, of his terrible plan to open the gates to the Lollards that they might throw the images in the river and force the prior to distribute his wealth among the poor. He went over in his mind all the undesirable things that clutched the hem of the Church—the services in an incomprehensible tongue, the Holy Bible that few could read, the whoring friars with whom no man's wife was safe, the professional pilgrimages, the worship of images, the schism in the Papacy, bishops fawning at court, priors dedicated to hunting, even the filthy Pardoner and the cruel Summoner—he viewed them all one by one, seeing them clearly in all their ugliness. He saw them and, in an act of faith, he took them to his bosom. Not because he loved them nor because he thought them good or desirable, but simply because he had seen that to criticize them led a man step by step into heresy. He saw what he had never noticed before, little devils lying in wait, ready to entice a man from one censure to another until he found himself a heretic, deceived and damned. No, he would tolerate all these small evils if the greatest evil could be avoided. If criticism of the wealth and worldliness of the Church meant the slippery slopes of heresy, let the wealth and worldliness remain. He would not touch it. Goodness lay hidden inside it, just as the prior's virtue lay hidden behind his opulent Church, just as Old Peter's faith lay hidden inside the wooden statue. To know God upon his tongue, that was the only truth that mattered. To say else was to plunge into a bog of falsehood. Fearfully he put a question. 'Your daughter? Does she believe as you, that the bread and wine suffer no miraculous change?'

Once again Philip seemed to have difficulty in thinking of his daughter. 'Nay, a woman got no head for thinking, my lord. Listen she do, but not understand. It's not a woman's place to think, like. Not but what I'll be telling her, mind, one day or another. I'll not be leaving her in darkness, as you might say, not now I knows the truth.' He too knew that what he believed was true, as surely as he knew he breathed. What a strong devil, thought Simon, to make him believe such a wrong.

'And Llewellyn ap Thomas? Him who brought the Lollard to the March? Does he believe as you?'

Philip did not know. He thought not indeed, although Llewellyn was a friend of the Lollard. A strange man, Llewellyn ap Thomas, not a man for religion but for magic and sorcery.

Simon gathered that Philip Win did not care for Llewellyn ap Thomas.

It was late. The rushlight burned low in a halo of insects. Already the table was thick with their dead. The Lollard was gone; if he returned Simon would have him driven from the town lest he drip more poison in men's ears. Eva stood in no danger, it seemed. Nor Llewellyn. Like himself, to the final heresy they would find the correct responses.

He sat with his hunched shoulder towards the open doorway and heard the priory bell ring for Matins. Past midnight already! He did not intend to leave the tailor's house that night for he would not sleep without Eva. Every bone in his body seemed to cry out for her. Nor did Philip move but sat staring at the dead insects, staring at his newfound truth. Simon watched him and, in all his longing and dismay, felt another burden drop from his crooked shoulders. One inner conflict was over. For years he had been tilting at the evils in the Church but now suddenly he lowered his lance and retired from the lists, feeling the blinding relief of one who knows he need fight them no more. What he must fight was devils, Philip's devils. To save Philip's soul, that was work God wanted him to do.

All at once the light flickered and went out. Overhead the hens were restless. The cow lurched against the laths, making the house tremble. Suddenly the night was shattered by a loud knocking at the south gate. On an impulse Simon got up and closed and barred the door. They waited, he and the tailor, in the stifling darkness, hearing a confusion of voices, then a long pause, then the running of footsteps, the Constable's voice, Richard's voice, and the unbarring of the gate. The chains rattled, the bolts rasped, horses' hooves clattered on the cobbles. They did not climb the hill to the castle but came across the market-square towards the house. Now the two men could hear the harnesses tinkling and see through the cracks the glare of torches. Simon held his breath, smelling trouble, and was astonished to feel the tailor clutch his hand. They waited. When the knock came they did not move. A terror seized them paralysing their muscles. The knock came again, an angry double knock made with a stick, and a voice cried: 'Open! Open in the name of the lord bishop of Llandaff.'

It was the Summoner's voice.

Simon's first instinct was fear. For an instant he and Philip clung together like children, then slowly he drew away his hand, limped to the door and drew the bolts. At first the torches dazzled him and he seemed to see hundreds of faces, anonymous blobs hanging in the globe of light as if on strings. He put his hand to his eyes and slowly the blobs came into focus. There was Richard, anxious and uncomprehending, the Constable assuming an unaccustomed authority, Huw gazing at him with irritating intensity; there were unrecognized bishop's men and, thrust close to Simon's own, the spiteful visage of Brother Gregory and the predatory eyes of the Summoner.

'You want me?' he asked in a steady voice.

'Not you, my lord,' replied the Summoner in obvious disappointment. What a haul to have netted the baron's son, he was thinking, but he could not arrest a man of such importance without evidence of the final heresy and even Brother Gregory would not swear to what he had not heard. 'It is the Lollard I am wanting,' he said, civilly enough, 'and the tailor.'

'You will not find the Lollard here,' said Simon, wishing with all his heart that it had been the father, not the daughter, who had taken the surcoat to Mamhilad. Let him but have Philip to himself, surely he could convince him of his delusion. But the Summoner ... Simon thought of the black knobby eyes and the way they had gleamed when the Summoner had showed him just what they would do to Stephen Oxted. He relished cruelty, this man, as another man relished a woman; he would be eager to see Philip burn. If he recanted, he would suffer bitter disappointment. He will recant, thought Simon fiercely. Now the Lollard has gone with his fiery persuasions surely Philip would see his error and creep back into the bosom of the Church.

'And the tailor,' said the Summoner, slapping his thigh with his whip.

'Here I am,' answered Philip, stepping out into the light. The bishop's men looked at him curiously, disappointed with his dumpling figure and apple cheeks. Here was a queer Lollard indeed. Although he held his head high and gazed steadily before him, he had not the look of a man for the burning.

The Summoner unrolled a parchment. It was so quiet they heard the scrape of his yellow nails. He cleared his throat, licked his lips and began to read. 'In the name of God, Amen. In the name of Walter Merton, the lord bishop of Llandaff, I do accuse thee, Philip Win of Abercibbi, layman of this diocese, of and upon the crime of heresy; whereby you shall answer for your crime at my court sitting at Mathern.'

The terrible words entered even Richard's brain and he cried, 'I cannot believe . . . He always seemed . . .' while Simon moved so that he touched Philip with his shoulder. 'You shall not take him tonight,' he said, knowing that to offer money were vain. Here was a crime too serious even for the Summoner to overlook. Now he was accused, Philip would have to answer to the bishop at Mathern.

'At first light,' said the Summoner, feasting his eyes on Philip's plumpness.

They took Philip to the castle and locked him in the cellar and the Summoner put the great key into his bosom. Simon begged to stay with him but the Summoner refused and not even the baron had the authority to order the bishop's officer. The bishop's men lay down in the rushes to wait for dawn and Simon sat watching the Summoner tearing lamb's flesh with his pointed teeth, thinking with a strange mixture of passion and pity of Eva's homecoming in the morning. How would he tell her? What would she say? Would she let him comfort her, protect her? Would her sorrow keep him from her bed? Her father would be gone before she returned. What last message would he leave for her, his only child? If only Simon had had time to speak to him alone! Now his chance was gone.

The Summoner said little. He licked his dirty lips and seemed pleased that the bishop was old and foolish. Once he mentioned Eva, without apparent interest, like a wolf that assumes innocence but watches none the less out of the corner of his beady eye.

'Where is the tailor's daughter, my lord?' he asked, wiping his fingers on his coat.

'What do you want with her? She has no hand in heresy, I can give you my oath on it.'

'No, no,' replied the Summoner pleasantly. 'Do not be so fiery, my lord, I did but ask. I should like to speak with her, that is all. Some little matter, you understand. I will be enquiring again when I return from Mathern.'

'Oh, you are returning to the March?'

'Indeed yes, my lord. I have yet to catch the Lollard. In the Welshry, I'll be bound. And I will be having a word with Eva Win, if I can find her.'

'You will find her,' said Simon. 'She did but walk to Mamhilad with a surcoat.' But he did not feel easy. What could the Summoner want with her? If he touched her, it could but be to hurt her.

At cock crow the big doors were flung open, the baron was carried from his chamber, sops were eaten and the horses made ready. Brother Gregory sidled into the courtyard with his nag, for he was to bear witness against the tailor at the bishop's court. A heavy haze hung over the mountains, the colour of the sky. When Simon limped outside to smell the weather he could not see the Welshry; it was as if it did not exist, as if the valley went on until it met the sky. He prowled restlessly, dragging his foot, then suddenly Huw appeared at his side and whispered: 'He is in the privy, look you, loose in the bowels by the sound of it. There's the tailor's sops going. Quick with you, now, and you may speak with him.'

He hurried to the cellar steps and was at the cellar door when the bishop's man came down with a bowl in one hand and the key in the other. A silver shilling changed hands and Simon was within, down on his sound knee in the straw. Philip was awake and accepted the sops without surprise.

'Recant!' cried Simon, frantic at the shortness of their time. 'Confess your error. It is all delusions, Philip, it is devils you hear. The Lollard has been dripping poison in your ears. The bishop is an old man but not cruel. He can have no longing to burn a man who confesses to delusions and asks the Church's pardon. Repudiate your error and you will be back in the town within three days, before your daughter need suffer.' Philip looked at him oddly and seemed to grow smaller. He took no notice of the steaming bowl, simply looked at the young lord with his breath coming short. 'Believe me,' urged Simon, 'the Lollard has lured you with deadly falsehoods into this heresy. He is speaking with Satan's tongue, trying to pitch you into hell. Draw back into the truth! No one will harm you if you acknowledge the truth of the Mass.'

Philip slowly shook his head. 'I knows the truth,' he said simply. 'I seen it clear. "In memory," that's what He said. He didn't go cutting no pieces off Himself for his friends to eat. It's not likely now, is it?'

'I beseech you,' cried Simon in horror. 'Listen to the teaching of the Church. Accept the miracle. "*Hoc est corpus meum*," He said. Listen to Martin if you will not listen to me.'

'Priest or no, it don't make no difference, my lord. I can't put my tongue to no lie.'

'But it is not a lie, it is the truth.'

'It's a lie for me, my lord. I will say what they like about the rest. I'll not be pressing it. But this now, this is the truth. 'Tis not God's flesh Martin puts into my mouth at the Mass and that's the truth.'

Footsteps sounded on the stairs and Simon heard Huw's urgent voice at the door. He rose reluctantly, aghast that Philip should be so stubborn. Surely no man could believe, not truly believe in the core of his soul, such a terrible heresy? Surely the devil could be made to loosen his hold.

'I will pray for you,' he said quickly. 'I will have Martin say Masses for your enlightenment. Do not worry about your daughter. I will see . . .' But he said no more because Philip threw himself forward on his knees and grasped Simon's legs with trembling hands.

'I am afeared,' he cried. 'I am afeared to go alone. Come with me to Mathern, my lord, I am afeared to go alone.'

Simon gasped. Leave the March? Have Eva return and find him gone? Sleep without her? Leave Blorys and the Welshry and the friend whose touch he could yet feel on his knee? Philip did not know what he asked.

'Please, my lord, please,' cried Philip, plucking at his coat. 'Do not leave me go alone.'

Something stirred in Simon's heart. He had never in all his seventeen years had an appeal like this. This man needed him, was appealing for his help and comfort. There might be opportunities on the journey to reason with him and drive his devil out.

'I beg you, my lord,' pleaded Philip, scrabbling in the straw. 'Come with me to Mathern.'

Simon looked down into his beseeching eyes. 'Aye,' he said slowly, making his act of renunciation. 'I will come.'

He sought his father's permission. He gave instructions for Merlin to be made ready and limped hastily down to the tailor's house with Old Peter at his heels. Neighbours had already removed the chickens and led out the cow to pasture but Simon caused the ladder to be raised and climbed up into Eva's chamber, the stifling upper room that had become a sanctuary from the distresses and disappointments of his life. It seemed much as before, the covers neatly folded and the jug and saucer on the chest. He laid his head on the bed, trying to smell Eva's skin but she was nowhere, nowhere. He placed the saucer on the ground but the milk was solid in the jug and would not pour, so he sent Old Peter for new milk and when it came poured it into the saucer and called '*Llyffant bach*' as he had heard Eva do. But no toad appeared, and when he shifted the chest with his one strong shoulder the space beneath was empty. The toad was gone. There was not a living thing in the attic save himself.

When the sun showed himself over the horn of the Holy Mountain they were ready. Six bishop's men, three baron's men, Philip, Simon, Brother Gregory and the Summoner. They could hear Old Peter crying in the cook's brawny arms because he could not go. The porter opened the castle gate and Simon turned in his saddle and looked at his home, knowing that when he next saw it it would not seem the same. They had reached the south gate when there was a rattle of hooves behind them and Huw appeared on his Welsh pony, riding as was his wont with a short stirrup and without spurs.

'You will be wanting me, my lord, I am thinking,' he said, ignoring Brother Gregory's scowl.

Simon drew rein. It was on the tip of his tongue to send Huw back, for Llewellyn and Eva between them had wiped from his memory all the years of Huw's devotion. Yet he did not send him back. Perhaps it was Brother Gregory's scowl or Summoner's open dislike. Perhaps it was the precise degree of Huw's aggrievement when he said, 'Who will be helping with your lacing, look you, if I do not come?' and Simon's feeling that he would die rather than let Brother Gregory touch him. Or perhaps it was God's will that he should have Huw at his side when he most needed him.

'So be it,' said Simon shortly, and they set off.

It was not until they reached Ysgubor-wen at noon and saw the forests of Wentwood rising before them like a green curtain that Huw came abreast of his master and thanked him, telling him that the baron had given permission because there had been a miraculous improvement in Seneschal's condition during the night. As the bell had rung for Matins it was as if an evil spirit had left him. Within an hour his head had become cool and he had sunk into a deep sleep, no longer moaning for his St Christopher medal. The danger was over. Seneschal was not going to die.

The forest came to their feet, sliced off as if by a sharp knife. Beyond it lay Mathern and the Severn Estuary. Summoner took a firmer grip of Philip's leading-rein and checked the ropes that linked his feet under the horse's belly. Brother Gregory rattled his beads and crossed himself. The bishop's men unsheathed their daggers, the baron's men unslung their bows. Huw drew nearer his master's knee. For Wentwood forest was dark and long, the refuge of bandits and outlaws. Here the trees met over their heads, shutting out the sky. All was cold and gloomy, with danger in every thicket. They climbed for an hour, bent over their horses' heads and keeping well together. Once only did the trees part, giving them a glimpse of the flats of Caldicot and, beyond, the gleam of the Severn. The forest was very still. They went on through a forest as chill as a church and great beeches as smooth and cold as pillars. Once over Troggy Brook they began to descend, crushing their vitals against their pommels; at the fourth hour they passed through the hamlet of Shire Newton and by Vespers had reached Mathern.

Philip amazed Simon by his calm. Within him devils raged, yet he sat his horse peacefully and his apple cheeks had lost none of their bloom. Once only did he lose his composure, when the Summoner snapped a twig between his fingers and said, 'Good faggots for burning here, Master Win, eh?' And sniggered.

Simon felt anything but composed. He had been prevented by the Summoner's skilful manœuvring from having private words with the prisoner. Once he had managed to whisper, 'Think, man, think,' and Philip had replied, 'Aye, my lord, I thinks hard,' but Simon was afraid that he was not thinking the right thoughts. For himself, every league that separated him from his father's March seemed to add weight to his shoulders until he rode into Mathern bent with weariness over Merlin's neck. He pictured Llewellyn waiting for him in the Welshry, watching for him with his dog beside him. He thought of Eva returning from Mamhilad to find him gone. Yet when Philip smiled at him he did not regret coming. All he asked was that they should get it over quickly, so that he might return to Abercibbi. Resolutely he pushed to the back of his mind the death that Philip would suffer if he did not repent. He must repent! He must!

They found the bishop awaiting them in the church with his court about him. He was an old man tired of life, anxious to get this business over so that he might return to his herbs and his splendid palace only newly built. He was a simple old man who had never recovered from the shock of seeing Glendower's torches at the gates of Llandaff nor the ignominious hustle of getting away by the postern gate. Glendower had burnt his palace and all it contained, so now he was spending his last days in his new palace at Mathern, well away from the wicked Welsh who did such terrible things in the name of their golden dragon. He sat like a wrinkled old doll on the altar steps with his deacons and archdeacons ranged in the choir stalls on either side. Archdeacon Huntley rose to welcome them as they walked stiffly with straddled legs up the nave. Evidently there was to be no eating or drinking until the trial was over. It was dark in the church, and cold. The altar candles were lit but they burned with a tiny cold flame. The clergy rustled and whispered, looking at Simon out of the corners of their eyes, wondering if he were the heretic. Philip gazed steadily at the archdeacon, knowing instinctively that this man held the strings of the bishop's will. Stools were placed, the bishop nodded his head once like a puppet, and business began.

'William, by the sufferance of God, bishop of Llandaff, to all gathered here today, greeting, grace and blessing. Forasmuch as Lollards, under a certain cloaked show of holiness, do run abroad through divers places of our diocese and endeavour to cut asunder the Lord's unsewed coat, to rend the unity of the Holy Church and of the Catholic faith . . .' The archdeacon's voice boomed like an organ through the lofty church and Philip gazed upwards as if he expected to see it bounding among the vaulting . . . 'these children of wickedness have wickedly presumed and do presume from day to day many things heretical, blasphemies, schisms and slanderous defamings . . .' Here Philip gave a slight smile as if amused that he should be guilty of such high-sounding crimes. '. . . They expound to the people the holy scripture as the letter soundeth, otherwise than the Holy Ghost will needs have it, where the words wander from their proper significance and appear to bring in, by guessing, new meanings. . . .' He means '*Hoc est corpus meus,*' thought Simon, and wished heartily that the Lollard had never come to the town with his false interpretations of scripture. '. . . The words must be judged not by the sense that they make, but by the sense whereby they be made. . . .' He must make his act of faith, thought Simon, but he could not see any yielding in Philip's placid face. '. . . Have caused Philip Win, layman of Abercibbi in this diocese, to be brought before me that many cases and articles concerning the Catholic faith may be ministered to him, that he may answer to the same at this day and at this place.'

The archdeacon let his parchment roll up with a snap and sat down. Philip was pushed forward and the shaven heads in the stalls crowded together with whisperings. Again the puppet nodded and the archdeacon rose to begin the questioning.

'Do you, Philip Win, believe that a prelate, being in deadly sin and hearing the confession of any under his hand, in giving him absolution does nothing?'

'No, my lord,' said Philip readily, and Simon breathed a sigh of relief. There was more whispering and the Summoner bit his nails savagely.

'Do you, Philip Win, believe that only contrition puts away sin and that auricular confession is superfluous?'

'No, my lord, I do not believe that.' More whisperings and Simon shifted to a more comfortable position. All would yet be well.

'Do you, Philip Win, believe that the Pope cannot grant indulgences and pardons?'

'No, my lord.'

'Do you, Philip Win, deny the august powers of the Pope?'

'No, indeed, my lord.'

'Do you, Philip Win, believe that a priest who sins should be deprived of tithe and living?'

A pause here, while the Summoner looked up hopefully from his nails. Then, 'No, my lord.' And Simon breathed again.

'Do you, Philip Win, believe that images are idolatrous?'

Another pause. 'I did think so, my lord, but my mind can be turned, if you follow me. I'm not set on it, not now.'

'Do you, Philip Win, believe that the Holy Scriptures should be read by the multitude in the vulgar tongue? Likewise that the services should be said in the vulgar tongue?'

A longer pause, while Philip searched his conscience for the truth. At last he said, looking from one cold candle to the other: 'Not so as to die for it, my lord. It's better, to my thinking, but I'll not stick at it now.'

'Do you, Philip Win, believe the heretical doctrine that the Church should be stripped of all goods and property and returned naked to the state of apostolic poverty?'

A very long pause indeed. Then very slowly Philip shook his head. 'No, my lord.' And Simon's heart leapt. If he recanted his views on property surely he would recant his views on the Mass. 'I did think so,' said Philip, 'but something tells me no, sudden like, not without the Church wills it, that is. Force never did nobody no good, that's what God tell me just recent. I had a dream see, but then I had another dream, and the second dream were better than the first. In God's own time, the angel tell me, angry at me for speaking hot words.'

The archdeacon had reached the end of the roll. He cleared his throat. 'Do you, Philip Win, layman of this diocese, believe the abominable heresy that after the sacramental words uttered by the priest having the purpose to consecrate there is not made the very body and blood of Christ in the sacrament of the altar?'

Silence. They waited like waxwork figures, their eyes on the dumpling figure in their midst.

'Yes, my lord, I do.'

Simon was aghast, too appalled to move. He heard Huw

draw in his breath sharply behind him. The Summoner chuckled in triumph.

'"Do this in memory of me," my lord, that's what He says to His friends. It's not likely He'd be cutting bits off Hisself for His friends to eat, is it?' The archdeacon closed his eyes as if in pain. Slowly the bishop's wrinkled lids lifted and little pale eyes peered out at this hardy Lollard. 'I knows the truth, my lord, and I wishes you could be seeing it too. It's bread and wine before and it's bread and wine after, no matter what words is said over it. In memory, that's what——'

He stopped as a Bible was thrust into his hand and he was told to take the oath. Then the questions were put again and answered as before. Again and yet again. Then Brother Gregory gave his evidence, then the questions again. But although his words might vary his meaning was plain. The bread and wine did not change their nature during the ceremony of the Mass. 'Take a rat now,' he said persuasively, and the bishop looked in alarm about his feet. 'Say a rat do come sneaking out now and finds the lid of the Pyx open and eat the wafer, what then? Do he eat the flesh of Christ, a dirty rat what hasn't never been baptized into the Church?'

'Of course not,' said the archdeacon crossly, annoyed at having to cross swords with a tailor. 'The nature of the sacrament is miraculously changed before the rat can eat it.'

'But what if . . .' began Philip obstinately, but he was not allowed to finish. Unexpectedly the bishop spoke, leaning forward over his dry hands. He spoke to Philip as to a friend, an obstinate friend whom he wished to convince. 'Believe,' he said in his cracked old voice. 'Only believe, Philip Win, believe the teaching of the Church. It is older than you. It speaks the truth. It is the mouth of God. If you do not believe it, you are casting yourself into outer darkness, where devils will eat your soul.' He peered at Philip from under his creased lids and the Summoner cursed him under his breath.

But Philip met the old eyes steadily and said, 'If I burn for it, my lord, I believes the bread stays the same.'

'You will burn,' muttered the Summoner gleefully, 'you will burn.'

The bishop seemed to shrink and he became suddenly very much smaller. The archdeacon handed him a parchment. He put on an astonishing pair of metal spectacles and unrolled and read in a quavering voice the condemnation of the court.

'In the name of God, Amen. We, William, bishop of Llandaff, do accuse you, Philip Win, being a layman of our diocese, of and upon the crime of heresy and do decree that you be taken from this place'—here the Summoner smacked his lips—'to the archbishop's court sitting in St Paul's in London, that you be tried anew by the archbishop's court.'

The Summoner hissed in fury, balked of his burning. Simon took a deep breath, thankful for this reprieve. There was time yet for Philip to see the light of truth. If it cost him ten silver shillings he would speak privately with him tonight before he and Huw and Brother Gregory and his father's men left for the March. Already he felt his melancholy lightening. The very candles seemed to burn brighter. Tomorrow he would return and sleep in Eva's bed. The following day he would ride up into the Welshry and have speech with Llewellyn. Only one night of absence. It was not so much after all.

Suddenly he sensed a stir. The old bishop was shuffling towards the south door on the arms of two deacons, with Archdeacon Huntley in the rear. Simon was all at once aware of an almost numbing fatigue. Even his strong leg felt weak and he staggered when he rose to bow to the bishop. Through a haze of weariness he saw the Summoner approach Philip and rope his hands. But Philip broke away and flung himself at Simon's feet, bringing them both to the ground with a crash. The Summoner swore and leapt but Huw put out the flat of his hand so that the Summoner ran his face against it. For Philip was not trying to escape. He clutched Simon's withered shoulder, digging his fingers into the flesh, and cried: 'Come with me to London, my lord. Don't leave me go alone. For the love of God, don't leave me now.'

10

SIMON's world spun round him. He gasped and threw up his hands like a man in a whirlpool. He felt as if Philip were sucking him down into bottomless despair. Surely God could not ask it, that he should turn his back on Eva and Llewellyn and take this man, this tailor who meant nothing to him, on the long and hazardous journey to London. It was not a journey that could keep him from the lordship for less than three weeks; it was a journey full of hardship and danger and with what end? That he might hear Philip Win deny the miracle of the Mass in the archbishop's court and that he might witness the horror of horrors, a living being roasted in the fire. He could not endure it. He could never witness such suffering and retain his wits.

'No, no,' he whispered, crouched at the foot of the pillar with his hands before his face.

The Summoner grasped Philip's collar and lugged him to his feet. He pulled his hands behind him and secured them with rope and paused an instant while he wound the rope round his wrist and got a firmer grip. In that instant Simon looked into Philip Win's eyes and knew in a rush of fury and reluctance that he would have to go. He could no more leave this tailor, a man who meant nothing to him, than he could walk past a drowning man. Although he could not swim he knew that he would have entered the water. So now. This man Win was riding to London to face the most terrible death a living being could suffer and he could not let him go alone, a little dumpling figure in a posse of surly bishop's men. Thus twice in two days did Simon Beaumont put his own desires behind him and yield to the desire of another, a man too for whom he had no love. God had willed it, for the good of his soul, that he should accompany Philip Win to the archbishop's court. So be it. Although it meant for him nothing but suffering and despair, he would go.

'Do not fear,' he said, as the Summoner twitched the rope. 'I will come with you.' And he saw the tailor's face transformed in the dim light into the face of an angel.

There was much to do. He wrote a letter to his father and sent it back into the March by one of his own men, with instructions to return at once with an answer and, if the baron sent money, to hire an escort for the journey through the forest. The man left at dawn with Brother Gregory; he could not possibly return before the following day. The Summoner locked Philip into the bishop's prison and departed on his unpleasant business the following morning, having reluctantly handed over the custody of the prisoner to the archdeacon. He did not go, however, without a final word to Simon.

'A pleasant journey, my lord,' he said, with a glance of relish at Simon's thighs, as if he could see the sores through his hose. 'I return now to your father's March to hunt the Lollard. If I find him there will be another burning, eh? Maybe this time my lord bishop will order the faggots and not leave all the pleasure for the men of London. The Baron Striguil would have held the torch and glad to do it.' Simon said nothing, willing him to be gone but he had not done yet. 'And Eva Win, my lord. Shall I find her, do you think? I am not a man for gossip, as my lord well knows, but I have heard talk of the lovely Eva that has made me prick up my ears.'

'You can want nothing of her,' cried Simon hotly. 'There is no heresy in her. She is not tarred with the same brush as her father.'

'Who speaks of heresy?' said the Summoner softly, picking his nose. 'Your mind runs so on heresy, my lord, you can see nothing else. Just a little matter between Eva and myself. You will be knowing soon enough, if I find her.'

He lashed his horse and left Simon troubled with unnamed fears.

For two days he awaited his father's reply. He strolled in the bishop's sunny garden, crushing herbs between his hands.

He went to Mass in the church and had God put into his mouth by the archdeacon. He talked long and earnestly with Philip in the prison room but Philip could see only one thing. He looked at the Church through a leper's squint and could see only the Mass and the delusion into which the Church had fallen. 'It can't be so,' he would say over and over again. ' 'Tain't reasonable, my lord; when He says, "Take, eat, this is My body," you don't mean to say he takes a knife and cuts off some of His own flesh? Or lets His blood drip into a bowl as for the letting? I can't put my tongue to a lie for no man, and that's all there is to it, my lord.' At other times Simon had Huw rub ointment into his chafed thighs and ordered shoes for the horses and at night he tossed on his mattress or played chess with Huw to try and keep himself from sleep.

On the third day came his father's reply with a bag of money for the journey.

Son, I greet you well [he wrote] *and send you God's blessings and mine. You have my permission to go with the man Win to London. Take Huw and my men with you and exhort Master Win to repentance, for never let it be said that the Baron Abercibbi cared not for a tailor of his lordship. Item, beware of loose women lest they be bearers of the pox. Item, pray you buy Seneschal a St Christopher medal in London, for his own has not come to light. His health mends slowly but he does not speak. Item, Philip Win's daughter has not returned to the town and no man knows her whereabouts. Item, Llewellyn ap Thomas came to me from the Welshry this day and spoke civil words offering his master's help if I needed it in your absence. I told him your absence was like to be long and he asked to be mentioned in my letter, that he sent greetings and was your servant at all times. Methinks we are taming the Welsh falcon at last! Item, if the money does not suffice, apply you to the Bishop of London, with whom you will sleep. There is much liking between us, for we fought as young men together in the French wars. Item, Old Peter mopes like a dog at your absence. Item, it is well there is not any great bustle now until the corn harvest. The grain ripens well. Item, your lady mother bears herself as always. Your brother Richard sends greetings. Alice does not seem like to whelp. You must see what you can do for us, my son, after Lammas. And God be with you. Written at Abercibbi in right great haste, the 24th day of June, two days after the feast of St John, by your father, William Beaumont.*

They could not set out for two days, for three falling stars had been seen in the east, an unfavourable omen. But on the third day the portents were good and Simon reluctantly turned Merlin's head to the east. Long after, he remembered how he had turned his head to look at the Welsh mountains, knowing that when he saw them so closely again he would not be the same man. He did not want to go into England. He had no wish to cross the Wye at Chepstow, pass over Offa's Dyke and set Merlin's hooves on English soil. He disliked England, which he had seen as a child through the curtains of a litter on his many journeys to English shrines in search of healing. He had been jolted two hundred miles into Norfolk to see the marvellous shrine of Walsingham, with the phial containing the Virgin Mary's milk; he had travelled nearly as far to pray for a miracle before the bones of St Thomas à Becket at Canterbury. He had been taken to the tomb of Edward II in Gloucester, to the Glastonbury Thorn and the Holy Gospel Oak, to a hundred different tombs and shrines, and because these journeys had been vain he had come to hate the ground they had covered. He did not know England; he simply disliked it. It was a place where lived a leprous king who had taken hostage a thousand Welsh children during the Glendower rebellion. There also lived his son Harry who had crushed Glendower's rebellion and whose burning desire was to leap to arms the moment his father died and who longed only for foreign conquest. Such a man cared more for martial glory than for his people; such a man would never bother, no more than his father, about Simon or the March or a little heretical tailor. For years Simon had been shut up in the March like a beetle in a box, obsessed with the lordship like his father but with the wrong half, the brown half of the map instead of the green. He could not even love the Englishry, was it likely he would love England? No, he could see nothing good in England, a tame land of manors and hillocks covered with flocks of silly sheep and stupid peasants pulling their forelocks before the king's judges.

They set off at Prime, for they had to make Gloucester before dark, a forty-mile ride that boded ill for Simon's buttocks, even though Huw had smothered them with goose-grease before they started. Philip rode with his legs free, for he had taken his oath not to escape and the deacon was no summoner. He was a big jolly man, this deacon, who was to see the heretic safely to the archbishop's court and be the representative there of his master the bishop. He was a Somerset man and a man of the world, who had entered the Church as another man enters trade and whose ambition was so vast that no one could beat the bounds of it. He had an eye for the main chance, had Deacon Henry Fulbert, and he meant to sniff the wind at Gloucester and again at Oxford to see if it was like to blow him into any profitable place. He was a man of good humour and sang loudly, not always songs of devotion. For the rest, there was Simon, Philip and Huw, six baron's men in green and six bishop's men in stripes, all well armed and mounted, and three packhorses. At the hour of Prime they clattered out of the bishop's courtyard and began their long journey to London.

For Simon it was a nightmare. He felt he never could have endured it, save for Huw. There were hours of toiling in a choking cloud of dust under a merciless sun, for it was a splendid midsummer and the sun burned fiercely from dawn to dusk in a cloudless blue sky. The ruts of the road were baked as hard as iron and they had to watch without let for the horses' legs. Their only hours of coolness were in the forests and here they sweated not with heat but with anxiety lest they be attacked by robbers. They muffled the harness, the trappings and even the money in the bag, lest robbers should hear it. At Chepstow they crossed the Wye and entered England and for fifteen miles they rode along the flats of the Severn Estuary, within sight and smell of the globs of grey mud that low tide had revealed. They passed many wagons creaking under loads of wood and flour and once they saw a litter with drawn curtains, carrying perhaps a sick soul to the shrine of St David's. They kept a sharp look-out for robbers, and Simon's heart lurched when a figure leapt out of a thicket and seized his bridle. But it was only a beggar, a poor creature with running sores and foam on his lips, and Simon threw a farthing into the dust that he might scrabble for it.

They were now in the Severn valley, riding up the west bank of the river with the Forest of Dean away to their left and the Cotswold Hills a faint outline to their right, with the fair town of Gloucester lying snugly in between. The valley looked smug and prosperous in the rich evening light and for the first time in his life Simon began to realize how pinched in comparison was his father's Englishry in the valley of the Usk. He had always thought of the Englishry as rich compared with the Welshry, and he had been used for so long to his father's struggle to get in his rents and make good the damage done by Glendower's army that he had lost the power—until this moment—to appreciate its bitterness. But now, riding up this sleek and prosperous Severn valley, it was born in on him league by league that the Englishry had indeed been unfortunate to come under Glendower's lash. He had been so used to burnt acres covered with dock and thistle, to seedling trees a different green from their neighbours and to the relics of smashed millstones knee-deep in nettles, that he had forgotten—until this moment—that all valley lands were not the same. Some of those half-heard conversations at the high table drifted into his mind: 'Begs time to pay, my lord . . . twelve acres at Penperlenni still not reclaimed . . . three acres of woodland replanted . . . burnt by Glendower's men . . . begs time to pay, my lord . . . all his sons murdered by Glendower's men and no man to guide the plough . . . the only oxen at Mamhilad hamstrung by Glendower's men, the draught horses stolen . . . time to pay . . . two fields of wheat trampled by Glendower's men, a scanty harvest and no seed saved . . . sluices opened at Llanfoist and two fields of barley washed away . . . begs time to pay. . . .' For years Simon had listened as to a boy who shouts Wolf!; now for the first time he began to see that the complaint was real. He began at last to feel faint stirrings of sympathy for his father's Englishry.

At Compline the horses stumbled wearily across the river by the wooden bridge and they entered Gloucester through the west gate. The cathedral reared its square head before them in a cluster of smaller churches and they rode into the precincts to claim the hospitality of the bishop. The usual bustle ensued. Monks ran hither and thither in great excitement, craning their necks to see the heretic, who watched them calmly but kept as near Simon as he could. They dismounted painfully, feeling as if their legs would never come straight again. Well might the priests offer prayers for the suffering of travellers! The horses and the heretic were led away, the men in livery sought the common hall and the deacon and his party with Huw in the rear were conducted ceremoniously to the bishop's house where they were to lie that night.

For Simon the scene was misted over with pain and unhappiness and longing. He felt as if he were looking through a befogged window in which a tiny circle had been cleared as by a finger, through which he saw only Philip, although he was shut up in the prison room. Of the bishop he saw nothing. Huw stood in a mist. The deacon was merely a voice fishing for preferment. He was aware of a rawness in his groin where sweat had rubbed. His face was blistered with the sun, his throat parched. The reins had worn a groove between the second and third fingers of his left hand. He noticed how the monks stared at him and crossed themselves, but although he felt his difference, his body no longer obsessed him. It was but a poor thing to be the cause of such melancholy. But his mind, his poor mind, was tortured by longing and passion and homesickness and a horrifying sense that the worst was yet to come, waiting for him at the end of the journey.

Every night of the journey he dragged himself after meat to where Philip lay and pleaded for his soul, trying to drive the devils away. At first he pleaded as much for his own sake as for the tailor's, that he might return to the March with the repentant sinner and not press on to London. But as the days passed and the quiet night hours in Philip's company sank into his soul; as he travelled further from the Welshry and from the Welsh spells that still bound him; as the discomforts of his body became so acute that they took up space in his mind that hitherto had been filled only by his unhappiness—then gradually he began to lose sight of his own desires and plead with Philip because he loved him and could not bear to see him descend into hell. Long before they reached London Simon could never again say that the tailor meant nothing to him. He loved him. Without spell and without magic, he loved him. Here indeed was the love of man for man that the Church blessed, the love of David for Jonathan. He loved him for his honesty and his obstinacy and his simpleness, even his heresy could not prevent his love. He simply could not be with him and not love him. And the tailor returned his love. He was calm so long as the young lord were near him and Simon's hand on his shoulder could take away his dread, the faintness that came over him whenever he smelt wood-smoke. But he would not be persuaded. God had told him what to believe; God had shown him the truth and to this truth he clung.

After early Mass in the church they mounted stiffly, with groans, and rode out of Gloucester by the east gate, ducking their heads under the swinging signs and the barbers' poles. The sun was relentless. Even the deacon sang but little, distracted by his bruised bottom. Simon set his teeth and endured the pain in his thighs without a sound. Although Huw had stuffed sheep's wool into his hose every movement was like the rasping of files on his skin. Philip said little, content to be near the young lord. Although he was not used to a horse he was as tough as an ox and rested in his wooden saddle as comfortably as in a chair, dozing or looking about him and closing his mind to his thoughts. Ten miles out of Gloucester they came to the foot of Birdlip Hill, steep but not as steep as Blorys. They climbed slowly, bent over their horses' necks with their tail-bones jammed against their saddlebags. They came out of the trees into sheep country, hundreds of acres of rolling grassland with scarcely an arable patch to be seen. Almost like the Welshry, thought Simon, save that they grow sheep instead of cattle. Yet it was a world away from the Welshry, as a second glance showed. This was prosperous land. The churches were stone; even the houses were stone, many with tiled roofs. The sheep were fat even after their shearing, unlike the skinny mountain sheep of the Welsh hills whose ribs started through their skin. The people too were different, more like his father's English tenants, fair, with sunburnt skins and cropped heads and lanky legs, as different from the Welsh as men could well be. Yet because he loved Philip, who was fair and ruddy, Simon could not feel the old contempt for these English peasants. They seemed friendly enough and they did not stare more than he could withstand and Huw bandied good-humoured words with them as freely as if he were back in the March. They had no mystery, no appeal; they could not compare with Llewellyn's black and white magic nor Eva's unearthly beauty, but they suddenly seemed to him to be living people and once, when a girl smiled at him at a crossroads, he found himself smiling in return.

On the descent they passed an overturned cart and had to

pick their way over scattered logs, white with spilled flour. Once Merlin shied at a herd of swine and but for Huw's arm Simon would have fallen. At two villages they passed men in the stocks, all they could see of them their anonymous hands and feet stuck through the holes. At one crossroads a felon dangled under a swarm of flies. A mile from Cirencester they met a posse of jurymen hastening to the Assize at Gloucester lest the king's judge be there before them. Then Simon felt he was indeed in England where no baron had the powers his own father had in his March, but where a prisoner's guilt or innocence was settled by the oath of twelve men. A strange justice, he had always thought it, to take the verdict of twelve ignorant men, bribed like as not, with their thoughts on their deserted fields or their empty shops. A stupid justice, what one would expect of stupid English peasants. Then suddenly a new thought struck him, inspired by these new surroundings and this new horizon. What if the baron were a bad man, his justice bad justice? What if the baron were not like his father but like the Baron Striguil, a bad man who would have leapt to put the torch to Philip's pyre, who hanged men for misdemeanours and who had had a woman stripped naked and whipped for refusing his bed. With child, too. The baby had been born with the marks of the lash across his back. Perhaps after all, he reflected, a jury was better than Baron Striguil. Thus much more had this strange journey done for him. It had put a wedge, thin but tapering, into his obsessed mind. He had come but sixty miles and already the convictions of a lifetime were beginning to soften at the edges.

The sun beat fiercely down and they lay that night at Cirencester, worn out with heat and sores. The abbey was rich and powerful, the abbot gone to London to the House of Lords, but they were welcomed by the prior, a lean aescetic man as unlike Simon's prior as he could be, with marble eyes like a cat and lips so thin that when he closed them his mouth disappeared into his face. Here the story was repeated. Philip was put in the prison room, Huw did what he could for his master's hurts, Simon pleaded long into the night for Philip's recantation, but he received always the same answer: 'I can't see my way to it, my lord, really I can't. Say what you like now, and I knows you wishes me well, I can't put my tongue to a lie. The bread don't change into flesh and the wine don't change into blood, and that's the truth.' When he heard the bell tolling for Matins, Simon limped to his bed, dragging his foot, and Huw sat beside him until he fell into restless sleep, ridden by his dreams. Once he dreamed that he held Eva in his arms and a man with a mask and devil's horns came and pulled her away and ravished her before his eyes. Then the mask fell away and he saw that it was the Summoner who straddled her, and he woke, shouting, in Huw's arms.

Next day they went on, through Burford and Witney, to Oxford. Before Witney the light changed. A dullness came over the sky like lead. Queer winds blew. A black cloud shaped like a goat appeared before them in the east. The men crossed themselves and muttered while Simon fingered the crucifix round his neck. The deacon stopped singing a roundelay and started a psalm. At first the rain fell in great drops that kicked up the dust and lay strewn on the ground like pennies: then more pennies appeared and soon the rain fell in buckets, making streams of the ruts and ponds of the holes. They were miles from shelter so they pressed on, streaming with the wet, to Witney. As they crossed the bridge into the village they felt its stones shake beneath them and as the last hoof gained the far bank the bridge subsided with a roar into the rushing stream. A miracle, a miracle, they muttered, and climbed painfully from their horses to give thanks on their knees in the thrashing rain.

They reached Oxford with their hair plastered over their faces and sought the Mitre Inn, for the deacon wanted his clothes properly dried and there were no fires in a monastery, save for cooking, between Easter and Martinmas. The men stared at the scholars in their queer caps and gowns and the scholars stared at Simon. At the crossroads the sound of pursuit reached them above the sound of the rain and a panting wretch darted between their horses' legs and plunged into the maze of houses. But Simon to his surprise did not automatically swing his horse to cover his tracks, as he would have done a month before; when the hue and cry came into view he did not point the way the man had gone, but neither did he point another way. He simply urged Merlin on and wondered what the man had done.

That night he sat wrapped in blankets and talked with Philip while their clothes steamed downstairs and a bear whimpered in the courtyard. He spoke of Eva, trying to reach Philip's devil through his fatherly love, but he found a surprising thing. Philip did not love his daughter. 'Not but what I always done my best for her, you follow,' he said, cracking fleas between his nails, 'but she don't seem to want the best done. Nineteen years and not married. Martin speak to me often and says it's time she wed. Ripe at eleven she were, fit for childbearing sooner than most. But no, put her by here and she would go by there, like her ma, now. There was a strange one. Welsh, she was.' He considered his dead wife, drowned in the Usk eighteen years before and found at Nant-oer with her back against the fish-traps. 'Drowned,' he said at length, and Simon murmured his sympathy, thinking it were better his mother had drowned like Eva's mother than lived to fall into such terrible sin that two of her children were born deformed and her tongue seized by the devil.

'Drowned?' he asked. 'Was she setting fish-traps then?'

Philip shot him a queer look and seemed to hesitate. 'Nay, she fell from the bridge. There was some could not like her. Some did even point the finger at me, but it wasn't my doing.'

Simon stared. 'At you, Philip. Why at you?'

'She had borne a child. The milk was still in her breasts when she drowned.'

'But why should you——'

'It weren't my child, my lord, for Eva's not my daughter. Married me with child, her mother did, and said nothing. But God punished her, like, by throwing her in the river, and I didn't never hold it against Eva for all her queer ways.'

'Who was her father?'

'She never tell. A Welshman, it seems.'

Since Philip had no feeling for Eva, Simon's appeal could not touch him. 'She can tailor same as me,' he said. 'If she does not marry she can keep herself. I learned her to sew soon as she could hold a needle.'

'But she must marry,' said Simon, mindful of his father's words. 'The Church says so.' And wished with all his heart that she could marry him.

Philip looked at him. 'There's not many will marry Eva,' he said, but he would not say why.

The deacon was absent, gone to pay his master's respects to the lord bishop of Oxford and find the way of the wind. The men were drinking in the common room, banging the table with their mugs. They descended to the fire and found Huw turning over the clothes in a smell of scorching. Philip bent forward for his shoes, which were roasting near the flame, and at that moment a log fell on to his wrist in a shower of sparks. He shouted and leapt back, twisting with the pain, and they were suddenly frozen, their faces ashen white, seeing with horror how this journey must end. He will burn, thought Simon. He will not flare like the glow-worm; it will not be a merciful death. And he sent up a frantic prayer that he would not be doomed to watch it.

Later Philip slept, his wrist bound with a rag. Simon turned the key on him and wandered out into the courtyard. At one end the bear slept with his muzzle between his paws; at the other torches flared and a girl danced on her hands, showing her drawers. There were laughs and shouts and he leant against the wall.

'Come to bed, dear?' said a voice in his ear. It was a woman, a loose woman with paint on her face and thin stuff, freshly damped, clinging to her breasts. 'Not strange, are you?' she went on, when Simon stared at her stupidly. 'You like a woman, eh? Not but what it comes more, now, seeing as . . .' She eyed Simon's withered leg, then looked at his face and said: 'Pretty boy, ain't you? Like to see me, eh?' And she pulled at the damp stuff while the bear shuddered in his sleep. She caught Simon's left wrist in a vice and made him feel with limp fingers. 'Nice, eh?' she wheedled, bending forward so that he smelled the ale on her breath. 'A shilling now and you shall have the rest.' She loosed his wrist and began fumbling at her laces, but Simon was gone. He could not take a whore to his bed, if he never slept again. Better the terrible dreams, the frantic waking, than this dreadful creature. Better even Eleanor with her big breasts and freckles, than this.

At dawn they left the town, with its whore, its sleeping bear and its weird scholars. Their clothes felt stiff and the folds sharp and Philip's wrist troubled him. Simon noticed that his cheeks had hollowed in the night, as if he were sucking them in. The deacon sulked because the bishop had not been cordial and he could smell no place for himself in an Oxford stall. Only Huw had his accustomed good humour.

The nearer they approached to London the more silent they became. Even the bishop's men stopped ogling village girls and fell to spitting between their horses' ears. They crossed the river at Thame and rode in silence through the lush valley that cut the Chilterns in two, a valley in which the grass was longer, the sheep fatter, the cows bigger and the corn thicker than anything in his father's March. Soft as butter, he thought angrily, as if someone had compared it favourably with the Usk valley. At the mouth of the valley they found a hermit, a holy man with eyes like pools who sold holy water from the well to travellers. Unlike the Pardoner, he made no extravagant claims for his ware. 'Madness and melancholy, my lords,' he cackled, mumbling his lips and scratching his armpit, 'that is all it will cure. Drive away evil humours, that is all it will do.' Simon threw him a penny and Huw emptied his water-bottle. The hermit dipped a ladle into the sweet water and emptied it into the bottle but Simon had no great faith in it. He was not surprised when he felt no change after drinking it. Yet it was cool and sweet and chilled his burning forehead.

The heat returned and with it the dust and the flies. Five miles short of Wycombe they heard screams from a thicket and found two ruffians raping a woman, turn and turn about. Simon was so stiff with sores that Huw had had to lift him into the saddle at the holy well, yet he leapt from Merlin like a goat and, seizing his dagger with his sound hand, plunged it between the shoulders that covered her. The other leapt but fell with Huw's sword in his throat. Justice was done. No need for juries now. They dragged the man off the senseless woman and buttoned him up for decency's sake; then they laid his companion beside him and left them, flies already busy about their eyes, for the sheriff's men. The woman they laid across one of the packhorses, where she slumped like a sack. At the abbey the monks received her with kindness, but she died at the last Angelus and Simon dreamt of her in the night, that it was Llewellyn who raped her and whose back he had stabbed. It was the first man he had killed, he who looked upon violence as on a raging bull and could not bring himself to crush a beetle. Huw could not believe his eyes. Was this the man who grovelled in his own vomit when the bear was torn by the dogs? Was this the man who lost his senses when Sarah Saddler's baby had its legs taken by the scythe? Who had moped as a child because he could never bend a bow? This man had leapt from his horse without hesitation and had struck strongly in the right place, straight between the ribs into the heart. Simon Beaumont could do mightily, if he wished!

They lay at Wycombe Abbey that night, heard Mass sung for the dead woman's soul and journeyed on towards London. Philip scarcely spoke but turned continually towards Simon as if to renew his strength. The deacon talked much of the bishop of London and of what he would say to him and how he hoped the bishop would reply, but at length even he fell silent, humming a tavern song under his breath. While still within the Buckinghamshire border they entered a stretch of forest, but with their goal only twenty miles distant they fell careless and forgot to muffle the money-bags. In the darkest stretch of the forest, where the light was sieved through the branches and there was not even a charcoal-burner within call, a band of robbers leapt out upon them, outlaws and desperate men with nothing to lose and all to gain. Stiff with sores, bruised, aching and tired to blindness, the deacon's party had but one advantage, their horses. Dirty hands clutched their knees and their bridles, clubs whirled about the horses' ears, as the robbers sought to unhorse them. But the horses were strong if the riders were not. If they could keep their seats they might save themselves. Huw was cut off from his master by two men who threatened to bring down his pony by their very weight. Merlin's first lunge would, he knew, bring his master down. The heretic would run, for the forest was God's gift to him and the robbers his angels. But the heretic did not run, not without his lord. With one sweep of his arm he plucked Simon from his saddle and flung him across his own, kicked his horse and was away with Merlin thundering behind him. The deacon slashed at the clinging hands with many unholy oaths, Huw broke a jaw with his foot and his pony cracked a thigh-bone with her hard hoof, the sound of a horn burst through the trees and they were free, tearing on down the track with the money-bags safe and the robbers fallen behind. On the edge of the forest they found Philip still with Simon's horn in his hand, a dumpling figure with the strength of an ox. They had hobbled the horses and sat together, the tailor and the young lord, as friends sit, knee to knee on a fallen log.

'Well, Master Win,' said Huw with a grin. 'There is soft you are not to run.'

'Run?' said Philip with a frown between his ginger eyebrows. 'Run? I don't run when I taken an oath, see?'

Simon said nothing but he put his hand on Philip's shoulder and swore in his heart that nothing save death should part them. Watching them Huw felt a stab of jealousy, but when he thought of how it must end and of the further suffering his master must undergo, he said, 'Come you now,' as to a child and lifted Simon into the saddle. Four hours later Simon drew rein and looked at the walls of London.

He, Simon Beaumont, had arrived. But he was not the same Simon Beaumont as had left the lordship of Abercibbi eleven days before.

II

OF THEM all, the deacon was the only one who had seen London. They sat quietly and looked their fill, while he told them how many serving men the bishop of London had and how he coveted one of the thirty greater canonries of St Paul's. Each canon held a manor, he was anxious to inform them, as became a dignitary of London's cathedral. The present bishop, he boomed, had risen to his exalted position by way of a cathedral stall. Let him but take the bishop's sleeve . . . Simon heard but did not heed him. The sinking sun was behind them with no mountain to hide it as there was in the March. Their shadows, men and horses, stretched out blackly before them. Far to their right they caught the golden gleam of the Thames and a flash of fire that was the spire of Westminster Abbey. Two miles ahead rose the walls of London, brought closer by the brilliant light and wavering in the heat. They were tall and grey and punctuated by towers and houses huddled up to them as if for shelter. There was a jumble of spires and towers against the deep blue sky and, above them, like a celestial finger, soared the great spire of St Paul's. This was the end of their journey. Here the bishop awaited them. Their beds were made in the bishop's house. The key to the Lollards' Tower was oiled. The great men of the church were already within the walls against their coming, all but the archbishop who lay at Lambeth. Bishops, abbots, chancellors, doctors of divinity, all awaited the little heretical tailor who had been sent by the bishop of Llandaff to be tried in the archbishop's court and who was the living sacrifice to the ambitions of Llewellyn ap Thomas.

The wrong man had listened and believed. The man, not the master, had taken the leap into heresy.

With their journey over, their hurts seemed less. Led by the deacon the men surged forward and, urged by ambition or curiosity, they pressed on towards the golden city. But Simon did not move. He was reluctant to arrive. Although he could feel the wet of his sore places and his tail-bone seemed to bore through his skin, he wished they had a hundred miles yet to go. He was afraid that what London had to offer he would be unable to take. Then Philip touched him with a ghost of a smile. 'Come, my lord,' he said, and the three of them, Philip, and Simon and Huw, set their horses' hooves upon Oxford Street. They went quietly through the village of Holborn. They stared at the grisly gallows. The waters of Tyburn were untroubled but the deacon told them that sunk deep in the muddy bottom lay women felons with stones round their necks. Soon they passed over the Holborn bars and entered the outer precincts of the city where the fields were edged with houses and the Fleet pushed its dirty water southwards to the Thames. They clattered over the wooden planks, heard the screams of a pig from behind the bloody walls of the shambles, disturbed a clot of flies feasting on something in the roadway, and rode up to the gate. Two traitors' heads grinned at them from the wall, for Henry IV was not yet so secure on his throne that he could deal kindly with plotters. Leprous or no, he had a short way with treachery. The gateman looked them over while faces peered down at them from behind the prison bars and a carefully aimed crust hit Simon on his humped shoulder. They paid their toll, took a last look at the fields behind them and clattered under New Gate into the city.

The noise hit them like a blow. The stench stifled them like a pillow. Even the deacon stopped thinking of the bishop and put his hands to his face. Simon stared frantically about him, as if this were hell and these the first of the torments. A hundred city bells clanged the Angelus, drowning them in sound. A beggar clutched at his knee and exposed his scabs amidst piercing whines. Two forges rang under the hammer in the next street, a dozen apprentices shouted their masters' wares within earshot. Three dogs fought almost under their feet, their yelps trapped under the overhanging houses. They had lost St Paul's. They could scarcely even see the sky, so narrow were the streets and so close the roofs. When they took their hands from their ears it was but to stop their noses. The smell of corruption stifled them, strong enough to taste. There was no breeze within walls to carry it away. They smelt not only what they saw but, more horribly, what they could not see, the blood and filth of five hundred years soaked into the London clay, the countless bodies rotting only three feet deep in the churchyards, the cesspool simmering under their horses' hooves. Choking in his kerchief Simon was suddenly tormented by a picture of the Welshry with its cool wind and its silence. Even the Englishry, in spite of its busy manors, seemed quiet in comparison with this inferno.

All at once the bells stopped, and they drew breath. Simon threw the beggar a farthing and they moved on behind the deacon's important back, ducking their heads under ale-bushes and bird cages. The horses trod all manner of rottenness into the cobbles that fell away behind them, overshadowed with houses that all but met over their heads and so narrow that their packs scraped the walls on either side. People were everywhere, swarming like ants in and out of little holes, giving them no more than a glance, too busy, Simon felt, to notice his deformity. Only one woman stared, a woman in the striped hood of a harlot with a split nose to show that once she had dared to wander out of her district. At one corner a beggar held up her deformed child, whining for pity, and Simon thought that if God had willed it that might have been his own mother, for had she not maimed her children by her terrible sin as surely as this beggar had maimed her child? For this was no accident. He could see the marks of the knife. Suffering and sin, suffering and sin, here as everywhere it crushed and crowded him, tearing at him with hideous fingers like that scabby beggar. It was the bear all over again; soon he would vomit, a weak and foolish man who would not accept what his fellow-men accepted but who must always be kicking against the pricks.

Suddenly without warning the deacon turned sharply to the right and light burst upon them. There before them in all its glorious majesty stood the cathedral of St Paul's, the seat of the Bishop of London, the archbishop's court, their journey's end. It was quieter here and once they had passed into the churchyard through Paternoster Gate they were a world away from the stinking streets. Philip straightened his back and stared at the house of God where next day he was to be tried. He looked about him and asked if that—and he pointed—was where they burned heretics, but the deacon said no, that was only a preaching cross. Heretics were burnt at Smithfield, outside the city walls.

They were expected, had been expected for three days. The advance messenger of the bishop of Llandaff had given tidings of their coming. The archbishop was at Lambeth and would cross the river in the morning. Such bishops and abbots as were in London for the sitting of parliament would take their seats at Nones the next day. The benches were already set in the choir and the bishop's throne shifted to the foot of the altar steps. The quills were sharpened, the sand prepared, the parchments cut. Prayers had been said in all the city churches for the enlightenment of the court. The tombs had been polished, the floor swept, the rushes changed in the Lollards' Tower. Everything was ready and awaiting the tailor of Abercibbi. When the word passed of the heretic's arrival the canons came running to view him for they were as curious as peasants, and more than one crossed himself at the sight of Simon, in the belief that he must be the Lollard. They were led round to the west porch, a huge edifice flanked on the right by the Lollards' Tower and on the left by the bishop's house. Here the bishop of London himself advanced to greet the son of his old friend and endeared himself to Simon for ever by proffering only his left hand. He was just such another man as his father, courteous and honest and a fair judge of men. He summed up the deacon in an instant and to his outraged fury gave him into the care of a lesser canon, to feed in the common hall. Huw dismounted and lifted Simon from Merlin's back, all in one piece like a wooden doll. They all dismounted, the men followed the horses, Philip was led away into the tower and the bishop himself conducted Simon, with Huw at his heels, into his own house.

The evening passed in misery, the night in torment. The bishop spoke kindly of his old friend and told tales of their adventures in France, and if he thought the baron's son discourteous he did not show it. He spoke of his Italian chessmen, mother-of-pearl inlaid with tortoiseshell, and invited Simon to a game, but Simon was too wretched to play. He spoke of the Lollards and of the archbishop's determination to stamp out their abominable heresies and he voiced the unanimous hope of the court that the heretic would recant and spare them the pain of handing him over to the sheriff for burning.

'Is it such a slow death?' asked Simon, and was told slow enough to satisfy the most orthodox.

Not slow enough for the Summoner, thought Simon.

'I saw Sautre burn,' said the bishop thoughtfully, spooning his blancmange. 'They gave him a soporific sponge, but I was sorry for it. Not that I wished to see him suffer,' he hastened to explain, lest Simon think him cruel, 'but I wished to hear him repent. It is wonderful what the flames will do. There is always hope that in the last agonies, even as death stops the breath, an act of repentance will drive the devil from the heretic's body and save his soul. I stretched my ears to hear Sautre's devil leave him but he was stupid with the herbs and I heard nothing but his moans. Who knows but that the devil was drugged also and could not be expelled?'

'Would not the fire burn the devil also?' asked Simon.

'No, fire is a devil's natural element. The heretic is not put into the fire to drive out the devil but to punish him for his wickedness and make him repent and to give an example to others that they do not listen to false whisperings.'

'But if the devil puts words into his mouth,' pursued Simon, intent as ever on the truth, 'how can you call the heretic wicked? Surely it is the devil that is wicked, not the man.'

The bishop looked at him, at the frown between his eyes so deep it was like a scar, and at the melancholy eyes. 'Your thoughts are too heavy for comfort, my lord,' he said at length. 'Whether it is a devil speaks or no it is wickedness to question the doctrines of the Church. Only thus can the fabric of the Church remain whole and strong. The Church is merciful to those that repent but terrible to those that persist in disobedience. Listen, when your tailor burns. Listen for a sign of repentance. If his very beard is alight we will have him from the fire.'

'He does not have a beard,' said Simon, and the bishop laughed.

'Do not grieve, my lord,' he said with kindness. 'Two priests sit with the tailor now, exhorting him to repentance. Everything will be done to save him. He has only to give the true answers tomorrow and there is not a man of God but will rejoice to hear them.'

When the bell tolled for Compline Simon dragged himself to his chamber. He did not sleep.

At cockcrow they rose but were not allowed to see Philip, who did not even appear at the Mass. Throughout the long morning Simon sat at one window looking out over the roofs of New Gate Street or at another looking into the west courtyard. All morning the great men were arriving, from the north through Paternoster Gate and from the south through Paul's Chain. All morning there were shouts and the whinnyings of horses, the querulous voices of chaplains and the calmer tones of the bishop of London as he welcomed his guests. Simon caught glimpses of splendid trappings and embroideries and the precincts swarmed with bishops' men, eyeing each other warily. Soon after High Mass the archbishop arrived from Lambeth in a train of men and priests that stretched from Billingsgate to the cathedral. Simon craned his neck but glimpsed only a crimson cap spattered with gold and a wrinkled neck before the porch swallowed him up.

At noon dinner was served but he was too sick at heart to go down. Huw brought him meat and broth but he could not eat. A terrible depression weighed him down. He struggled with his fears through the long, hot morning, hearing the life of the city but faintly over the churchyard wall and watching the men throwing dice on the tombstones. An hour after noon Huw came to fetch him, with a canon to show him to his seat. They came into the cathedral by the bishop's private door and walked past the font into the nave. Here Simon caught his breath, stunned by the beauty he saw. To his left the nave stretched like an avenue into the distance, lined and vaulted by a stone forest, and at the end the east window glowed like a sun. There were clergy everywhere, pacing softly over the brasses, and serving men leaned against the outer walls, but Simon had eyes only for this splendid house of God. He limped between the towering pillars, unconscious of his dragging foot, with his withered arm dangling unheeded at his side. At the chancel steps Huw had to leave him and he looked back at him with something like regret, for it was the first time since they had left the March that he had gone where Huw was unable to follow. Then the canon opened the chancel gate, Simon stepped through the screen into the choir, and splendour burst upon him. He was dazzled by colour. Light streamed through the brilliant rose window in a dazzle of blue and red and gold, turning the cold pillars into pillars of fire. The walls glowed with frescoes. Between each pillar lay a painted tomb, splendid with colour. Even the corbels in the roof gleamed with gold. But the splendour of the churchmen outshone the splendour of the church. The stalls had been extended by benches and on either side, from the screen to the altar steps, stretched the front row of bishops and abbots and behind them the great laymen, dukes, earls and barons and the officers of the king. The light sparkled on gold and silver thread, jewels and precious stones of all colours, on copes stiff enough to stand alone and mitres encrusted with pearls. It flashed on the rows of pastoral staffs, each standing upright in its niche. Gloved hands lay folded on ample episcopal laps or fondled the heavy pectoral crosses. Dukes leant over to speak with bishops, who turned stiffly to greet them. Simon could see only two seats vacant, the bishop's throne that awaited the archbishop and the wooden stool that awaited the heretic.

The canon edged his way to the left. Simon followed and found himself wedged into a space on a raised bench in front of John of Gaunt's tomb. By craning his neck he could see the bishop's chair and, he hoped, Philip's head. On his left sat the mayor of London, a portly man in scarlet cloth who kept fitting his podgy fingers into the links of his chain; on his right, by heaven knew what manipulation, sat Deacon Humphrey Fulbert. He had quite got over his chagrin at dining in the common hall and was eager to play the informant, airing his knowledge of the great ones' names as if he were in their counsel. He identified ten bishops in the opposite stalls, Shrewsbury, Winchester, Exeter, Norwich, Salisbury, Bath, Bangor, Lichfield, Ely and, surprisingly, St David's. For the bishop of St David's had seen all of sixty summers and could not have taken less than two weeks on the road. Even in his cope and mitre he continued to look dishevelled, as if his vestments had been too long in the saddlebags. The splendour of the bishops was relieved by the brown of the four abbots, Cirencester, Waltham, St Albans and Evesham, and behind them sat many great men, onlookers all. The deacon rolled them with relish round his tongue—Edmund, Duke of York, with yellow teeth that had left marks on his lower lip; Thomas Beaufort the Chancellor of England, a serious man with a beard cut in a fork, French fashion; Lord de Roos, Clerk of the Rolls; two assize judges and many others. Sitting together in black and white like magpies were the learned doctors of canon law and their doyen, the Chancellor of Oxford.

'The king?' asked Simon. 'Will the king come?'

'No, he dare not show his face. They say it is disfigured and his hair falls in handfuls.'

'The Prince of Wales then? Is York to be the only Lancaster present?'

'Save for Gaunt here,' said the deacon, jerking his head backwards towards the stone figure of John of Gaunt, who lay listening over his own bones.

Why would he have expected the Prince of Wales to come? pondered Simon. Why should a heretical tailor stir his curiosity or his pity? Harry of Monmouth had other things to do, bullying his father and trying on his father's crown, to bother with a little heretic. Yet, although it was what he had expected, Simon was disappointed. He had been more moved than he could express by the sight of the might of the Church met to reason with one poor heretic. He knew, none better, that dirt lurked between the toes of the Church and cruelties under its cloak; for all his faith he could never think without sickness of the Summoner's relish at suffering and humiliation. But he witnessed now, as he had never done before, the accumulated wisdom and goodness of the Church, with its truths that had an existence independent of the men who uttered them. The bishop of Bangor might drink more wine than was good for him, the abbot of Evesham secretly wear fur next to the skin, and the bishop of Lichfield have fathered a daughter in his old age but, seated in their robes of office in the archbishop's court, they were not merely men with human weaknesses but men vested by God with the power to make priests. Their failings did not rob them of their power to ordain any more than a priest's failings robbed him of his power to put God in a man's mouth. They were wise, these men of the Church, with the wisdom of the Church. In matters of faith they spoke with God's voice. To them one fallen sparrow was as significant as a dozen bishops. They wanted to save Philip and bring him back into the bosom of the Church, not only to preserve the Church from the threat of his delusions but also to preserve his soul from everlasting torment.

But not so the Prince of Wales. He was too busy watching his father's breath to come.

The mitres below him turned gravely from side to side, the podgy fingers tried first one link and then another, the deacon chattered in his ear. Simon gazed about him, watching for Philip with a heavy heart. He twisted in his seat and studied the tomb behind him, sad to think that his mother could never lie in the priory church beside his father, possessed as she was by her devil, and damned. He gazed idly over the two stone figures and saw two eyes gleaming in the shadows of the side aisle, in the angle of the wall. A rat? They were too widely spaced. A dog? They were too still. He stared and gradually saw that they were the eyes of a man, a bony-faced man with a hooked nose who peered through a slit in the north wall and gripped the edge with bony fingers. A man? In a dungeon? For the man's eyes were on a level with the floor and he peered up at Simon with eyebrows as bushy as his father's. Simon plucked the deacon's sleeve and pointed. But the deacon was not interested. The anchorite, he said over his shoulder. Had the lord Simon not heard of him? He had been walled up by his own wish for thirteen years, fed through the slit and left to pray his way directly into heaven. Cold? Aye, doubtless it was cold. In winter they could hear his teeth chattering from the nave. Dark? Aye, no doubt it was dark save when the sun came through the south window. Rats? It was possible. It was said he ate only half his daily crust and laid the remainder on the sill. Why did he do it? God and he alone knew. The deacon could not think of anything more foolish. Simon looked at the eyes again, and thought, not for the first time, how many ways there were to God.

There was a stir. Everyone rose, the copes more slowly than the magpies. The chancel gate opened and the procession appeared. First the bishop of London in green and silver, then the archbishop in red and gold, the archbishop's chaplain, a dozen subfusc priests and monks and finally the dumpling figure of Philip Win in a white gown that reached to his ankles and a hempen girdle. At the sight of him Simon felt his heart leap out towards him. He longed for Philip to see him but Philip looked steadfastly on the ground before him and when the archbishop was seated sat on his wooden stool. This stool was on the archbishop's left so that by raising his eyes he could have seen Simon but he did not look up. The bishop of London stepped forward and unrolled a parchment and the trial began.

To his dying day Simon had but a misty recollection of what was said. He concentrated his whole will on to making Philip look at him. Only let him look up, he prayed, and he would know. The familiar rigmarole proceeded but the words reached him faintly . . . 'to tear in pieces with their tempestuous blasts the power of St Peter . . . quite contrary to the sacred canons and decrees of the holy fathers . . . deceivers and horrible seducers among the people . . . sheep diseased with a terrible sickness going about to infect the whole and sound flock. . . .' The bishop's voice went on and Simon wished Philip were as conscious of his eyes as he was himself of the anchorite's, which were boring into the small of his back. '. . . Being indifferently learned, do inveigh against the determinations of the holy fathers with presumptuous boldness . . . to bridle malice and obdurate contumely.'

Eventually the bishop concluded his address and the magpies stepped forward one by one to question Philip. Philip rose and took the Bible in his right hand. He spoke. 'I swear,' he said, 'by Almighty God that I will speak truly.' And raised his eyes. Then Simon knew, and knowing he closed his eyes and began to pray. Philip had seen him and Philip would burn. It was the court at Mathern all over again. One by one the learned doctors stepped forward and questioned him. To all questions save one he returned the right answers, but to the one, the all-important, he gave the wrong response. 'Nay, my lord. Nay, reverend sir. Nay, your grace. The wine don't change and the bread don't change and that's the truth.' For three hours they fought for his repentance. Bishop followed bishop to his stool, abbot followed abbot, pleading for his recantation. They tried persuasion, they tried exhortation, they tried threats, they tried prayers. They even tried the anchorite, taking Philip to kneel by the slit and listen to the holy man's counsel. But they could not move him. God had told him what to believe, he said, and even their learned lordships could not make him change his mind. The Chancellor of Oxford harangued him until the Duke of York became restless. They brought the blessed wafer to him and begged him to admit its miraculous properties but he said he was sorry but he could not put his tongue to a lie. At length the bell rang the hour of Vespers high above their heads and the archbishop rose. Seated, he was but a cope, a mitre and a strip of white lamb's wool; standing, he was the tongue of the Holy Church. He spoke without rancour or hatred, more in sorrow than in anger, but every word was relentless. If Philip Win would not recant, he must burn. 'We, Thomas, by permission of God, Archbishop of Canterbury, sitting in tribunal seat, having God before our eyes, weighing and considering the articles by the aforesaid faithful Christians put up against the said Win in the cause of heretical perversity, with masters and doctors of divinity, do pronounce, decree and declare the said Philip Win to be and to have been a heretic, schismatic and as such is to be avoided of faithful Christians.'

I cannot avoid him, thought Simon. I love him. If I die for it, I will speak with him before he burns.

There was a long wait while messengers were sent to Westminster for the king's signature. Bishops went out to relieve themselves, lords strolled arm-in-arm in the aisles, a foot from the anchorite's eyes. But none was allowed to approach the heretic, who sat quietly plaiting his girdle and glancing at Simon from time to time as if to reassure himself of his presence. Simon stared at Philip, at the anchorite and at the pictures on the walls that showed devils tormenting lost souls with pincers and hanging them upside-down by chains. At last the messenger reappeared. The bishops hurried back to their places and eased their mitres. The archbishop read the king's declaration.

'We, Henry, king of England, Wales and Ireland, do command you Thomas Arundel, primate of all England, as much as you have by the consent and counsel of your co-bishops and abbots pronounced Philip Win to be a manifest heretic, to hand the said Win to the Sheriff of London that he cause the aforesaid Win, being in his custody, in some public and open place within the liberties of the city of London to be committed to the fire and him in the same fire really to be burned for detestation of his crime and the manifest example of other Christians. And hereof you are not to fail upon the peril that will fall thereupon.'

The archbishop paused after the terrible sentence, then read with slow emphasis the signature:

'Teste Rege, apud Westminster, 2nd July, *Anno Regni sui, Anno Domini*, 1411. Henry, Prince of Wales.'

So Harry of Monmouth had signed the sentence. Eager that Philip should burn, thought Simon, and his lip curled. And to think this prince would soon be king! It was his last coherent thought that day. Horror seized him, the horror of what he must watch. Philip was led to the chancel gate and surrounded by clergy and serving-men. The archbishop came slowly from the altar steps and stood behind, the bishop of London beside him. Two by two the bishops and abbots took their places in train and the great lords fell in behind them. The mayor rose. The deacon rose. Simon felt himself taken by the arms and escorted to his place in the procession. Doctors and clergy fell in the rear. The chancel gate was opened and they all moved forward, down the steps, down the avenue of pillars and out of the west door. Simon was dimly aware that Huw had joined him and taken the mayor's place. The churchyard was thronged with people who whispered and pointed and stretched their necks on the tombstones. The procession turned northwards and passed through Paternoster Gate, while rosary makers and text writers hung over the wall to see them pass. All Simon could see were two huge backs in front of him, one purple and one green. All he was aware of was a numbing terror and Huw's arm holding him up. They were hemmed in on all sides, they could not have fallen out had they wished. Philip he could not see. They crossed New Gate Street with people crushing them on both sides and went on down Chepe until they reached Aldersgate. Simon was aware confusedly of many things; of Huw's arm; of his fear of falling and being crushed by those following; of the muck flung from upper windows that was meant for Philip; of the burning sky, the dry kennels, the sound of cock-fighting from a courtyard, a hide stretched above their heads to dry. They came out of Aldersgate and turned left into Smithfield market. Here the crowd spread out over the caked dung and Simon saw Philip. His arms were bound behind him and he was turning his head slowly from side to side as if looking for something. Simon hurried forward, his foot scraping over the dung, and cried: 'Philip! Philip!'

Slowly, as a man who hears imperfectly, Philip turned his head and on seeing Simon gave him a smile of such sweetness that Simon felt his senses swim. He clung to Huw and cried: 'Repent! Repent! There is yet time.' But Philip carefully shook his head. Yet he looked at Simon, never took his eyes from him until the end, and Simon stood there to be looked at, clinging to Huw in the black depths of horror.

To his confused sight there seemed to be thousands of people about him. He recognized the mayor's scarlet cloth and heard his chain clink. He saw the sheriff order the barrel and the chains and the faggots and send a man for a torch. And all the while he stood where Philip could see him. Scores of copes dragged over the muck, hundreds of rosaries swung, there was a forest of coloured hose, a sea of velvet, whole islands of decent hessian and a fringe of fluttering rags. It was the seventh hour but the sun still burnt fiercely as if unwilling to sink before this lesser fire was lit. It was like a copper coin in the hard sky and the air was still and hot like an oven. Suddenly there was movement and out of St Bartholomew's came the prior and twelve monks, each bearing a torch and chanting the Miserere. The prior carried before him a golden Pyx and he came steadily on in the midst of his monks until he reached Philip. He asked him clearly and loudly what he bore in the box and Philip answered, still with his eyes on Simon: 'I knows what you wants me to say, your reverence, and I honours you for it, but I can't say a lie, and that's all there is to it. There's hallowed bread there and that's all. That's not God's flesh you got there and I can't say as how it is.' There was no more to say. The prior made the sign of the cross and retired with his monks to his priory, whose windows overlooked the market and were already thronged with spectators.

The stake was fixed into its socket and the bottomless barrel placed over the stake. Philip was lifted into the barrel and chained to the stake with iron chains. Faggots were piled about the barrel and a torch brought. Never once had Philip taken his eyes from Simon's face, nor did he now when a tall figure leapt from the crowd and cried: 'I implore you to repent. Be guided by the wisdom of the Church and confess your error.' Again Philip shook his head while the market buzzed with the royal name. ' 'Tis Harry, Prince Harry'; 'Harry of Monmouth, sure enough'; 'The prince! The Prince of Wales!' He was tall and lean, a handsome man with brown hair and red cheeks. Simon felt his eyes drawn to him by strings. He had no coherent thoughts but a feeling akin to gladness came over him that the prince should be there and should after all care for the soul of a little tailor. But he could do nothing. Philip shook his head again and the prince stepped back. No sponge was offered, no soporific drug. He must go to his death in his full senses. Simon shut his eyes and began to pray, no longer that Philip should be spared the fire but that the fire should make him repent. He remembered what the bishop of London had told him. One act of contrition and Philip was saved if not from death at least from damnation. But they would never know. If he said nothing, they would never know if the fire had saved him or no.

Suddenly Philip said to Simon, quite distinctly, 'Farewell, my lord,' and the torch was put to the faggots. The dry wood flared, and Philip shrieked. Instantly the prince leapt forward and kicked at the flaming wood. Men rushed to help him. The chains were undone and Philip lifted from the scorched barrel.

'Repent!' cried the prince again. 'Only say the word and you shall be taken from the fire.' But Philip, his hair singed and his face blackened, only shook his head and licked his cracked lips. He did not speak. 'Think, man,' cried the prince. 'Do not fear for your livelihood. Only repent and you shall have threepence a day until the hour of your death. Only confess your error and you shall never want.' Threepence a day! More than an archer's wage! The market buzzed with the prince's generosity. But Philip shook his head again, once, twice, three times and reluctantly the prince stepped back. Again Philip was lifted into the barrel. He grasped the edge with firm hands and they did not chain him. The smouldering wood was pushed back, more torches were brought and put to the faggots. And God was merciful; merciful to Philip in that the barrel flared like the glow-worm and death was quick; merciful to Simon in that, even as he sank in Huw's arms and lost his senses, he heard Philip's voice cry in his ears, 'I seen it, I seen it,' and he knew that Philip Win had seen the truth. What reason could not do the flames had done. In the midst of the fire Philip had made his act of contrition. He had driven out his devil. He was saved from hell.

12

WHEN all was done, Huw picked up his master and carried him through the gate of St Bartholomew. There he lay in the priory hospital for two nights and two days, senseless. Mercifully he was spared the sound of the scraping shovels as they carried away the charred remains of Philip Win and threw them in the river, leaving not so much as a pinch of ashes. They laid Simon in a private room away from the clamour of the market and for forty-eight hours he lay like a log. Twice the hospitaller brought a mirror to make sure he was still breathing. They could do little for him save anoint his sores, now slowly healing, and wait and pray. For two days Huw never left him but sat with his face to the light, so placed that when his lord opened his eyes the first thing he should see was his devoted servant.

At Vespers on the second day Simon woke. The first thing he knew was that his wits had not left him; the first thing he saw was Huw. He saw him clearly with the light on his face. He saw the wide mouth, the steadfast eyes, the hair greying at the sides. The fog was gone at last and memories rushed in: Huw toiling up the staircase with Simon on his back; Huw struggling down the Holy Mountain with Simon's wrists crossed under his chin; Huw unwrapping an apple bud and telling him what it was like to lie with a woman; Huw snoring at his bedside, playing chess to keep him from sleep, lifting him on to Merlin, brewing him herbs in the small hours; Huw rubbing him with ointment, walking in his footprints, breathing his breath. All the years of Huw's devotion came rolling over him like a great sea; Huw linking hands for his mounting, teaching him to use a dagger; Huw cutting up his meat, cleaning his face of vomit; Huw caring nothing for his deformity, fighting a man with his fists for calling Simon a cripple. The curtain Llewellyn had drawn between them had gone up in the flames.

Simon's eyes began to burn and something was hurting his throat; then his lips began to tremble and something wet ran down his face into his mouth. It was salt. He was crying and what he tasted was tears. He had never cried in his life; he had no memory of weeping. Tears had been a luxury denied him. Where others had wept he could only vomit. Accepting the miracle, he turned his face into his pillow and wept without shame. At first he cried in an awkward, unpractised way but gradually the tears came more freely and brought him comfort.

As he wept, cruelty and suffering suddenly lost their terrible power to torture him because he saw that they could have a purpose. Suffering had saved Philip, he was convinced; benefit had lain hidden in the flames. Was it not therefore possible that good lay hidden even in the bear's agony or the raping of the woman at Wycombe? Could not they, like Philip's burning, be parts of God's will, links in God's chain, pieces of God's pattern? That being so, who was he to question the divine ordering? Who was he to kick against the pricks? So he wept and thought, a new-born philosopher, in the hospital of St Bartholomew and found at last the right response to suffering.

Later he sat up and had Huw wash his face and he looked at Huw with pleasure, marking the lines at the corners of his eyes and the good-humoured lift of his mouth. He ate and drank and heard the bell ringing for Compline and soon he felt strong enough to ask Huw what he wanted to know. 'You heard it, Huw?' he asked, making a tight roll of the sheet. 'You heard the devil leave him? Did you, Huw? I did not dream it?'

Huw looked at him and loved him. 'Aye,' he said slowly. 'Heard it I did, there was a noise he made, look you.' And he crossed himself.

Simon sank back in relief. Philip was saved. The gates of hell were shut. The way through purgatory might be long and stony but it led to heaven. Philip was saved. Simon's journey had not been made for nothing.

For another day he rested in the hospital of St Bartholomew. On the fourth day they returned, Huw and he, to the bishop's house in St Paul's and made preparations for the return journey. The heat still held. The smells of London began to creep into St Paul's churchyard even up to the altar and the noises echoed in the streets like pebbles in a bucket. From dawn to dusk the sun burned without pity in a glazed sky until even the pigs sought the shade and big rats lay limply in the kennels. Simon saw four in Paternoster Row when he went to buy a St Christopher medal for Seneschal. They looked at him with dull eyes and did not attempt to move. He went little into the city. London was to him a monstrous sore, a blemish on a fair countryside, its only virtue the presence of Prince Harry, the king's son. Many things had happened to Simon in Smithfield market, not the least of them the realization that the prince did after all care for the little heretic, even to the point of offering him a handsome pension. If he cared for a tailor of a distant Welsh March, why should he not care for others of his subjects, English and Welsh? Was it after all untrue, simply another unfounded prejudice, that he cared only for fighting the French dogs and nothing for his people?

Thus as he rode beside Huw on the long journey home the first breath of patriotism blew on Simon. It was strange and somehow sweet. For so long had he been shut up in the March like a bug in a box, seeing only as far as the boundaries, that the sight of a fair country and a fair prince came upon him like a revelation. To his surprise, he found that he could not dislike the English, whose blood after all ran in his own veins. Their cruelties were no worse than the cruelties of the March. Their land might be richer and their life easier, but that did not make them either stupid or wicked. He had met with kindness at the monasteries; none had thrown filth; he had heard some of the greatest Englishmen in the kingdom plead with a little tailor for his salvation; no English Summoner could be worse than the bishop of Llandaff's; no English baron could be more cruel than the Baron Striguil.

In Buckinghamshire the ripening corn was as thick as a mat, with scarcely a thistle to be seen, and Simon compared it sorrowfully with the cornfields of Abercibbi where years of inadequate hoeing had given the thistles roots and where only half the woods were fully grown. In Oxfordshire he saw fat sheep with fleeces like summer clouds and thought how different were the tatty beasts of Penperlenni and Lywnd-u. With Philip's back no longer riveting his eyes he noticed not only the richness of the land but also the prosperity of the villages, with no wastelands and two working mills; he noticed mature orchards with no gaps in the ranks; tiled roofs with here and there a brick chimney, as many as eight oxen to a village instead of two as in his father's manors. He passed quarries in full working order, ironworkings that had never known a subsidence, millstones that had been grinding one against the other for a generation. These English lords had never needed to hound their rents, as his father had. These meadows had never been raped by a destructive army. These peasants had never lost a man from each family in a single night, as had the peasants of his father's Englishry. He who had never been able to feel its suffering felt it now; he who had never been able to share his father's concern for the green half of the map, he shared it now. He would make amends, he swore it. He would do what he could to lighten his father's burden. From a boy he had known where his duty should lie; he had always known that he was no free-lance but a man committed to serve only one master and that his father; yet only now did he begin to accept his duty with anything like grace.

He rode peacefully towards the Welsh border, thinking of what his father had said in his letter. *Please God we are taming the Welsh falcon,* he had written. It pleased Simon to think that the Welshry and the Englishry might draw nearer together, and when Huw told him that Prince Harry was well liked by many of the Welsh he longed most ardently for the old king to die. Better times were coming, he was certain; he felt the stirrings of optimism rising out of Philip's ashes like a phoenix bird. Little breezes blew and tempered the burning heat and one night it even rained, a soft rain that settled the dust and brought greenness back into the grass. Thankfully neither the deacon nor the bishop's men had accompanied them but had stayed in London on the bishop's business. There were only eight of them now, Huw, Simon, and six Abercibbi men, and eleven horses, Philip's riderless.

At Burford Simon noticed ditches dug criss-cross fashion

in a low-lying field and thought how such a plan might improve the arable at Penperlenni. Descending Birdlip, with the fork of his hose tight against the pommel, he noticed that the Cotswold hurdles were made of hazel and wondered if hazels would grow well in the Englishry. At Gloucester they stayed with the bishop as before and Simon found he could describe Philip's end without pain. Exhilarated by the nearness of home and Eva, he limped through the streets with Huw after supper, his toe bumping over the cobbles. Boys were nailing branches over the tavern door to show that the ale had arrived, but Simon turned away and strolled out of the west gate, his feet instinctively seeking the road for home. Presently they came to the river and the bridge and watched the trout making rings on the golden water. Under this bridge, in a cell stuck on to one of the uprights, lived a soothsayer, a wizened old man who claimed knowledge of the future and had a beard reaching to his waist. He peered up at them from the bank and offered Simon a cure for his humped shoulder, but the day was long gone when Simon would swallow raw snails or pay a shilling for a pot of green ointment. He no longer expected that kind of miracle. Then the soothsayer offered to tell his fortune and idly, for the diversion of the moment, he agreed. He climbed awkwardly down a set of steps cut in the bank for the convenience of customers and sat down on the grass with Huw beside him. A penny changed hands and the soothsayer brought out from his rags the shoulder-bone of a ram. It was polished with much use and gleamed in the dying sun. He laid it on his palm, the point towards Simon's navel, and stared at it thoughtfully, so still that they could see the lice crawling in his beard. Simon gazed at the river incuriously and was startled when the soothsayer spoke.

'Your brother will die,' he said, and then added, 'In a battle.'

Richard die? Fighting the French, by the sound of it.

'I cannot promise you happiness,' said the soothsayer. 'God did not make you to be happy seemingly.' And he turned the ram's shoulder-blade through ninety degrees.

'Shall I marry?' asked Simon, only half-believing.

'Aye, marry you shall, like all but holy men.'

Here Huw grinned and said he'd be damned if he would marry, say the Church what it liked.

'Shall my brother have a son?' pursued Simon, who had thought of Alice more than once on this return journey and remembered the fear in her eyes.

But the old man could not say this sooth. The bone would not tell him, not even when another penny changed hands. But Simon would marry. That was certain.

At Cinderford they hired an escort to take them through the Forest of Dene, for the outlaws could not know that their money-bags were all but empty. In the forest they heard their last English cuckoo and in the tiny church of Coleford, surrounded by charcoal-burners, they partook of their last English Mass. At noon on the twelfth day of July they came out of the trees and gazed at the Welsh mountains, which rose in the sky like giants; Blorys and the mass of the Welshry behind it and, far to the north-west, the beacons of Brecknock. Simon filled his lungs as if he were already breathing Welsh air. He was nearly home. It was perfect summer weather, hot not with the stinking heat of London but with a kindly warmth that ripened the ear without withering the root. The men began to chatter and laugh at the sight of the mountains and started down the hill to Monmouth with gaiety. But before they reached the town they saw a strange blackness gather in the west, not so much clouds as an inky mist that hung in the sky above Blorys and came no nearer. 'Rain,' said Huw, but the men muttered uneasily and said they had never seen rain-clouds like that. So they lay at Monmouth overnight, for not even Simon's eagerness could disregard such an omen, and in the morning the mist was gone.

They went by way of Usk, although it added five miles to their journey, for Simon had business there that he did not wish to delay. He had not seen his little sister Blanche for more than a year, not since he had taken her with Richard, her dowry clinking in his saddlebags, to be shut up in the Benedictine nunnery because no husband could face her. Since Philip's death he had thought of her more than once, more than in all the year of her absence, and it occurred to him that he had no knowledge of her welfare, whether she was happy or not.

When she came to him in the parlour she looked much as she had always looked, save that her hideous lip was the more prominent for the white linen that framed it. She kept her eyes to the ground like a good novice and answered him shyly. Yes, she was well. Yes, she was content. No, she did not find the services arduous. Yes, she had had a holiday. She had been the youngest novice on the last Innocents' Day and had played the prioress from sunrise to sunset. Yes, the nuns prayed for Simon's healing and had a wax image of him in the chapel that they might the better fix their minds on him for whom they prayed. Yes, she thought perhaps the prioress would have Masses said for Philip Win's soul if he paid for them. Yes, the Summoner had been much about and had led a weeping nun away to the bishop's court. No, she had no news of the lordship.

Then the prioress herself appeared, anxious to do the honours of the nunnery, and into her hands Simon pressed all his remaining money to be used for the shortening of Philip's purgatory. The prioress promised that the chaplain should say a Mass each day and Simon told her that he would send more money, if he was able. Blanche was permitted to accompany him to the outer courtyard and for all his fever to be gone he lingered to look at her. She had sent her duty to her father but her mother she had never mentioned. He found himself wondering what she thought of her mother, whether she hated her for conceiving her in mortal sin. She did not know, any more than he, what her mother's sin had been, but did she harbour secret hopes that one day her mother would confess it? Or had she, like himself, abandoned all hope for their mother, that she would ever speak or confess or lie in hallowed ground? Did she pray that her mother's devil would leave her? He did not know. Blanche seemed content enough, with her services and her brother's wax image and her holiday on Innocents' Day. Before he left her he kissed her on the forehead and she looked round quickly to see if the prioress were watching.

At Llangattock they saw men in the river fishing for the statues that they had drowned at the Lollard's instigation. A mile from the town, with the dust a white cloud at their horses' rumps, they saw a figure crouched by the side of the road. It was Old Peter, looking as if he had taken root in the baked ground. He saw them and shambled towards them on his heels, waving a bit of bracken. Simon's instinct was to ride past him and spur on to the town and Eva, but one glance at Old Peter's adoring face changed his mind and he drew rein. Old Peter said nothing, simply clung to Simon's foot and kissed it, the purpose of his life returned. They hoisted him on to the spare horse and trotted forward, their aching buttocks forgotten in their eagerness to be home.

It was the fourth hour and the sun was still high. It sparkled on the river and made short shadows of the oaks. It lit up the crown of Pen-y-val and bathed Blorys in radiance. The wheat was pale gold, the whorls and ridges of the ploughland a rich red, even the waste was gay with yellow charlock and purple loosestrife. The sky was a deep blue, the road a dazzling white, the sun a burning copper disc. Nature had hung out all her flags for their return. From the bottom of the slope they looked up at the castle, perched forty feet above the river on its bed of rock. The town gates were open, men and women came running to greet them, children cried a shrill welcome. Huw was surrounded, the men invisible in the crowd. But Simon did not dismount, nor wait for greetings. He rode straight through the gate, turned right along the south wall, passed the priory and came with beating heart to the tailor's house.

It was empty.

He knew it as soon as he saw it. Eva had not returned. Weeds sprouted on the threshold. The ladder was gone, the shutters close shut, the cabbages wilting with thirst. No hens roosted in the thatch. All was dry and deserted, like a husk, the only fresh thing a bunch of St John's Wort nailed over the door.

'Looking for Eva Win, my lord?' said a voice, and Simon looked down to find the Summoner at his knee. When he did not answer the Summoner went on: 'Lusting for her, eh, my lord? Maybe you can smell her out better than me. Passion do have a long nose, so they say. Not that I'd be saying no myself, you follow, but I'd not presume to lay my seed over the seed of such a man as your lordship.' He squinted at Simon with his face to the sun and put his hand on Merlin's bridle. 'You find her for me, now, and the bishop will be thanking you.'

The bishop? What could the bishop want with Eva?

'I have told you,' said Simon shortly. 'Eva Win has naught to do with heresy.'

'Am I saying she has, my lord?' said the Summoner softly, drawing something from his pocket and holding it up in the sunlight. Simon saw that it was a wax image of a man with a silver medal hanging round its neck. The surface of the wax was rough and the head had been fashioned clumsily with a dent in the crown. The Summoner put it into Simon's hand and he saw that the medal bore the image of St Christopher. He looked his enquiries and learned that the Summoner had found it in Eva's room, hidden under the bed. But still he could not see. The St John's Wort meant nothing to him. The image was just such another image as the nuns had in their chapel at Usk, for the efficacy of their prayers. Even when he saw the initials scratched on the back they meant nothing to him. Seneschal was simply Seneschal to him. He had never heard him called by his proper name.

The Summoner did not explain. If the young lord was left in the dark, he was the more likely to lead him to the woman. For himself, he did not care about the Lollard, who was doubtless dodging the officers of another diocese by now. Only let him get the woman . . .

'Have you ever seen a woman pricked, my lord?' he asked, returning the image to his pocket.

Pricked? What for was a woman pricked? Was it one of the Baron Striguil's tortures?

'Nay, pricked for insensitive places, not for sport, my lord. They'll not bleed, so they say, go the pin never so deep. God's work, you understand, that a bishop's officer should be permitted to witness. I have never been at a pricking.' And he licked his lips like a jackal over filth. 'But a searching, now that I have witnessed.'

A searching? What could the man mean?

'Why, a searching for supernumerary paps, my lord. Very secret, some are, hidden in secret places. Two dugs has God given a woman and she has no business with more. If a woman has an extra pap, it is for no good purpose, but to suckle devils and familiars. There was a woman in Garndyrrys, the wives said no, but I found it, my lord, I found it in . . .'

There was foam on the man's lips and Simon jerked Merlin's head away in disgust. He saw nothing but that this brute liked to torture women and had taken a fancy to Eva Win. If she stood in danger from this beast, it was well that she was not in the town. But he would find her, find her and protect her. He would ride up into the Welshry the next day and seek Llewellyn's counsel. Llewellyn would be able to help him find her, maybe already he knew where she was hidden. It could be but a night, two nights at most, before he lay with her.

So he picked up his fallen hopes as best he could and began to climb the cobbled slope for the castle. The Summoner shouted after him that he was off to Llandaff—a matter of a nun taken in childbed that did not brook delay—but that he would be back and hoped the lord Simon would have news for him of the woman. Simon did not turn his head. He tried to shut the Summoner's mocking laughter out of his ears. He looked up at the castle and knew that he was not the same man as had left it three weeks before. When he saw his family gathered in the courtyard he knew that he was seeing them with different eyes. He saw them now as he was to see them until the hour of their deaths. His father sat in his great chair with his back bent like a bow, peering up at his son from under his bushy eyebrows. His face was alight with welcome but Simon saw that his shoulders were bent, like Atlas's, by an insupportable load. He was carrying on his own back all the struggles of the Englishry, the fight to pay their rents, to reclaim their waste and to restock their farms after Glendower's rape. At a time when a man expects to lean on his sons he was carrying the March alone.

Richard could not help him. He stood behind his father's chair with his face stretched in a grin and his moustaches drooping. His eyes were empty. As ever, his will was waiting to be led. Alice stood beside him, nervously plucking her lip, her stomach as flat as ever, without life. His mother waited a little apart with her squirrel on her shoulder. Margaret touched her arm and pointed but not a muscle of the white face moved. She knew her son but she showed no enjoyment, for the devil held her as fast as ever. In the background was Seneschal, a shadow of a man leaning on a stick. 'They need me,' thought Simon, his eyes suddenly opened. He could take much responsibility from his father's shoulders, if he tried. To Seneschal he could be at least his three missing fingers. Richard valued him because he could take from his brother the tasks that were beyond his capacity. Although his mother only clucked in her throat she found pleasure in this son, for she took the necklace he offered her without Margaret's prompting and showed it to her squirrel. To Alice he could mean salvation. If he married and got sons his father would not have to get papal dispensation for Richard's remarriage and Alice would be saved from the cloister.

The talk that night was hopeful. First his father spoke of the wedding, which had been postponed until the feast of St. Bartholomew, six weeks distant. The Lady Eleanor was pleased with the gifts and begged the Lord Simon to come into Wentloog to visit her and see the estates that were her marriage portion. When Simon did not respond, his father went on to the Lollard. There had been no more trouble with heresies, it seemed. Once the Lollard had fled, men's minds had returned to normal and the statues had been fished out of the river. Where the girl was no one knew. The Summoner wanted her, had indeed been searching the March these three weeks past, but none knew for what. Strange stories flew about but no man knew for certain. The Welshry? Ah, the Welsh had done many kindnesses. Twice Llewellyn ap Thomas had been to the castle, before Seneschal came out of his stupor; both Blaen-avon and Pwll-du had offered men to help with the corn harvest and the shambles. The Welsh falcon lay quiet. Seven years of distrust was giving way to seventy years of peace. Such was the baron's news.

Despite his sore thighs Simon told Stephen Oxted to have Merlin ready at dawn the next day, that he might ride up into the Welshry to seek Llewellyn, whose touch he still felt on his withered knee. Llewellyn would help him, would give him advice and comfort. All night he lay sleepless, with Huw dozing on the floor at his side and Old Peter snoring across the threshold. At cockcrow he was up. Today he would find her, he felt it in his bones. He sent Old Peter into ecstasies by promising that he should come with them. He astonished Huw by putting on his own hose and trying to tie his laces with one hand and his teeth. It promised to be a splendid day. From one of his narrow windows they could see the Holy Mountain, its horn black against the rising sun; from the other they looked at Blorys shrouded in mist, at its feet the lovely curve of the river. They ate their sops standing, impatient to be gone, while Merlin stamped his new shoes in the courtyard. Old Peter tied rags round his feet. Sparrows fluttered in the roof. The cook cursed sleepily in the kitchen. It was on just such a morning that Simon had been sent to view the church roof and had fallen with his head under the herring cart; it was on just such a day that Llewellyn had first linked hands for his mounting.

Soon all was ready. They came out through the big doors and Huw bent to lift his master into the saddle. Suddenly there was a scream, a sound of terror that froze their blood. There were shouts, the air was filled with fear. A soldier came running to tell them that a man had fallen in a fit, William Parsons who had been on the journey with them to London. Parsons? Ah, the tall, thin one without teeth, who had been last off the bridge at Witney. He was stretched out in the lower courtyard, senseless. Simon went down on his sound knee and called for water. He pulled at the man's laces that he might breathe more freely and exposed a hairless chest. The man's skin was white but planted upon it was that which made terror leap in Simon's belly and sent the bystanders back against the wall.

It was the black print of the plague.

13

THE plague! The dread word was on every tongue. They looked at William Parsons' livid face and at the black mark of death and crossed themselves. Here was the sign of God's anger and they were defenceless against it. They grunted and whispered, their eyes full of fear. The plague! The dreaded pestilence that had struck down every second man in England some sixty years before and which lurked yet like a wild beast in a thicket, ready to pounce! There had been no plague in the March for a generation, although news of it was frequent from the port of Cardiff; for twenty-five years the air of Abercibbi had been pure and sweet. To the young men the plague was but a calamitous tale for the fireside, a spine-chiller for winter nights; for the old men it was a memory of which time had robbed much of its terror. They remembered a summer when they had stuffed their ears with rue, when the churches had never been empty and when a man might fall in a fit even as one talked to him, yet like all remembered horrors it was the excitement they recalled rather than the suffering. It was not until they saw the black spot on William Parsons' chest that the horror came back to them. Then indeed they remembered and were afraid.

What the young men saw was a tale made fact before their eyes. One spot would, they knew, become many. The man would spit blood and then he would die, if not today then tomorrow or at most the day after. If he rallied enough to make the sign of the cross, he was lucky. Others would follow, first the young and strong, then the aged and then the babies. The pestilence would rage until God chose to withdraw it.

They had no more appeal against it than against storm or drought. There was no remedy. There was no treatment save the lancing of the boils, and many preferred to die in peace.

Simon knew it as well as any. His father had seen plague in Warwick and in France. In four months six hundred had died in Calais alone and the stink had been so great that the ships had moored outside the harbour. He knew what was to follow as surely as he knew that hail ruined the young wheat and that corn reaped on a Sunday turned mouldy in the bin. The March would be untouchable, like a leper or a Jew. They would be shut up within their boundaries as closely as an anchorite within his cell. There would not even be a slit for the passing of food. While the plague raged they would have to live on their own resources. Many would die. There might not even be enough hands left to bury the dead. The ripening corn might never be harvested. The pestilence might presage the end of the world or it might only be God's punishment for sin, but whatever it was they had only one weapon with which to fight it, their prayers. And God's anger could be softened, they might yet survive.

All this went through Simon's mind as he crouched over William Parsons and his terror gave way to reason. There would be no time now for melancholy, time only for work and prayers. He could not go up into the Welshry nor seek Eva for fear of spreading the infection. For all he knew the pestilence was lurking even now in the fold of his tunic and he could not carry it to Llewellyn nor to her. But if the plague meant disaster it also meant salvation. There would be no wedding now on St Bartholomew's Day; the road to Wentloog would be closed indefinitely.

He was roused by the approach of his father, who came swinging his spindle legs from a chair and looked at Parsons without a word. All at once before Simon's eye he became an old, old man, shrinking and withering like an old root. For a long time he looked at the senseless man, then slowly he raised his eyes to those of his son and Simon knew that his father's authority was ended. With a gesture of his stiff fingers the baron passed it on to his son, not to Richard but to Simon. In that moment Simon became a man. He had not failed Philip, he would not fail his father.

The first thing he did was to have Parsons carried to his quarters and send for Thomas to give him the last rites. Next he had Huw call together all the men of the town that they might hear the baron's will. He urged his father to speak but even the great voice had failed and since Richard stood open-mouthed in terror Simon spoke in his stead. He spoke simply, so that all might understand, and with an authority that, while they wondered at it, all could accept. He was a queer one, this lop-sided lord, sure enough, but he did know his own mind. He would tell them what to do. His instructions were clear. 'Let no man leave the March and no stranger approach. Let no man go into the Welshry unless he has heard of the pestilence already there. If man, woman or child drops you must send for a priest at once. Eat sparingly, lest you come to want in winter. Pray for God's pardon and keep yourselves free from mortal sin. Bury your dead the same day, on the waste outside the east wall. Let no man enter the town. If you go out to your fields, you must not linger in the villages but return direct to your houses. Go now about your business and God have mercy upon you.'

William Parsons died that night and was buried on the waste-land. Next morning two more were struck, two more of the men who had made the journey to London. An uneasy week followed, with men eyeing each other suspiciously and none caring to go far from home. On the eighth day a woman screamed at the well and fell back in a fit, with blood spurting from her mouth. Within an hour the dreaded marks appeared and Simon knew the worst. The plague had come to stay.

Of two hundred souls within the walls twenty died in the next week. On Lammas Day, the day of Simon's wedding, a man fell behind the plough at Llanfoist with a black swelling behind each ear. Within days men were dying as far north as the Brecknock border and as far south as Mamhilad. Terror reigned in the town. In the castle fear was like a stinking rag, stifling the breath. The soldiers began to drop like flies in winter, the mourners following the dead often into the same grave. The wise woman's garden was stripped of rue to stuff into the ears. Everywhere herbs battled vainly with the stink of putre-faction. By the feast of the Assumption of the Blessed Virgin they were burying the dead in one grave, covering them not with earth but with lime for the quicker decomposition of the bodies. Martin was everywhere, giving the last rites to the dying, hearing terrified confessions, taking the Mass into the parishes when the village priests began to drop. When not out on such errands of mercy he was in his tiny church, offering prayers and stations for the lifting of the pestilence and giving what comfort he could to the terrified souls who crowded within his walls. The church was never empty now. When Simon went for morning Mass there were people clinging even to the font for lack of a place to put their feet. The walls echoed with the age-old words: '*Cesset iam manus tua, et non desoletur terra et ne perdas omnem animam viventem,*' and with the whispered supplications '*Salvum me fac, Deus.*' Martin had to send for more wine from the castle cellar and when the baker died make do with rough bread, for none but he had the art of making the holy wafers. By the end of August there were but five priests alive in the Englishry; Martin, the prior, Thomas and the priests of Llanfoist and Langattock. Then the prior and Thomas took to their horses, that the people should not lack the consolations of their religion, and with them went Brother Gregory who zealously lanced such swellings as would not burst, carefully wiping his lancet on a clean rag between operations.

There was not a living soul without a crucifix round his neck, be it only a rush twisted like a Palm Cross, but it was of little avail. No man knew where the plague would strike next. Women dropped with their babies tugging at their breasts and the wails of starving infants were added to the general lamentations. Men fell from ladders, from hayricks, at the milking, in the fields, even at the altar. Boys went to sleep healthy and never woke. Girls wept for their husbands, children for their parents. In many homes only an aged grandfather was left to yoke the oxen. Cattle strayed for lack of herdsmen or fell sick for lack of milkers. Weeds flourished for want of hoers. Many fled only to die on the roads. Within a month, of the four thousand souls of the Englishry, seven hundred lay buried in the lime pits, a hundred of them from the town of Abercibbi, fifty from the castle itself. Of all his soldiers, the baron had but ten left. Of all his retainers but twenty, of all his house servants only six. All the gate-keepers were gone save Rufus. Constable had died in the second week, John Upton and Margaret soon after. Richard was near to death with terror although the plague had not touched him. His mother moaned for Margaret but there was no one to heed her. Seneschal chafed at his weakness and did what he could to order the food. The baron sat alone in his chair at the high table, for there was none left to carry him out. The town lay defenceless, safeguarded only by its pestilence. If the plague left it, there were only its gates left between it and an enemy.

The days and weeks passed and there was no let in the sickness. The sun shone brilliantly in a clear sky, as if mocking their misery. A fine harvest was promised while the men who would reap it sickened and died. On the first day of September Martin fell with God's flesh in his hand and rallied only to take the last sacraments from the prior's hand. Henceforth the whole town, Simon among them, went to the prior for Mass and Simon had no inclination now to jerk his head away. Those fat white hands still smelt of soap, the piggy eyes still gleamed in plump sockets, but Simon had learned to look beyond appearances and while he mourned Martin as a friend he revered the prior as a holy man, who still gave his poor lepers the remnants of his crowded days.

So the burning, fear-filled days wore on towards harvest, with a hundred and fifty deaths a week. Every week a hundred and fifty healthy men and women were struck by the plague as if by the knacker's hammer, and the air above the plague pits was black with flies. There were no clouds, no rain, nothing but a pitiless burning blue. At last the day approached when the corn must be harvested for it stood stiff and ripe in the blazing sunshine and would droop if it were not cut. Two days were spent by Simon in riding from end of the Englishry taking the roll of the able-bodied. Huw rode with him, making marks on a tally, for John Upton had long since died and Thomas had no time for anything but baptism, confession and the Mass. Then Simon knew the horrible truth, that they could not hope to harvest the corn before it withered. He went over Huw's marks again and again but the acres and the men simply did not tally. If they harvested a quarter they were lucky. If they hoped to live through the winter, even allowing for fewer mouths, they would have to call help.

Now there was only one place from which to call help and

that was the Welshry, the brown half of the map that had never known injustice from its English baron and that had mercifully been spared the visitation of the pestilence. At the thought of the Welshry Simon's heart leapt. Perhaps God would grant him a sight of Llewellyn and news of Eva. Llewelyn would not refuse him. Llewellyn was his friend.

On the second day of September they set out, he and Huw with Old Peter ambling behind on John Upton's horse, for there were many horses but few riders. The road was deserted, the fields empty, the cattle watched by a solitary child. Simon urged Merlin forward regardless of the baked holes. A broken neck, a stroke of the plague, what did it matter? Death awaited them all in one form or another. Perhaps after all death was preferable to life. The ironworkings were silent, the workers stricken or fled. The forges were cold and quiet. Yet surprisingly the pile of iron at the side of the road had dwindled to a heap. What need had people of iron, he wondered, when they could not smelt it? Then it occurred to him that perhaps the smiths had lasted longer than the diggers, and he wondered what was to happen when new ploughshares were needed. In the whole of the Englishry there was but one smithy working and that at Mamhilad, nine miles downriver. Well, they must do the best they could. If the worst came, the Welshmen must lend them tools. Llewellyn would arrange it. Llewellyn would not refuse.

They plodded up the hard track, grateful for the coolness but sad to see the charcoal domes smokeless and groups of swine wandering herdsmanless among the trees. There were no gleaners, no happy children playing hide-and-seek among the tree-trunks. 'Quiet, is it?' said Huw, and Simon nodded, thinking how not so long before he had found fault with the forest for being too noisy and had thought of it as a prison closing round him. He did not think so now. At last light gleamed ahead of them and they urged their horses forward to come out of the trees into a blaze of sunshine. They saw the track divide into two in front of them, one leading straight ahead into Pwll-du, the other striking off to the left to run for ten miles along the boundary of the Welshry until it met the only other upward way into Lasgarn. All was as Simon had imagined it, the pure arch of sky, the fresh breeze, the bright expanses of pasture and the yellow patches of corn. Behind him the forest stopped as if cut off by a knife, before him stood a boundary cross sunk knee high in a mound. Simon put his hand on his horn and urged Merlin upwards that he might blow it from this height, but he had not gone three paces before a line of men rose silently from the bracken, fitted arrows to their strings and drew their bows. There were twelve men and of those twelve four aimed at Simon's heart, four at Huw's and four at Old Peter's. Simon looked at them and saw that they were all men of Pwll-du. Evidently Caraddoc ap Rhys was taking no chances.

'Men of Pwll-du,' he cried, letting his horn fall to his side, 'have no fear. I do not come to cross the boundary. I would have speech with Llewellyn ap Thomas, if you will fetch him.'

To his surprise the bows were not lowered, although he could see more than one forearm quiver with the strain. A gnome spoke to him in English. 'There is nothing you can be wanting with the Welsh,' he said, squinting against the sun. 'There is nothing we are owing you now the cattle is paid. Go you now before your stinking disease creeps up behind.'

Simon sat motionless with Huw a pace behind him, swallowing his anger. 'I pray you fetch Llewellyn ap Thomas,' he said again with civility. 'I will give you my oath neither I nor my servants shall stir from this spot until he comes.' And he prepared to dismount. The arrows did not waver except to follow their dismounting. Huw tethered the horses to a thorn bush and the three of them sat on a hummock a stone's-throw from the Welshmen and waited. At last the bows were lowered and a lengthy Welsh argument began, ending, as Simon knew it must, in a man being despatched into Pwll-du. The Welshmen could not approach them, neither could they kill them. In their view the quicker the English went the better.

It was a long wait, long and anxious. Simon felt the sun on his neck and drank the sweet air. The Welshmen squatted in the bracken and watched them out of the corners of their eyes.

The sun climbed higher, so that they were forced into the shade. The stream murmured and swallows snapped at flies. They fanned themselves with bits of bracken and Old Peter undid and did his rags, asking nothing more than to be out of the stench of the pestilence and at the side of his lord. They nibbled sour apples that were too bruised for keeping and drank water from the stream, a drink they would be having much of, when winter came, for whatever barley they salvaged would go into bread instead of beer and every undamaged apple was to be laid by for the lean months to come. At noon there was a stir. The Welshmen rose, pointing, and before there was time even for a Paternoster Llewellyn was among them. He slipped from his pony and came forward to the boundary cross and stood there with his face to the sun, his hand resting on the stone. 'Llewellyn! Llewellyn ap Thomas!' cried Simon, and but for Huw's hand would have run forward. Here was the man, the friend, whose image he had had before him for so many weary weeks. Here was the man he loved, who could help him find Eva and relieve the distress of the Englishry. 'Llewellyn,' he cried again. But although Llewellyn looked at him with the same hot dark eyes, they told him nothing. He could read no welcome there. Perhaps he fears these Welshmen, thought Simon, excusing him. Perhaps afterwards . . . He forced his private thoughts to the back of his mind and proceeded to business. 'We need your help,' he said, 'the help of the Welshry. You can carry the message for me, to the six commotes. If you do not help us, we shall starve. The baron asks for a gift of corn from each commote, as much as can be spared, and salted meat in the barrel, and ploughshares. They could be left on the boundary for our wagons——'

'There is no tribute we are owing,' said Llewellyn suddenly, in a foreign voice. 'My lord Caraddoc sees no call for further payment.'

The words were like a blow in the face.

'I do not ask for payment,' Simon pleaded. 'I ask for a gift. I ask for Christian charity, that we may not starve.'

Llewellyn lifted his hand to shade his face, so that Simon could no longer see his eyes. 'My orders I have,' he replied. 'There is not in my power to disobey my master.'

'But would you have us starve?' cried Simon desperately, unable to believe his ears. 'Give us what you can spare. Your men are young and healthy, can they not give up their beer that we may have barley bread?'

Again Llewellyn spoke, automatically now, as if, Simon

suddenly thought, his heart was not in his words. 'There is no more I can be saying. There is nothing for you in Pwll-du.'

'But Blaen-avon? And Lasgarn? What of Tillery and Llanhilleth and Carn-y-cefn? You will pass on the message, since we may not enter?'

'Aye, my lord, the message I will send.' But to Huw it did not sound likely that the message would get through. Not for nothing had Huw spat into his bosom and made Old Peter do the same.

Simon gazed about him in bewilderment, his hopes crashing about him. If Llewellyn failed him, to whom could he turn? If Llewellyn were deaf to his appeal, who would hear it?

'Lasgarn,' said Huw in his ear. 'We must be trying Lasgarn. There is the only other commote we can reach.'

Simon ran forward a pace, dragging his leg, desperate to look into Llewellyn's eyes and find some spark of encouragement, but at his movement half a dozen bows were drawn and Llewellyn cried: 'Back, my lord. There is foolish you are to come forward. Shoot any that cross the boundary, such are my lord Caraddoc's orders if we would save ourselves from the plague. Pass your message I will, my lord. More I cannot do.'

Simon fell back, stricken. Now every arrow was strung, pointing the way back into the trees. Huw brought the horses and lifted Simon into the saddle, thankful that Llewellyn could approach no nearer. Yet Llewellyn did approach. Huw turned to help Old Peter with his rags and with a sign to the bowmen Llewellyn came down from the mound until he stood within five paces of Merlin's head. Then indeed Simon looked into his eyes and what he saw made his heart leap. Llewellyn was yet his friend, he saw it at once. He could not help his orders. He spoke but for his master. If he disobeyed, who knows but the arrows might be turned upon himself. Llewellyn spoke low, too low for any but Simon to hear. 'I cannot help myself, my lord,' he said softly. 'Bleeds my heart does for your distress, but there is powerless I am to disobey my master. But news I have, my lord, of Eva Win. Well, look you, and safe hidden for the time. If you would see her . . .'

See her? How could he see her, if she lay in the Welshry?

'Keep a stout heart, my lord,' murmured Llewellyn with

his eyes on Huw. 'Wait you for a message and I may yet bring you to her.'

'But the pestilence?' urged Simon softly. 'What if I carry the plague to her bed?'

Llewellyn looked at him and held his gaze while a man might count to ten. 'There is a risk the woman will be taking . . .' He hesitated for an instant. 'For love.'

Huw tied the last knot and turned to his horse and Llewellyn noted the spittle on his breast. 'Tell the Seneschal,' he cried, 'that the lord Caraddoc will be hanging his own felons 'til the plague be gone. Good Welsh justice, look you.' But he smiled at Simon as they turned away.

Before Simon stripped his coat for the harvest, he tried for help once more. He rode up to the Lasgarn boundary with Huw and Richard only to find the track guarded as in Pwll-du. But not by the men of Lasgarn. It was twelve men of Blaen-avon who rose from the bracken at their approach and a Blaen-avon voice that told them to go back whence they had come. Of the Englishmen in the Welshry there was not a sign, not of the bailiffs or the foresters or the reeves. There was to be no help from the Welshry.

A plan was thrashed out at high table. Simon would not follow Seneschal's suggestion of reviving the old labour service —dead now for two generations—nor would he demand that the able-bodied should harvest first the baron's corn. 'Can we eat and watch the peasants starve?' he asked. 'Let each man harvest what he can, cut it and thrash it and lug it to the mill as best he can. God has spared us two millers, let us be thankful for so much.' So the harvest began, surely the weirdest harvesting that Blorys had ever watched. Every soul that could crawl came to the fields, to work from dawn to dark under a burning sun. Those too weak to wield a sickle chopped at the corn with billhooks. Children cut with scissors, girls and boys with shears. Even the idiot worked, breaking the stalks carefully one by one. Men were left dying in their houses while their wives and children worked in the fields. What each family cut, so they lugged and thrashed, while in their wake crawled the orphans gleaning what they could. The baron sat in the castle, chained to his chair by his affliction, but his family sweated beside their servants in the fields, blistering their hands and burning their skins. Richard worked like a Trojan, happy that here was something he could do. No load was too heavy for him, no day too long. Beside him toiled Alice, thankful for the first time in four years that she was not with child. Old Peter carried sheaves to the ox-carts until he was told to stop, then hobbled before them to the thrashing floor, unloaded and led back the empty carts. He was as happy as a man could well be, to know that he pleased his master. Huw had thought to be his lord's right hand but to his amazement Simon did not seem to need one. His deformity was forgotten. He cut with one hand, lugged with one hand, thrashed with one hand until his palm was raw, but nothing seemed to tire him. He was buoyed up with hope, the hope of seeing Eva. Llewellyn was his friend, Llewellyn wished him well, Llewellyn was trying to bring them together. What was this labour with such a reward waiting?

Even Simon's mother came to the fields, with her squirrel in her pocket. She seemed to find pleasure in wiping the sweat from the brows of the cutters, that their eyes be kept clear. Seneschal was too weak to hold a sickle but he apportioned the grain fairly, keeping back a third for the spring sowing, and saw the grist to the mill. As they came to their last gasp, they could grind the seed, but they must think of the next year and save for the sowing if they could. From time to time a worker dropped with the black marks of death on face or breast and was dragged into the shadow of a tree for Thomas's ministrations, for the prior was busy in his own fields, spurring on his brothers with his gown tucked round his fat thighs. From north to south of the Englishry the scene was repeated. Golden fields awaited reapers who would never come. Those that worked toiled like ants in a desert of corn, making but little impression. The sacks at the English mills increased but slowly, while up in the Welshry a fat harvest was brought in, with sheaves to spare to decorate the churches.

In ten days they harvested one-tenth of the crops. On the eleventh day the weather broke and a furious rain drove the rest of the grain into the ground. Within a week it was mouldering and they knew that winter would indeed be a hungry season. As if the storm were too much for his weary spirit, the baron laid down his head to die. He had seen death coming.

His wax image was made, his coffin ready, his tomb waiting in the priory church. The plague did not smite him, he simply felt that he had lived long enough. He lay on his bed and watched death approach, no longer reluctant to leave the March, that had been his first care for so long.

The prior came to give him the last rites and anoint his eyelids, nostrils, lips, palms and soles with holy oil. On the feast of St Cyprian at the hour of Compline William Beaumont died. His sons knelt beside him but it was to the younger that he commended his possessed wife and his stricken lands; it was Simon's hand he felt for even as his eyes were closing. 'Look to them, Simon,' he murmured. 'I am leaving them in your hands.' And Simon swore at that merciful deathbed that he would serve the March as his father had done.

So William Beaumont died. So bent was he that they had to break his back and his legs before they could get him into his coffin. On a day of thrashing rain they buried him, laying him in his stony tomb in the splendid church. In spite of the infection people came from all parts of the Englishry to pay their last respects to a just master whom all had revered and many had loved. There were veterans of the wars who had fought with him in France, men who had served under him at Calais, peasants whose roofs he had thatched, children whose godfather he had been. They lined the cobbled slope from castle to priory and those that had the strength climbed to watch from the roof-trees. Some even scaled the walls by the scaffolding that they might see the better. By midday the street ran with water and the mourners waded as in a stream, while the sound of the Miserere vied with the lashing of the rain. First came the monks with their snuffed candles, for not one would stay alight and even the torches spluttered and went out. Then came the prior with his gown held high in one fat hand, his surplice streaming with the wet. Next came the coffin, carried by the six sole retainers with the image of the dead man fashioned in wax upon the lid. He lay wide-eyed over his own body, painted as in his youth with blue eyes and golden hair and straight limbs under his velvet robes. This was a William Beaumont Simon had never seen. Behind the coffin walked the baron's two sons, Simon's lame foot making splashes in the stream. Then followed Huw leading Merlin, although it was so many years since the baron had ridden him that he could scarcely be said to be the dead man's charger. At Merlin's heels came the lady Phillipa, the widow, her squirrel still in her pocket. She was dressed in black and her head was covered with a black veil but Simon did not think she knew that her husband was dead. She gazed about her incuriously, as was her habit, and stroked her squirrel's tail while Alice vainly tried to keep her skirts out of the wet.

The meagre procession came down the slope and disappeared within the priory gates, followed by a draggled train of mourners. Amidst the glorious brilliance of the priory church and after due rites and ceremonies they placed William Beaumont in his tomb, let fall the stone lid and laid upon it his wax image, arranging the velvet folds as carefully as if he were alive. Alice led the widow away, the onlookers departed and the monks withdrew to their quarters. The white hoods of the lepers vanished into the gloom and the brothers were left alone beside the tomb, the new baron with the empty head and the young lord with the full heart. Suddenly Richard seized his brother's hand, struggling with his incoherence. 'You must do it, Simon,' he managed at last. 'You must help me. I cannot . . .' Here he stuck and shook his great head. 'I do not —I have not the power. Fighting now, that is different, but to read and do figures like our father . . .' He seemed to find confidence in Simon's touch, for he went on: 'God has not given me the brains, boy, I did not ask to be the eldest, and Alice . . .' He grinned feebly and ran his free hand over his moustache. 'Alice do pester me so I cannot spill the seed. Afraid, you understand,' he added with a sudden illumination as if this were a truth he had but just seen. 'I am not wanting another wife, boy; if I had sons they would be stupid like me and . . .' He tugged at his hair in a fury of frustration but Simon knew what he wanted.

'I will help you, Richard,' he said quietly. 'Have no fear. This evil will pass and good will come of it, you will see.' He put his sound hand through his brother's arm and led him out into the rain.

The rain fell without respite. The ditches filled and overflowed. One by one the roads out of the March degenerated into mud and potholes, impassable to horse or cart. The river came out and flooded twenty acres of ploughland and the water lapped the foot of the castle rock. Three bridges were washed away but the bridge that led to the Welshry remained firm. Soon the rain forced its way through the thatched roofs but no straw could be spared to patch them and the rushes were under five feet of dirty water. Cattle squelched hock high in the sodden pastures and the carcases of sheep were piled up at the bridges. Even the plague pits filled with water and the bodies dropped into a liquid mess.

It was still raining when the time arrived for the shambles. Now indeed Simon learned to kill, he who had been used to vomit at hangings and had never even set his foot on a beetle. He learned to slit a belly or a throat with his strong left hand and to turn back the hide from the raw flesh without sickening. He learned to hold the bolt steady against the forehead while Huw swung the hammer. He learned to disregard the filth through which his lame foot dragged and the agony of salt on his raw hand. Obsessed, as were they all, with the fight for survival, he laboured day after day under a leaking roof to kill as much meat as their supply of salt would cover. Such meat as could not be salted was smoked, such as could not be smoked was turned out on to the short pastures to live as best it could through the approaching winter. They thanked God it had been a good hay harvest. At least the oxen could be saved. They would be needed as soon as the floods withdrew, for no amount of men, even if they had them, could pull a plough through that waterlogged ground.

So the Englishry laboured to save itself, so that those not already dead of the plague might live through the winter. The young lord laboured as hard as any, astonishing his people by his endurance; and his reward was not far off. One cold day in mid-November, when the rain had stopped and there was frost in the air, a ragged man came to Simon with a parchment. Simon wiped his bloody hand on his apron and slit the seal with the roll in his right armpit. It was from Llewellyn. The man had found it tied to a tree in the forest of Blorys, with the Beaumont arms roughly drawn upon it and a man with a short leg so that he might know who it was for. It was a letter, telling him, if he wished to see Eva Win, to come by night at the full moon to the shepherd's hut in Garndyrrys that he had known from a child. He must ride a Welsh pony and bring no man but

Old Peter. Simon cracked the parchment across and across and dropped the pieces in the offal.

'Huw!' he cried across the mass of blood and bones. 'Come new moon I shall be needing your pony.' And Huw thought that never in all his years of service had he seen his master so near to happiness.

14

SIMON no longer asked himself about the future. He was to see Eva, that was enough. He hoisted that certainty in his mind like a banner and bore it before him until the moon was full. The moon came to its fullness on the feast of St Cecilia, five days after the last brine tub was nailed. The frosts had already set in and every night the soil grew harder. It was a race to get the arable ploughed before the ground broke the ploughshares, but there was so little seed that enough was once turned at least for the spring wheat.

They set off at Vespers, the master, the servant and the two Welsh ponies, with a sprinkling of snow under their feet. They heard Rufus shoot the bolts of the north gate behind them, then they turned their ponies' heads northwards. It was dangerous riding for the road was frozen into ruts and holes as deep as a man's elbow and there were treacherous patches of ice; but the moon shone brilliantly and they had flint and torches for the forest. With Old Peter behind him, Simon walked his horse over the stone bridge and along the road to the iron-workings, using the verges that had been shaved by scavenging sheep. He did not turn into the trees by the usual track for he knew that Caraddoc ap Rhys' men were bivouacked at the head of it. Instead he rode cautiously on until he reached the Clydach, a shallow stream that came tumbling down from the northern boundary of Pwll-du and flowed into the Usk three miles from the town. Here Simon nodded over his left shoulder and said, 'This way, Old Peter,' and Old Peter grunted. It was bitterly cold and their teeth chattered, but the moon shone brightly on the valley of the Clydach into which Simon now turned his horse.

It was more a gorge than a valley, with thick forest growing almost to the banks of the stream. The best foothold was in the water, for here there were flat stones for the nimble Welsh hooves and the water was too fast for ice.

For a mile they picked their perilous way up the bed of the stream, the slipping of hooves echoing from one side of the gorge to the other until they thought it must wake the Welsh. Despite his gloves Simon's fingers froze round the reins and he tried vainly to warm his withered hand in the breast of his coat. More than once he all but slipped into the rushing water, for his balance was precarious, but he clung as best he could with his uneven legs and in an hour they came to the brook. This was a tiny rivulet, no more than a trickle in summertime, that crept down through the forest on their left and had its source in the heights of Pwll-du.

Here Simon dismounted stiffly in order to light the torch. Old Peter had dry tinder in his rags but it was many minutes before Simon could make his frozen fingers hold the flint. At last he had a flame and the next instant the torch flared, lighting old Peter's face like a gargoyle and throwing fantastic shadows on to the trees. It was a weird scene, the stillness, the moonlight, the rushing stream and the dark forest and the brilliance of the torch that made everything beyond its reach as black as pitch. They mounted and began to climb the bed of the brook, thankful to find it almost solid with goose-grass. Old Peter went first, for he had a spare hand for the torch. Once Simon's pony went down on his knees but Simon saved himself by flinging his sound arm around the horse's neck and suffered no hurt beyond a bruised groin. The branches shut out the sky like a roof, except where here and there a chink let a ray of moonlight through. It was deathly still, the only sound the squelching of their ponies' feet and the faint hissing of the torches. There was no snow under the trees and they followed the green of the goose-grass until at last the branches parted to show them the stars. There were on the edge of the tree line at a spot called Blaendyar, a desolate area of scrub and bracken with a tarn the shape of a pear.

It was desolate but also beautiful, for the moon and the sprinkling of snow cast a spell over its poverty and the mountains rose like great boulders into the sky, crowned with snow. The water shone like a mirror reflecting the dark outline of a shepherd's hut and a spiral of white smoke. They dismounted and led the ponies forward over the broken ground. Simon's heart beat so loudly that he wondered Eva did not hear it, and something had happened to his belly. Yet before he opened the door he remembered to speak to Old Peter. 'Hobble the horses, Old Peter,' he said, 'and come to the fire when you are done.' Then he lifted the latch and entered.

There was a fire smouldering on the hearth and a rushlight on the table but the shadows were so deep that at first he could not find her. She was standing against the far wall, as he had seen her long ago in the tailor's house, and her black hair hung to her waist. She was just the same, just as lovely, with a skin as white as the snow and eyes like black coals. He looked at her without speaking, feeling a man's love. As he looked at her he felt that there was nothing that she could ask that he would deny her. She possessed him without even laying a finger on him; he felt his will tied to her with strings so that she had but to jerk them and he would do her bidding. When he hesitated in the doorway, making the smoke swirl in the draught, she came slowly forward to where he stood and wound her long white arms round his neck. She kissed him between the lips and held him and seemed to melt him with her fire. How long he stood there with the cold at his back he did not know, but presently Old Peter came behind him and made his way to the hearth.

She brought them food, smoked meat and bitter oatcake and a mess of peas, and never had food tasted so good. They drank thin Welsh beer and it was like wine. She made much of Old Peter and unwound the sopping rags from his feet and made him thatch them with straw. She showed him the hay for the horses and made him a nest in the lambing fold, gave him a hunk of cheese for his waking and shut the heavy door behind him. She drew Simon to the fire. 'There is long you are coming, *cariad bach*,' she said softly, pleating her gown with her long fingers.

'I could not bring you the pestilence,' he answered, never taking his eyes from her face. 'Nor did I know where you were until Llewellyn sent me word.'

'Ah, Llewellyn.' She considered Llewellyn a moment and said: 'There is a clever one, *cariad*, sharp to prick a needle and loves you, too. There is something to shout for indeed to have Llewellyn love you.' She moved to his feet and sat with her hair falling over his knees. She took Simon's sound hand and began to play with his fingers, weaving them into her own until he could not tell which was her hand and which was his. He had thought to talk to her, to tell her of all that had happened to him, of what was happening in the Englishry, of his father's death; but once he touched her he did not want to speak. She knew without telling all the thoughts in his head. He wanted to take her and then to sleep, not the drugged sleep of exhaustion nor the broken sleep of dreams, but the sweet sleep of yearning satisfied. He wanted to lose in her body all the accumulated weariness and sorrow of the past months, Philip's suffering, the raped woman, the harlot and the bear, the dead in the lime pits and the living stalked by hunger, his father's death, his mother's madness, the threat of his marriage, even Richard's incompetence—he wanted to pass them into her body with his seed and not carry the burden of their memory alone. He wanted oblivion, be it only for a night. If it was the last thing he did on this earth, he wanted to come to rest between her thighs.

The rushlight burned out and Simon threw sticks on the fire that he might see her in the light of the flame. She made a bed of hay on the hard earth floor and there he lay with her the night through, while Old Peter snored on the other side of the wall. But before she came to him she put some mess into a saucer and called, '*Llyffant bach*,' as she had done in her attic and Simon was amazed to see the same green toad crawl out of a dark corner. She crouched over him while he fed and stroked his back, nor did she come to Simon until the toad was finished. She lay down beside him and took his head to her breast, where he saw as of old the curious crimson scar. Her long white fingers inched over his body, right side and left side as if they found no difference, but his reason did not go down without a struggle. Something nagged him, a thought scratching at the door of his mind. Something the Summoner had said when he showed him the wax image and asked if he had ever seen a pricking. He worried and groped—and was lost. For Eva wound her white legs about him and pressed him down into a fiery darkness.

He awoke in the dawn, rigid with cold save for his withered hand that lay between her thighs. In the cold light that crept under the door he could see Eva sleeping, so still and remote that her body seemed empty, as if her spirit had gone on a journey. He woke her with kisses but her spirit did not instantly return. For a moment she stared at him almost with dislike, as if she resented his summons. Then she smiled and far away in his house Llewellyn heard the deep sigh of Simon's surrender.

Presently she let him go and he fed the embers with twigs, blowing them into a flame as he had seen Martin do with the Pope's pardon. There was no bacon but there was a cabbage in the pot and he ate it as he thought of Martin in his cold churchyard and of how he had wanted to guard Simon from the temptations of heresy. Old Peter took his breakfast out in the open, for a weak sun was struggling over the Holy Mountain and no more snow had fallen in the night. While they ate, Eva spoke with calculated horror of the Summoner.

'He lusts for me, that one,' she told Simon, her eyes huge with terror. 'Wanting me, he is, for his own pleasures.'

'He will not find you here,' Simon reassured her. 'He will not be abroad now until the spring,' and he wondered what God had in keeping for the spring.

Eva shuddered and drew closer. 'There is fearing him I am,' she confided. 'His nose is long with him, like a vulture for smelling. He has been in Wentloog, look you, sniffing along the border of Bedwelty. I had it of Ivor ap Lud that he would be finding me if he had to crawl into Pwll-du on his hands and knees.'

'He knows you are in Pwll-du?' asked Simon, appalled at the man's tenacity.

'Guesses he does. Not much credit to that, I am thinking, for he found my mother in Pwll-du and there is no credit to seek the flower where the seed was laid.'

Simon's thoughts went back to Philip's voice saying, 'A Welshman seemingly.' 'You are not . . .' he began, then remembered with relief that the Summoner was not a Welshman. He was not Eva's father. If he were, he would not be seeking her to torment her.

'Shall I be telling you what he did to my mother?' said Eva. 'Stripped her, he did, and tied her hands behind her and searched her.'

Searched her? Why?

Eva's eyelids fell like shutters between them. 'That searching,' she said. 'It is women's work, but they said they could find nothing and the Summoner would be searching for himself, look you. With child, too, she was.' She stared at the fire, forgetting how she had wished to curdle his blood. 'He found it, too, that one, but the bishop would not convict on the word of one man. There is holy he was then, not to condemn my mother.'

'Condemn? Why should she be condemned?'

Eva did not answer. She sighed and went on: 'Marry my father she did then and gave birth to me, but there was many that pointed at her, see, and she did jump in the river. Her heart was sore with her and she did jump in the river. Found her they did in the old river, with her back against the fish-traps.'

'But what had she done?' urged Simon. 'What for did the Summoner want your mother?'

'For torment,' shrieked Eva, clutching her head. 'For torment and pricking and foul lusts.' She twined her fingers into her hair like snakes and cried, 'There is what he will be doing to me, if he finds me.' She flung her arms about Simon. 'There are dreams I have, *cariad bach*, dreams that the Summoner do catch me and do me terrible harm.'

I, too, thought Simon, remembering a nightmare of Eva raped by the man with the devil's horns.

'Save me,' she screamed. 'He'll not leave me be. There is frightened I am of the Summoner.' She clung to him with astonishing strength, with arms that were like iron bands. She brought her lovely mouth to his ear and whispered: 'Hide me, Simon, if he comes after me. Hide me in the castle. A good thing it will be indeed to have a stout wall between me and the Summoner.

Simon thought of the Summoner's knobby eyes, lit with lusting, and of his mouth tearing the meat from the chicken. He remembered the yellow nails rimmed with dirt and the sickening talk of pricking. He would never let him touch her! Better anything than that he should have the chance to torment her, as he had tormented her mother. She moved her mouth to his and breathed: 'Open the gates now if I come asking, *cariad bach*. I'll not be coming unless the Summoner is after me.'

'Come,' said Simon. 'If you have wind of the Summoner, come at once. If you come after curfew I will open the gate and hide you safely. No one shall harm you while I live.'

The frost held and slowly the pestilence died away. But now hunger had come to take its place and the weak and the old began to sicken on the scanty rations. No food was put over the boundary. No carts came from Herefordshire or Wentloog or Warwickshire, for the roads were impassable. In the second week of December snow lay three feet deep, hiding the holes under a white blanket and sending the coneys deep underground. The cattle they had turned loose in the autumn were frozen stiff in the fields, too hard even for the crows to peck. Of all the two thousand able-bodied men and women in the Englishry, barely seven hundred survived. In the town only fifty souls remained, half of them children. They began to run short of fuel, for there were not enough to cut wood and the saws needed new blades. Already a third of the flour was eaten. The hens stopped laying. The calves were brought into the common fires. Men shot crows for the pot and one by one the dogs were made into stew. They had salt meat to last until February, then it would be the turn of the horses. In the priory church the prayers to survive the pestilence changed into prayers to survive the winter.

In the midst of his preoccupation Simon began to notice a change in his mother. The devil still possessed her but she no longer withdrew to the solar and she began to watch the muted happenings of the hall with more attention than usual. Her chin was still raw with drooling, but now and again she opened her mouth curiously and once, when they brought in a sheep to be thawed by the fire, Simon had the odd impression that she was going to speak. She became restless at night and Simon spent many of his sleepless hours sitting with her in her chamber admiring her squirrel and telling his mother stories of London. She showed no great sign of understanding but she used to hold up her squirrel to greet him and she was always waiting when he came after Mass to take her for her airing on the battlements. Not for nothing had Simon sworn to look after his mother. He was not afraid of her, as his father had been. She could harm him no more than she had already done. Although to his dying day he would carry the stain of her sin, yet he could not hate her.

On the feast of St Thomas he walked with his mother on the western rampart. It was noon and bitterly cold with a sharp wind off Blorys that whipped the fallen snow into powder. The light was hard and cold, the sky like lead. A shroud of snow lay over the lordship, relieved only by the dark carpets of the forest. Forty feet below them the river unwound its black coils. There was no colour anywhere. Even the squirrel had lost his lustre. Simon dragged his foot along the parapet and blew on his fingers, while his mother clucked in her throat and held up her squirrel, who was attached to her right wrist by a golden chain. Suddenly he seemed to leap out of her hands. The chain broke and he scampered along the wall away from her, hopping up and down the buttresses with a flash of his tail. Simon looked round, saw his mother run after the squirrel and instantly sensed her danger. He shouted to her and began to run. The squirrel reached the turret and leapt ten feet up the sheer stone. His mother began to clamber up after him, her black veil whipping about her head, and immediately the little beast jumped down over her head. But she did not follow him. She stood clinging to the turret with her eyes on the chasm at her feet, almost as if she saw something there in the snow. The squirrel was forgotten.

'Mother!' screamed Simon, seeing her purpose. 'Mother! Mother! Mother!'

When he was still a pace from her skirts she turned her head, cried, 'God forgive me,' and leapt into space. They were the first words she had uttered for seven years.

Simon knew at once what he must do. He did not waste time in rushing to peer over the battlements, but heaved himself to the stairway and shouted for Thomas. He jerked himself down the narrow stairs shouting as he went until his ears felt crushed by his own voice. By God's mercy Thomas was within walls and came scurrying across the hall to meet him amongst the scattered, anxious faces. 'She has spoken,' gasped Simon. 'The devil has loosed her tongue. Quick, man, if she has breath to confess she may yet be saved.'

Thomas stared at him stupidly, not comprehending his haste. He made slow gestures and murmured, 'My surplice—

let me but find my surplice and I will come to your lady mother——'

But Simon grasped his arm in a frenzy of impatience. 'Quick, there is not a moment to lose. Even now we may be too late.' Only then, as he dragged Thomas towards the door, did he realize that he had not told them what his mother had done. 'She jumped,' he gasped, 'from the west wall. Even now——'

Pandemonium was loosed. Alice screamed and wrung her hands, Richard came running from the stables with his mouth open, the men scurried for wood for a stretcher. In an instant the courtyard changed from white to grey as their feet kicked up the snow. Thomas clutched his rosary and ran, with Simon labouring at his heels and Huw not far behind. They ran down the swept slope, out of the south gate on to the dirty road and plunged to their right into the virgin snow. It was well over their knees and Thomas pulled up his cassock to his waist, exposing his skinny legs and coarse drawers to the bitter cold. Huw went ahead of his master and endeavoured, by dragging his own right leg, to plough a furrow for Simon to follow. They laboured through the snow like ants, trailing their fingers along the south wall and came at last to the south-west corner. Here the wind nearly took their breath from their bodies. If his feet had not been anchored by the snow Simon felt he would have fallen. They could see his mother now, a black stain in the snow at the foot of the west wall. Her head was against the stone and her feet towards the river and her skirt fluttered in the wind. Simon could think of only one thing. 'Pray God she is alive,' he muttered to Huw. 'Pray God she can confess her sin.' He had no hope that she would live. The snow did not lie deep enough to save her.

They struggled on with their heads bent and came to the fallen woman, who lay peacefully as on her own bed, with snow for her pillow. Her eyes were shut and they went down hopelessly on their knees about her. Suddenly it seemed to Simon of overwhelming, indeed of the utmost importance, that he should rouse his mother. The devil had left her, unchaining her tongue after seven silent years; here was her chance to save herself from the everlasting torments of hell and to free her children from the stains of her sin.

'Mother!' cried Simon with his mouth at her frozen ear.

'Mother! Mother!' The eyelids did not move. 'Mother! Mother!' he screamed, shaking her arm.

Suddenly her eyes opened and she looked not at him but at the priest beside him, with his crucifix held upright in his numbed hands. Her voice which the devil had held for so many years came in a whisper from white lips. '. . . *Confiteor, Confiteor* . . .' she whispered and Thomas waved them away. They waded to where the others stood with the litter and waited in a frozen huddle, watching the priest bend his ear to the woman's mouth. He was no longer the Thomas they all knew, with his spite and his jealousies and his timidity. He was a holy man ordained by the bishop and invested with the power to grant God's pardon and absolve from sin. He alone could shoot the bolts of hell against this dying woman.

Time passed. Slowly the cold mounted their legs until they stood petrified to the knees. They could see Alice peering over the battlements forty feet above them and the little squirrel watching them from one of the buttresses. And still the black priest crouched over the black woman, motionless in the trodden snow. A pair of crows circled over their heads, scenting death. The river moved blackly behind them. The wind blew bitterly from the mountains, icing their eyelashes and whipping away their breath, yet no man moved. Not even Richard blew on his fingers. Simon watched in an agonized suspense, willing Thomas to lift his hand in the act of benediction. Suddenly they saw him move. His arm was raised in the age-old gesture of remembrance. Forehead, breast, left shoulder, right shoulder, even Old Peter knew what it meant. Thomas held the cross to the dying woman's lips and his words were carried to them on the wind. '*Deinde ego te absolvo. . . .*' God's grace poured over her.

She was saved.

Thomas rose stiffly to his feet. The men staggered forward with the litter, walking on dead feet, but Simon did not move. When Thomas's blessed words had reached him he had fallen forward on his icy hands and knees, his forehead pressed into the snow. Something had happened to him, something awful and good. The stain of his mother's sin, that he had borne all his life, was washed away. Almost he looked for traces of it on the snow. Her devil had left her, her act of contrition was made, her confession heard and absolution given. By her sin she had set him apart from mankind, by her confession she had returned him.

When they lifted his mother on to the litter she was already dead and stiffening fast. Simon tried to rise but found himself powerless, so Old Peter hoisted him on to Huw's back and Huw carried him, scarcely warmer than his dead mother, in the wake of the forlorn procession. But before they turned their backs to the wind there was a soft plop and a smudge of red appeared at their feet. It was the squirrel. Seeing his mistress carried away, he had leapt into the air forty feet above them and, sailing down like a queer red bird, had struck his brains against a hidden rock. Old Peter took out his knife and cut off the tail, that it might lie on the dead woman's coffin.

So she rested after all in hallowed ground. They buried her in the tiny churchyard beside Martin, using picks to open up the ground. They warmed a clod of earth for the prior to throw into the grave and as he heard it pattering on the coffin Simon sent down with it the last of his bitterness. What would be, would be. God's will be done. '*In nomine Patris et Filii et Spiritus Sancti,*' said the prior and the men seized the shovels.

But as the frozen hungry days crawled by, with no drop in the biting wind and the hinges of the gates iced solid in the night, Simon still longed for Eva. When he looked down the grey avenue of days he could not see her there, yet his present was obsessed by her. His body was cold without her, his mind lonely. Of Llewellyn he had heard nothing. Daily he sent men on foot to the boundary to look for supplies, but nothing was put out for them and, although the plague had gone, Caraddoc's men still camped at the top. Llewellyn had not been able to persuade his master, it seemed. Once Huw struggled with two men as far as Lasgarn, only to find the Blaen-avon men still bivouacked in the snow and to hear the same answer. 'Why should they keep us out now the pestilence is gone?' wondered Simon, and could only think that the Welsh were afraid for their corn-stocks.

Christmas came and went. In the Englishry men dined off dogs and apples, in the Welshry they made merry over goose and ale. At last the day came when Simon could bear his longing no longer. He would go into the Welshry to look for Eva.

They waited, he and Huw and Old Peter, for a full moon, for the way was treacherous and one of them would have to walk before the ponies with a stick to prod for holes.

They took the same way as Simon and Old Peter had taken at the previous full moon, but their pace was slower for Huw walked in front with the prodder and guided them round the pitfalls. At last the wind had dropped. The world was frozen silver, with black forests looming on their left and black shadows lying over the snow. Their bellies rumbled with hunger and the ponies' girths were in by a notch and the cold was almost tangible in its iciness, but they plodded on until they reached the Clydach, which they found frozen over. Even the Welsh ponies could not walk on ice, so they dismounted and led them up the gorge along the bank of the stream, testing every footstep for potholes and snags. The only sounds were their own breathing and the water gurgling under the ice and an occasional snort from one of the horses. When they reached the brook they found the going easier for the snow was packed tight in the runnel and they could follow the scanty green needles of the goose-grass. Here they lit the torches and made their way through a white underworld roofed in darkness, their only contact with reality the faint green prickings of the brook unwinding before them. When they saw the first moonlight ahead of them they doused the torches and Simon urged his pony forward with his numb knees. But the shepherd's hut was dead. There was no smoke and when they opened the door they found no fire on the hearth. The bed of hay still lay on the ground but the toad was gone and the cabbage frozen in the pot. Simon stood uncertainly in the doorway, remembering Eva's welcome. He had been so sure of finding her that now he did not know what to do. Outside, he gazed over the black tarn at the moonlit uplands of Pwll-du and longed to go on. Yet even he could scarcely have done so had not Old Peter grunted and waved. He had strayed to the other side of the tarn and found strange marks in the snow. They were tracks, shapeless blotches that came from the south towards them and turned westwards short of the hut. 'Snow-shoes,' said Huw, and pointed to where they led, straight into the heart of Pwll-du. There were many of them, mingled with the sliding tracks of foot runners and the punctuations of sticks. 'Fresh tracks, look you,' said Huw on his knees. 'There is funny, to be abroad in such weather, I am thinking.'

Simon decided to go on. 'Where they can walk we can walk,' he said hopefully. 'Perhaps I shall have sight of Eva.' They tethered the horses at the hut, gave them hay from the fold and left Old Peter to mind them, then they turned their faces westwards and set off. Their travelling was a nightmare. Although they had the tracks to follow, they had no steps in which to tread, for the Welshmen had only skimmed the surface of the snow. Simon heaved himself lopsidedly in Huw's wake with sweating face and frozen feet and the moon had sailed over an ocean of sky before they came to the end of the tracks. They came to the summit of a little hill and found themselves looking down upon a scene from fantasy. It was a sight that chilled their blood and broke the bonds of Llewellyn's magic like cobwebs, that cured Simon for ever of his obsession with the Welshry and turned Llewellyn before his eyes from a friend into an enemy.

What they saw was treachery.

Before them lay a natural arena, ringed by hills and lit by a hundred torches, each stuck in a pool of melting snow. It blazed with light like a Christmas procession but there was no charity here. There must have been a hundred Welshmen, a man to each torch, and they were viewing their weapons. What Simon had stumbled upon was a secret armoury. Instinctively they dropped back a few paces to be off the ridge and sank on to their knees in the snow, peering at the hell below them.

'There is amazed I am at such weapons,' whispered Huw. 'Where will they be having the iron for those, now?'

He was puzzled but Simon knew; from the ironworkings at Govilon, that was where they had had it from. What he had been blind to for so many months suddenly became clear. The Welsh had stolen the iron and hidden it in the herring carts and trained extra smiths to forge it. He had looked at the truth in the summer and not seen it clearly, but now it was as if scabs sloughed off his eyes.

'They stole it,' said Simon, and they both peered at the weapons.

To their left torchlight gleamed on the sharp blades of the lances, standing upright in neat rows like soldiers, each with death at its head. Looking at them Simon suddenly remembered the click of Welsh lances on copper coins and how the Welshmen had out-thrown the English every time. Then he had thought they were for spearing polecats; now all at once he knew they were for spearing Englishmen. Over to their right were the great bows, laid out in the snow like bodies, each six foot of yew carrying destruction in its gut. There were scores of these bows, whose predecessors had proved their worth on French soil sixty years before. Now it seemed that they were to be turned against their English masters. Beside them sprouted their arrows, each a cloth-yard long with a goose-feather flight, a tip of burnished iron and the power to pierce even Richard's armour at fifty paces. They said a Welshman was born with his fingers crooked and for a century they had been the best archers in the world. No Englishman stood a chance against them.

On a pile of brushwood lay the shortswords, beside them the spiked maces with leather thongs for the wrist. 'For the priests, see,' whispered Huw. 'They'll not be breaking Church law by wielding swords, but a mace now, that's the weapon for a priest. Kill a man without shedding blood, that's what their priests hope to do.' There were no daggers in the snow for every man carried one at his belt, but they flashed in the lights as their wearers moved.

At first Simon was confused not only by his clamouring thoughts but by the gleam of iron and the soft intensity of the men's movements, but gradually he found a pattern of activity emerge from the chaos. A man might wander from side to side, fingering the weapons. He might test the sharpness of a lance with his thumb, twang a gut as if he were tuning a harp, or try the balance of a sword, but sooner or later he would drift to the far side of the circle where the torches were set in the slope of the hill and where there was a carpet of brushwood for sitting. Soon there were only a few figures in the grey circle of trodden snow and in the torchlight Simon could see their faces. There was the old, old man who had sung in Caraddoc's house; there was Caraddoc ap Rhys himself, his short beard jutting blackly against the white hill; there was the little boy with the mark on his forehead; and there was Llewellyn ap Thomas. Crouched beside Huw in the moonlight Simon wept hot, aching tears that ran down his cheeks and pitted the snow. What Llewellyn had meant to him no man had ever known; not even Huw could appreciate his bitter sense of loss.

Afraid to move, they watched Iolo step into the centre of the arena. He struck his lyre once and men came running with a banner that they laid at his feet, a white banner with a great golden dragon that seemed to leap across the snow.

'Glendower!' breathed Huw.

On to this banner stepped the little boy, a fairy figure with his long black curls and regal head. There was a great shout and the name 'Glendower' came to them across the snow, repeated many times. '*Glyndwr we di'i eni eto,*' the Welshmen shouted.

'Glendower born again!' whispered Huw with ashen face.

Iolo struck the lyre again and began to sing, but Simon found in his voice none of the fairy magic of Caraddoc's feast. The song was treacherous, the man a traitor. They were all traitors to turn against their English lord who had given them nothing but justice and fair consideration.

'Come you,' murmured Huw. 'My legs are like stones with me. If we do not move now we shall be turned into statues.'

They crawled cautiously backwards down the slope, their clothes crackling with ice. Iolo's thin voice followed them as they struggled back over their own tracks, hoping the Welshmen would not notice them. Long before they saw the hut Simon's strength failed and Huw lugged him on to his own back so that he sank knee deep under his weight. Well might Simon thank God for his faithful friend and servant. When at last they reached the tarn Huw could scarcely drag his feet and Simon was sleepy with the cold. Huw stuffed hay into his master's clothes, made him suck some of the frozen cabbage and hoisted him on to his pony. He threw the horse-droppings under the trees, prayed for a fall of snow to hide their tracks, lit the torches and led the way into the trees. How they reached the castle he never knew, but he felt falling snow in his face at the ironworkings and as the first signs of the winter dawn crept up behind the Holy Mountain he beat feebly on the north gate and Rufus opened.

They were home. They were safe.

But for how long?

15

THEY plodded wearily along the snowy street to the castle, pushed open the castle gate and rode past the stables and the empty soldiers' quarters to the door of the hall. They found them all dozing round the hearth, worn out with anxiety and hunger; Seneschal, Richard, Alice, Thomas, four retainers, two soldiers and the cook. Eleven souls. Fourteen with themselves. Fourteen hearts beating in a great castle built to shelter a hundred heads. They were awake in an instant and Simon was carried to the fire and stripped of his icy clothes. He told what they had seen.

'A hundred men!' gasped Richard in consternation. 'Holy Mary, what can we do against a hundred men?'

'There will be more, I think,' said Simon, while Huw worked on his legs with hot towels.

'Will they attack soon?'

Simon glanced at the east windows where snowflakes whirled in the dawn light. 'They will want darkness,' he said. 'But they will come soon.'

'Tonight?' pressed Seneschal.

'It is possible.'

'Yet what can they hope to do?' mused Seneschal, staring into the fire; and Richard, thinking he was expected to say something, said, 'Aye, aye, what can they do, Seneschal?' And grinned at his brother.

'If the gates are fast shut, how can they hope to enter? In this snow they cannot bring siege machines——'

'They could be cutting a battering-ram by here,' put in one

of the soldiers. 'There be elms big enough outside the north wall. . . .'

Seneschal frowned. 'It is no easy matter wielding a ram in snow,' he said. 'Can they intend a siege? Nay, they would have to control the weather. How can they tell there will be no thaw, with relief from Herefordshire or Wentloog? We have water in the brook and we could slaughter the horses. Surely they cannot expect to starve us out?'

'What of grappling ladders?' asked Richard unexpectedly, his brains goaded into unwonted activity by the consternation he saw about him.

'Or the burning of the gates?' urged Huw. 'A hundred men, look you, and we have but a score within the walls.'

Here the cook began to beat his hands together, crying, 'God have mercy on us,' and Old Peter, transfixed by the sight of his old enemy in tears, began to howl in sympathy. The men muttered and moved about and Alice sat silently twisting her fingers. Fear had entered the hall. Seneschal felt it and dragged himself to his feet. Even Richard felt its icy fingers on his spine and began muttering about his sanding-tray. They glanced here and there, seeking a leader.

'This is what we will do,' said Simon Beaumont and they sighed in relief. Here was their leader.

He led them to the priory church. Brother Gregory rang the alarm bell to summon the people of the town. Here Simon spoke to the piteous handful of souls who now came trampling snow into the nave. Before he spoke he counted them. Eleven able-bodied men from the castle, beside Alice, Seneschal and himself. Six religious, counting the prior. Fifteen men of the town, one with his left arm missing at the shoulder and a second so old that he crept on two sticks. Ten women, two pregnant and three aged. And twenty skinny children, the youngest not eighteen months old.

'I have bad news for you,' he said. 'There is an attack coming from the Welsh of Blorys, an attack on the town. They may be here tonight, if the moon is not shining. We must all defend our town, if we die in the attempt. If the Welsh take the town they will hold it against all comers and ravage the Englishry like Glendower's men. It may be the sign for other Welsh rebellions, that I do not know. All I know is this. Every man, woman and child must, if needs be, give his life to stop the Welsh from breaking down the gates or scaling the walls.' He waited for the frightened murmurings to die down, then continued: 'Do not be afraid. God will be with us, fighting on our side. Go and wash and come to Confession, so that you may enter battle without sin. When you have finished Mass, eat. When you have eaten, leave the young children with the aged and come to the castle, to receive orders.' He paused, then cried, 'Andrew Hewitt, I want a word with you.' There stepped out the one-armed man. Simon drew him aside, away from the floods of lamentation. 'Get into Herefordshire. Your strong legs will serve us well. If the Welsh sit down in the snow to starve us out, we shall be glad of relief, when the thaw comes. Make for the baron's domain and raise the alarm. Perhaps word will get through to Prince Harry of our danger. Go now and God go with you.' The man touched his forehead and was gone, his sleeve flapping like a broken wing.

Mass was celebrated. The people gathered round him.

'First,' said Simon, 'we must send to the nearest villages to the south and east and bring what men we can find into the town. Let their families come, if they can get over the snow, but they must bring food. They must be in by Vespers or the gates will be barred against them.'

'Leave me go,' said Huw, and went.

'Next,' said Simon, 'is food. The Welsh may try and starve us out, although I do not think so. But we must have food, inside the walls. The hay must all come in and the oxen. Better nothing to pull the plough than a town full of dead men. Get the children to lug, and the women.'

The cook rose to his feet and looked at Old Peter. 'Come you, Old Peter,' he said, healing their long breach, and they went out together.

'If they do not intend a siege, they will attack,' continued Simon 'The gates will take the brunt, for grappling ladders are hard to throw and even a man with one arm can cut through the ropes with an axe. The north gate, now, that will be the place. The drifts are deep to the east and south and they can launch no attack from the river. If they split their forces they will lack strength, even with two hundred men. If they move from gate to gate, we shall be there before them. Bar, bolt and chain all the gates but assemble the tar and the mats and the scaffolding and build the fire at the north. That is my advice.' It was good advice and they took it without demur. 'As to numbers, we counted close on a hundred, but there may be more. We can but fight until we die. If the gates hold, we may yet survive. He hesitated. 'There are but two men to fear, Llewellyn ap Thomas and the bard. They pull the Welshmen's will with strings, those two. If you have either within range, shoot. But shoot to kill, for we do not have unlimited arrows. The bard you will know by his white beard and his red cloak, and Llewellyn . . .' Ah, how to describe Llewellyn? 'He has black eyes like coals and the power of a magician. If he lives, they will never give up.'

'The boy?' asked Seneschal. 'Glendower's heir, will they bring him, do you think?'

'Aye, they will bring him, for he is to be their golden leader, like Glendower before him. But do not shoot him. Although he carries the sins of others he is innocent. I would not have his death on my head.'

Under the promise of action they brightened and the long toil of preparation was begun. By God's mercy both sockets and bars were in good order, the bolts sturdy and the chains strong. Each gate was ten foot high, with a gatehouse over and a grille the height of a man's eye; each was made of stout English oak four inches thick and was studded with great nails. Each gate was double, opening out from the middle on enormous hinges; from each side bolts a foot long shot into the ground and into the stonework overhead. In addition there were cross bolts and chains to stretch from side to side. Across the whole went four iron bars, nine feet of cast iron that it took four men to lift and drop into the sockets. It was indeed a strong ram that could batter the gates of Abercibbi. The four stoutest men were set to the barring of the gates, all but the south through which Huw was to lead such men as he could find in the villages. Hearing the thuds, Simon was reminded of the day, nearly eight years since, when he had seen the torches of Glendower's army approaching from the north. Then Huw would not fight his kindred; now he had a dispensation from the prior and could shed Welsh blood without sin.

The mats were dragged out but, alas, only one was serviceable.

It was made of plaited reed and hide and was to be hung from the gatehouse, to protect the wood from firebrands or soften the blows of a ram. By God's grace there was tar within reach, two barrels in the priory against the sheep scab, which the monks dragged up to the north gate. Already, at noon, the prior was superintending the chopping of two empty houses for the boiling of the tar.

'Shall we light it tonight?' he asked, for even the great prior deferred to Simon in matters of defence.

Simon looked at the sky where a dense mass of clouds was gathering. 'Yes,' he said. 'If the clouds do not clear by Vespers they may well come tonight.' So the fire was lit and the tar put to simmer, that those who tried to scale the walls or who came under the grating in the gatehouse might receive it on their heads.

They had weapons in plenty but few men to wield them. Every one, all but the youngest children, was given a dagger and told to use it if he need. Swords and axes were put to the grindstone and lances stacked near the north gate. Leather jackets were doled out even to the women, with chain throat guards and helmets for those on the battlements. These were the archers who were to pierce the attackers from the top of the twenty-foot wall, standing in the shelter of the buttresses and shooting through the slits, with just sufficient room to lean their weight on their bows. But of all the men and boys in the town, but six had the art of the long-bow.

'I will take a bow to the wall,' said the prior. 'It is only a hunting bow, but it will kill a Welshman if he comes within range.' Three boys brought their coney bows to join him and four monks were deputed to man the gatehouse, to tip rocks or tar on to the Welshmen if they came at the gates with a ram. They had not the time to lug rocks from the river so they harnessed an ox and dragged the tombstones from Martin's churchyard, broke them with sledge-hammers and raised them with winches to the top of the gatehouse.

All afternoon the children dragged hay from the frozen haystacks and the aged man crept to and fro with ox reins over his shoulder until six oxen stood patiently in the churchyard taking their hay from the tombs. Children were set to greasing the wheels of the scaffolding with lard, so that it might glide where it was wanted. Whoever had no immediate task set himself to the clearing of the snow round the gates, lest the handling of buckets be hampered. Even the silly old woman had her faculties roused by the bustle about her and rocked the babies until they cried to be still. Brother Gregory brought his pincers and bandages to the north gate and his iron for cauterizing arrow wounds. Thomas ran here and there with his rosary in his hand, testing things that had already been tested. Richard flexed his arm muscles, thanked God that he had practised so dutifully at the butts and hoped that in seven years he had not grown too stout for his armour. Alice tucked up her gown about her knees, thrust her feet into clogs and set the pregnant women to polishing arrow-shafts. Simon was everywhere, his foot trailing unheeded over the frozen ground, his useless arm forgotten. He dragged himself up the northern scaffolding to view the buttresses and see the bows and arrows laid out in readiness by the slits. He cheered the children with apples, praised the old man, smiled at Brother Gregory and watched anxiously for Huw. There was not a soul in the town but rose to the occasion, finding unsuspected strength and hope drawn from them by the young lord's smile.

Soon, too soon, the hour of Vespers drew near and the light began to fail. The white snow became grey, the grey sky grew dark, and still Huw had not come. They gathered at the south gate, straining for a sight of him and—they trusted—of the men with him. He did not fail them. He was never to fail them. As the bell for Vespers stopped he came into view with a black caterpillar of followers crawling after him up the snowy southern slope. He had a girl on his back and a baby tied to his waist with rags. Behind, their skirts lifted to be clear of the snow, were a dozen women with children clinging to them, and in the rear trudged ten strong-armed men with sacks on their backs and full sheafs of arrows bumping on their hip-bones. Ten men who could bend a bow! Ten more men for the battlements! God be praised and send a blessing on Huw's head! They all crowded about him. Willing hands took the children from him and fetched fresh thatching for his feet. Hot food was brought, quarters allotted, the men carried to the north gate to be shown their stations. Thud, thud! went the south gate behind them. The bolts shot home, the chains rattled, the great bars were dropped into their sockets. The town was enclosed. Let the Welsh try and crack the nut! They would find Abercibbi ready for them.

There was no sleep that night. The archers sat huddled in blankets on the battlements, their eyes smarting with the strain of staring into the darkness to the north, but they saw nothing save the ghostly glimmer of the snow. The moon was hidden. They saw nothing and heard nothing. The others crouched on brushwood round the great fire, watching the tar bubble and murmuring supplications. It was bitterly cold, save in the circle of the fire, but none sought shelter. They talked softly and blew on their fingers and watched with awe while the monks said Matins. So the night wore on in prayers and watching while Simon, who had had no sleep for two nights, dozed restlessly and dreamt of Eva. An hour before Prime the sky began to lighten over the Holy Mountain and a cock crowed in the priory yard. Suddenly there was a shout from the battlements and an arm pointed towards Blorys. Men leapt to terrified attention. Weapons were snatched. Simon awoke and hastened to the grille and stood on tiptoe to look through. Were the Welsh attacking at last? But it was only a single figure, a black shape on a Welsh pony, coming with reckless haste over the snow.

'God's body,' gasped Richard in his ear. 'He'll break his neck.'

'Only one?' shouted Simon.

'Only one,' came the answer. 'No tracks but this one.'

The rider came on, glancing over his shoulder as if fearful of pursuit. A warning? Did the Welsh follow?

'Only one?' cried Simon again.

'Only one,' was the reply from above his head. 'Nothing else to see.'

The rider flogged his pony on, oblivious of the potholes lying under the snow, and on the way the horse sank up to his knees. Every bow was trained upon him until he disappeared under the gatehouse and there above the grating stood Brother Mark with a steaming pail of tar in his hand. But he was not to use it. The rider flung back his hood. It was Eva.

Seeing Simon's face at the grille she urged her pony closer and fixed him with her terrified eyes.

'Open, my lord,' she gasped. 'Let me in! The Summoner is after me.'

Already Simon's hand was at the chain. 'Open! Open!' he cried in a fever of fear and longing.

None hesitated save Huw, and he said nothing. Why should they hesitate? There was nought but this woman, and their young lord's word had become their law.

'Only be quick, my lord,' urged Eva, casting terrified glances over her shoulder. 'I had word he was after me. A man came to the hut——'

'Open! Open!' cried Simon.

Men climbed up the bars and pulled back the top bolts. The bottom bolts were frozen, so hot water was brought to thaw them. The chain fell back. A wooden platform was dragged for the four stout men to stand on. They climbed upon it and raised their arms to the bar. A grunt, a heave, and they had it out of the sockets and, stepping cautiously down with it across their arms, laid it to one side on the frozen ground. They mounted again for the second bar and laid it beside its fellow. Simon had been forced to step aside but he could see Eva peering in at the grille over her pony's head and he could hear her frightened voice urging them to hasten. The platform was dragged away. The men struggled at shoulder height with the third bar, while cries of 'Nothing to see' floated down from the battlements and Brother Martin left his cooling tar to peer inwards from the gatehouse. As the men bent their backs for the last bar the archers leant backwards from their perches on the wall, curious to see this woman whom their lord was so anxious to protect. Of them all only Huw, standing a little behind his master, had recognized her voice. And he said nothing.

The last bar was laid down. The last cross bolt was pulled back. Half a dozen hands tugged at the knobs and slowly, with a scraping of ice, the gates opened from the middle. Without haste, Eva turned her pony's head towards the widening gap, as if waiting for it to be wide enough for the beast to pass. Simon started forward with arm outstretched, seeing her about to cry out. But she never uttered. Something sang in Simon's ear and an arrow buried itself in Eva's breast. She fell forward on the pony's neck so that the butt of the arrow pricked him. Goaded, he leapt forward through the gap with the woman hanging on his neck and at that instant the first Welshman reached the gate. They were there then. Stupefied, Simon caught a glimpse of Huw with his bow still raised and heard above the hub-hub his servant's words.

'She was a witch,' he said.

There was a bloody shambles at the gate. A score of English rushed forward and hurled their weight against it. Two Welshmen were through already but they fell like polecats to the lances before they could make a stroke. The gap was a struggling mass of men. Shouts and screams filled the air. From the battlements came the irregular buzz of arrows as heads appeared within the archers' sight. Women and children leant their puny weight against the Englishmen's bodies and inch by inch the gap began to narrow. The Welshmen began to jab with their swords between the gates but as the Englishmen fell their comrades trampled on their bodies, using the corpses as chocks for their feet.

Suddenly Simon's senses unfroze. 'The tar! The tar!' he screamed and Brother Mark tipped his bucket. Three gallons of black stickiness fell on the Welshmen's heads and with a deafening thud the gates slammed home, with a Welsh arm caught between them. They could hear the wretch screaming behind the wood. In an instant the first bolts were shot, the chains on and the first bar laid in its sockets. They heard the sickening sound of iron on bone as the Welshmen cut off their comrade's arm, then they pulled the stump from the crack and tossed it on to a heap of snow. Now came the turn of the archers. The Welsh came from under the wall, and made for the copse that stood by the side of the snowy track, three hundred yards from the gate and safely out of arrow range. In the weird light there seemed to be hundreds of them, scrambling and slipping with their weapons over the frozen snow. But hundreds or no, their plans had gone awry. They had expected a sleeping town and they had found it wakeful. Under the cover of darkness they had crept up to the west wall from the river bank, crawled like ants along the base of the wall until they reached the north side, then lain concealed under white sheets until the witch-woman came riding up to the grille. They had expected no resistance, for the English could not know of the attack and the woman had the young lord in her toils. She had but to ask and he would open to her and the nut would be cracked. But something had gone awry. The witch had been shot before the gates were open by more than a yard and the gates had been slammed in their faces. The English were ready and waiting.

Furious and shaken, the Welshmen followed Llewellyn's call to the copse, but not without loss. Of a hundred and fifty men, twenty fell to the English arrows before the trees were reached. They fell in grisly attitudes, staining the snow with their blood, and began to stiffen at once. Eight men lay dead at the gate in a mess of tar and blood, another was raving with a shorn arm and two had disappeared within the walls. Over thirty lost and the gates fast shut!

Meanwhile Simon crouched over Eva's body and watched the life ebb out of her. He had undone her bodice when he pulled out the arrow and before his eyes he saw the crimson mark fade on her breast. At last he knew her for what she was. She was a witch. She had enchanted him, hoping to make him into a traitor. She was Llewellyn's tool as surely as the Lollard and the bard. He had brought him to her bed in the shepherd's hut that her spell might be strengthened. She had never loved him any more than Llewellyn had loved him. Now at last he knew why the Summoner wanted her. At last he understood the sickening talk of prickings and searchings. He would have had her tried as a witch, tried, condemned and burned like Philip. 'Thank God,' he murmured over her cold body. With one arrow Huw had saved her from the fire and Simon from her spell. Hell awaited her, he knew, and the everlasting flames that had so nearly claimed his mother, but it was beyond his power to help her now and his passion was dead. Huw's arrow had killed it. The last spell was broken.

When at last he rose he saw movement in her lovely hair and out crawled the green toad, her familiar. He bent down, took it by a hind leg and flung it into the glowing heart of the fire, under the simmering tar buckets. Huw came towards him. 'She was a witch,' he said again. 'There is your pardon I am asking.'

'Aye,' said Simon, 'I know. You did right,' and the last of his burdens fell on to the frozen ground, the burden of his sinful passion.

'Now,' said Simon Beaumont, 'we must prepare for a fresh attack. They will never give up so easily.'

Already the air rang with the sound of Welsh axes chopping a tree for a ram and in the intervals of chopping they could hear Iolo's thin voice urging them on to feats of bravery. 'Fight to the death, they will,' said Huw straining his ears for the words. 'They'll have no going back now.'

He was right.

'*Fe dreiwn y boncyff*,' shouted the Welshmen, and presently out of the wood laboured a strange monster, a young elm some twenty feet long, base first and lopped of its branches. It was slung in a cradle of ropes and each rope went over a man's shoulder and round his waist. There were ten men on each side and the thing struggled over the snow like a monstrous caterpillar, bent on the destruction of the north gate. On either side flanking cover was given by fifty Welsh archers each with a sheaf of arrows on his hip, a bent bow, and an arrow trained on one or other of the buttress slits. For these were men who could pierce a falling apple at a hundred paces and even in this uncertain light the slits in the English walls were possible targets. It was come to this, then. The lances were abandoned in the snow. Sword, dagger and mace slept at their belts. It was the north gate they had to fight, and the archers on the walls. Ram and bow—these were the only weapons of use to them now. They had not even brought fire.

On crept the wooden caterpillar, until it was but two hundred paces from the gates.

'Aim!' shouted Simon, with his eye to the grille, and the archers raised their bows.

'Mat!' and the hide mat unrolled from the gatehouse with a snap, blotting out Simon's view.

'Tar!' and men began to mount the scaffolding with simmering destruction on iron bars between them.

'Rocks!' Huw and half a dozen boys climbed up to help the monks heave the tombstones.

All was ready. They had but to wait.

On came the ram with its heaving, panting bearers and its watchful guard. The sky was lightening fast, but no man turned to see the sun. Simon heaved himself up on to the wall and crouched beside Richard with an axe in his left hand. 'Have they brought ladders, think you?' muttered Richard. 'I do not know,' was the answer. 'But the axe fits my hand. I have use for it.' His eyes were fixed on the foremost figure, a Welshman with long hair to his shoulders and a short sword in his hand. He was burdened neither with rope nor bow, but came on steadily at the head of the ram and encouraged his men with cries. It was Llewellyn ap Thomas and Simon's hand tightened on the axe.

Nearer crept the Welshmen and Richard shifted his feet, his muscles quivering. 'Now? Now?' he whispered, but Simon answered, 'No. Wait.' He glanced once over his shoulder at the waiting figures twenty feet below him, then back at Llewellyn, now scarcely fifty yards from the gate. 'Shoot!' he shouted and twenty arrows shot through the icy air in the direction of the ram. Ten found a target and the tree trunk sank down on to the snow but ten archers dropped their bows and seized the slack ropes and the ram jerked back into life. The English restrung their bows, but now the Welsh returned fire and two screams from the buttresses told that a pair of Welsh arrows had penetrated the slits.

'Shoot!' shouted Simon again and Richard's arrow sped past his ear into a Welshman's side. Welsh arrows pattered on the stone a foot from their heads but Richard, impatient with the restriction of the slit, stepped from behind the buttress to get a better aim. Immediately he dropped with an arrow in his throat that not even his armour could protect. He fell backwards, toppled over the parapet and fell twenty feet to the ground. Out of the corner of his eye Simon saw Brother Gregory and Thomas run towards him, but he knew they were too late. The baron was dead. The soothsayer had spoken truth. Richard had died in a battle. Simon Beaumont was the lord of Abercibbi.

The Welsh fell to right and left but still the ram came on and two more Welsh arrows pierced English flesh. One man had an arrow through his left arm, another had taken it full in the chest and lay with an arm and a leg hanging over the parapet. Only thirteen archers left and now the ram had reached the gates. Crash! The oak shook and jarred the bars in their sockets. The chains rattled. Crash! Now all but the end of the ram was out of range of the archers and the gatehouse sprang into life. 'Heave!' shouted Huw, and half a tombstone toppled over the gatehouse wall and dropped with a ghastly thud at the side of the ram. Two men disappeared beneath it and before their ropes could be seized another stone dropped. This missed the men but hit the tree, so that the great elm jumped like a fish and sent the Welshmen sprawling. 'Tar!' shouted Huw, and half a dozen steaming buckets were emptied through the grating. There were terrible screams as the tar covered ram, men and ground in a scalding, clinging mess and sprayed even the archers, so that many were forced to tear off their gloves lest the gut be defiled. 'Again!' cried Huw and another tombstone splashed in the muck below them. Llewellyn had disappeared from view. Another English archer had gone.

It was impossible to tell how many Welshmen were killed. There were but two stones left and four gallons of tar. If the Welsh had enough men to wield the ram, soon there would be nothing to stop them. Through all the clamour Simon heard Iolo's ghostly voice and immediately afterwards the crash of the ram again. This was followed by a sickening splintering of wood and the women ran for lances. Another rock went down from the gatehouse and then another—the last—but Llewellyn's voice rose triumphantly above the tumult, '*Mae'n rhoi, bois. Unwaith eto.*' The Welsh bowmen had closed in now almost out of the archers' range. They must have been packed in the gateway like flies. The Welshmen were swinging the ram over a bed of dead bodies. The mat was torn down and already the cook and Old Peter were jabbing through the grille with lances. Crash! Splinters of oak began to flake off the gate and the bolts rocked in the ground. Crash! They were striking the ram between the bars and even the last gallon of tar did not stop them.

'*Mae bron trwodd,*' shouted Llewellyn's voice.

'Down,' shouted Simon, and the archers scrambled down the scaffolding. The monks threw down their empty buckets and followed Huw to the ground. This was their last stand. They had only twelve fighting men left. For the rest there was a cripple, a sick man, five monks, two priests and a score of women and children. They would be hard put to hold even twenty Welshmen, when they had Llewellyn ap Thomas at their head. But they would give them a good fight, if God pleased. The monks came tumbling from the gatehouse and seized short swords. The archers took up their positions in front of the shuddering gate and strung their bows. The children brought out their daggers, the prior took a lance, Seneschal a sword. Even the aged man propped himself against a wall and grasped a cudgel in both hands. Crash! The wall itself seemed to shake and a dead man on the parapet fell dully to the ground.

But Simon did not descend. Instead he ran along the wall to the gatehouse, his axe in his hand. Below, Huw stood shoulder to shoulder with the archers, as his grandfather had stood at the battle of Crecy waiting for the French charge. If the wood gave, the Welshmen had yet to crawl between the bars and he hoped to pick them off. Yet there were but ten bows all told and but for Old Peter many would already have been shot from the grille. Crash! A few more blows and the wood would be through.

At this moment Simon shouted from the gatehouse: 'Lances! Quickly! And a crowbar. Huw!'

Brother Gregory and the novice Laurence leapt for the scaffolding with a lance dangling from each wrist. Huw slung his bow across his shoulders, seized an iron bar and climbed after them. They crowded into the gatehouse, keeping their heads well below the parapet, and the panting of desperate men rose up to them like the breathing of cattle. The grating was clogged with tar. 'Break it!' cried Simon. 'We can pierce them from above.' Huw fitted the bar into the iron mesh and leant his weight. Nothing happened. The iron was made to stand the weight of many men and had been embedded in the stonework for three hundred years. 'Again!' Huw and Laurence threw their weight on the bar, but they could not shift the iron. Crash! The gatehouse trembled. 'In God's name, how many men are there ramming?' muttered Huw. They could see nothing for the tar on the grating and they did not dare peer over the parapet for fear of the bowmen. But Simon dared. Suddenly he hauled himself to his feet and leant over, then got his left knee on the coping and pulled himself up with his sound hand until he stood on the narrow stone with his axe in his armpit.

An incredible sight met his eyes.

Ten men were wielding the ram. Ten men alone were swinging an elm twenty foot long. They had set their feet on the faces of the dead who lay so thick that the ram was battering at the height of a man's head. The ground was a morass of tar and blood and bodies. There must have been nearly a hundred corpses, dead from the rocks and the tar and the press of men. Crushed, burnt or suffocated, they were now no more than foothold for the ten who still lived. Nay, eleven. For there was Llewellyn, with his hand on the ram. He had no rope. He was taking none of the weight. But by his touch he was giving these ten men the strength of twenty, of fifty.

'*Unwaith eto!*' The men heaved again, slipping in blood and brains, and Huw heard the grille go, shot out of the wood like a stone from a catapult.

'Come you, my lord,' he entreated. 'There is need of us at the gate.'

But Simon did not move, save to take the axe from his armpit. He kissed the blade, crossed himself with the handle and jumped. He landed squarely on Llewellyn's shoulders and the axe went through the man's skull like butter. By God's mercy he missed the ram and rolled without hurt in a welter of arms and legs. An instant later Huw landed beside him and snatched his dagger from his belt, but he found no need to use it. As the axe cleaved Llewellyn's skull the Welshmen had sunk like dead men, without the strength even to keep their legs free of the tree-trunk. They lay pinned under its weight while grimy English faces peered at them through the hole in the gate.

It was over. Not a Welshman lived but these ten and they were hanged from the gallows the same day. Iolo they found frozen in the snow with the golden banner clutched in his stiffening hand. But the boy lived. They found him shivering and crying behind a thorn near the river bank. When they asked him his name he did not answer but cried piteously and said, '*Mae eisiau bwyd arna'i.*'

'Hot porrage for you, is it?' said Huw. He lifted the child in his arms and carried him with his face against his shoulder lest he should see Llewellyn's ghastly head.

16

ON A sunny morning in April Simon Beaumont sat with the boy Davydd on the slopes of Pen-y-val and viewed the March. The thaw had come early and on the feast of St David relief had come from Herefordshire with a company of royal troops sent by the special command of Prince Harry. But they had found no enemy to fight. The enemy was dead, all hundred and fifty, buried in a communal grave outside the north gate. With that hundred and fifty had died Llewellyn's dream of Welsh independence. Had they taken the town, who knows what ancient ardours might not have leapt in respectable breasts, as they had done seven years before? He had made a dragon of the English, like Glendower before him, and he needs must ram his lance down its throat. He had charmed a hundred and fifty into following him and with the boy, Glendower's son, at his side, who knows but that he could have revived the old dreams, if he had taken the town and dominated the valley?

But he had failed to crack the nut. The witch was buried deep in the forest and he and his followers jostled each other in their unhallowed grave, as became traitors. No one had risen to support them. Even in Brecknock, where the lord scarcely let his Welshmen breathe, there was quiet.

Two days after the attack the chiefs of the Welshry had come alone and on foot to the town to renew their oaths of homage. Caraddoc ap Rhys and Islwyn ap Morgan of Blaenavon had been slain in the snow, but the chiefs of Lasgarn, Tillery, Carn-y-cefn and Llanhilleth bent the knee to their new baron and swore on the Sacred Book to be his men. Simon could have been savage with them. He could have doubled their payment of cows, and hanged, on a pretext of perfidy, those of their families that he did not trust. But although his old love for the Welshry was gone, seared by the treachery of Llewellyn and Eva, yet he was merciful. Let them bring seed for the English fields and a gift of cow or ewe, let them send men to plough the English fields and to help with such harvest as God allowed them, and it was enough. He did not command, this queer lop-sided lord, he besought them instead, and there was not one but carried loyalty back up the track to the upland pastures.

The Welsh had been carefully examined before burial and the tar scraped from their faces, if they had faces, so that they might be identified. Men were brought from the Welshry to testify on oath to their identity, with the prior promising them eternal damnation if they spoke a falsehood. They were all, every one of the hundred and fifty, men of Blaen-avon or Pwll-du. The lands of such as could be named reverted by the law of escheat to the baron, with their herds and pastures. Simon intended farming these as his domain, under bailiffs even now on the road from Warwickshire. If the Welsh shrank from settling in the valley, let Englishmen settle in the hills. Only so could the two halves of the map be joined in peace and friendship. Let the old king but die and when he rode to Westminster for Prince Harry's coronation Simon might yet carry with him the loyal address of his Welshmen.

Meanwhile . . .

Meanwhile there was much to be done. The Lady Eleanor was expected any day, for the marriage was fixed for May Day and her dowry of two thousand acres would be a godsend to the impoverished Englishry. This quarter's rents alone would restock the domain farms with calves and buy a bull for stud. There was indeed much to do. Simon looked down the path of his days and saw endless endeavour ahead. There were new gates to be made, Richard's tomb to be ordered and blocks of freestone to be lugged from the Dundry quarries, with masons for the effigies. He prayed God his brother's body was well preserved, for they had been able to make no wax image from life. He must find a husband for Alice, a priest for the parish church and five others for the empty parishes of the Englishry.

He must bring settlers from England to take over the lands of the dead, that next year at least he might get rents. He must find homes for the orphans and husbands for the widows. He must see to the burial of the cattle and sheep that had been mouldering in the fields ever since the thaw. He must burn the tailor's house, where the witch had lived, lest any of her magic lingered in the thatch. The Welsh priests must be questioned for Lollardy, not by the Summoner but by the prior whom he had learned to think a merciful man. He must bring men from the Welshry to plough and sow the spring wheat and he must start the criss-cross draining at Penperlenni. He had schemes for increasing the sheep pasture, for it took fewer men to grow sheep than corn. All these plans hummed in his head as he sat with Davydd on the mountainside and felt the sun on his neck. He must get sons too, strong sons to help him as he, alas, had never helped his father. Above all, he must make Davydd ap Glendower into a loyal subject. Already the boy looked at Simon kindly and he had ceased to cry for Llewellyn in the night. Huw he loved, but then who did not love Huw?

Simon saw the busy days stretching ahead of him and he sighed with relief to think that it led him along a safe path. The miracle of conformity had taken place. He perceived the pattern of life at last.

It was a beautiful spring day, with white clouds in a blue sky. He touched Davydd's shoulder and studied the child's dark face. His hair hung about his neck in black curls and the sickle on his forehead glowed in the sun. He smiled.

'*Duw,*' said Simon, pointing up to the heavens.'

'*Duw,*' said the child.

'*Duw*. God,' said Simon.

'God,' said the child, trying to get his tongue round the stiff English word.

'*Eglwys,*' said Simon, crossing himself.

'Ah, *Eglwys,*' said the child, crossing himself likewise.

'*Eglwys.*' Church,' said Simon.

'Church,' said the child, thinking it an ugly sound but strong.

'*Dyletswydd,*' said Simon at a loss for a gesture.

'*Dyletswydd,*' said the child, puzzled for its meaning.

'*Dyletswydd*. Duty,' said Simon.

'Duty,' repeated the child, smiling but uncomprehending.

Simon rose awkwardly to his feet and surveyed his March. He turned his face to the south, whence Eleanor would come and where the great river gleamed silver in the sun. He turned to the east to the horn of the Holy Mountain which hid the gentle hills of Herefordshire. He turned northwards towards Brecknock and the Black Mountains of Wales and then westwards to the Welshry and the noble slopes of Blorys. He stretched out his arms, the strong and the weak, and turned slowly through the points of the compass.

'*Lloegr*,' he said.

'*Lloegr*?' asked the child, looking westwards.

'*Lloegr*,' said Simon Beaumont. 'England.'